Patriots and Rebels

John C. Bush

For Louise —
I hope you enjoy
the read!
John C. Bush

This is a work of historical fiction, and represents the actual experiences of individuals involved in the events described. It is based on records from the National Archives in Washington, DC or information otherwise publically available. In some instances, people, places or events described have been fictionalized. Any similarity to living persons is purely coincidental.

Typesetting and cover design by FormattingExperts.com

Cover photo: "The Battle of Nashville" by Kurz and Allison (1891), LC-DIG-pga-01886. Library of Congress, Prints and Photographs Division, Washington, D.C. 20540.

Contents

Acknowledgements

I am grateful to all those who have had a hand in shaping *Patriots and Rebels* over the three years or so it has been in progress. Their time, energy, feedback and encouragement have combined to make its completion possible. Special appreciation goes to my ever-patient wife Sara, who has endured hours, days, weeks and months – years, even – of my preoccupation with the project. Writers' group members Judy Mitchell Rich, Joyce Pettis Temple and Paige Maxwell McRight have given invaluable support, encouragement, criticism and suggestions, as have granddaughter Sara Jane Bush, friends Ron Simmons and, early on, Houston Hodges. The suggestions and affirmation of Kent Wright, Program Manager for the Tennessee Valley Civil War Round Table, gave just the right "push" at just the right time. The long distance and "virtual" friendship of Glenda McWhirter Todd provided a great deal of information and insight into the people and events involving the First Alabama Cavalry, United States Volunteers. Her several books about First Alabama Cavalry, U.S.V., are essential tools for anyone interested in this neglected piece of Civil War history.

I must express special thanks to a person I know only through limited email correspondence. Norman Peters is a researcher in the Washington DC area, whom I came to know through the good offices of Glenda Todd. When Norman provided me with the military records of Thomas Benton Files from the National Archives he appended a note that said, simply, "Looks like there might be a book in this one." Thereby he provided both the impetus and the raw material for me to get serious about writing a story that had been niggling at me for several years. If any single person is responsible for making the telling of this story possible, Norman Peters is that person.

Editor Amelia Morrison Hipps of Lebanon, Tennessee gave the manuscript careful attention, and it was her observations and insight that helped develop the distinctive voices of the primary characters, especially that of Mary Francis (Fannie.) Thanks to friends and acquaintances far and near, including myriad Facebook friends, who have followed this project over the years and urged me on to its completion.

Thanks to one and all!
J.C.B.

Foreword

In the years of the great crisis within the American states it was common for Southerners with Union loyalties to call themselves Patriots, and to reference their ancestors who fought in the Revolutionary War. It meant that the bond their grandfathers made with the United States was not to be broken, even at the cost of their lives. Those who sided with the secession movement were called Rebels or sometimes more derisively, Secesh, many of whom were equally willing to die for Southern independence.

The Patriots who joined the Federal Army to preserve the Union faced personal dangers on and off the battlefields. Continually mistrusted for their Southern accents and place of birth, their loyalty was always under suspicion and could be challenged at any time. If suspected of being a spy, a person could be summarily executed without trial. The families left behind were in personal danger too from brutal Confederate home guards and roving bands of guerillas, sometimes less politely called outlaws and freebooters.

Author and North Alabamian John C. Bush tells a marvelous tale of a family, actually his wife's ancestors, caught in the clutches of war in North Alabama. The father in the story is Thomas Files, a North Alabama Patriot and the great-great grandfather of John's wife, Sara Fulton Bush. That being said, this is not by any means a "family history." Factually, however, ancestor Tom was a proud descendant of Captain John Files, a hero of the Revolutionary War Battle of Cowpens. In the First Alabama Cavalry, United States Volunteers, he was First Sergeant Thomas Files. While serving, he gained the unpleasant distinction of being made a prisoner of war by *both sides*.

Meanwhile, his family was left to struggle under the same hardships of virtually all Southern families caught in the grip of the war—except for one thing—as Patriots in a hostile region they were at the mercy of the occupying forces, whether uniformed in blue or gray. Worse still, the anger and killing did not stop with Grant and Lee's handshake at Appomattox in April 1865; vengeful partisans and unforgiving neighbors would threaten private citizens for many months to come.

This novel by John C. Bush is built upon ancestral stories and official historic records. John has carefully fictionalized a story of real people, a family of Patriots, into the time and place of actual historical events. His praiseworthy research uncovers military facts relatively unknown except by persons who were there. In fact, rather ironically, the intimate knowledge of certain military facts was cleverly woven into the story as the critical element which saved the life of Sergeant Files. Equally ironic perhaps, for Mr. Files and his family, the worst of times may have come after the war was officially over.

This book is a must-read for anyone interested in the struggle *within* the American South and the mixed loyalties that helped to bring down the Old Order in the United States. It stands in total contradiction to the usual stereotypes and misconceptions of white Southerners during and long after the great struggle to define American ideals.

Kent Wright, Program Director and Member of the Board of Directors
Tennessee Valley Civil War Round Table
Huntsville, AL

Chapter 1

Rebel Yells shattered the quiet North Alabama night like the yowl of wildcats, jerking us awake. The thud, thud, thud of bullets hitting the house added to our terror. Both of us girls went running from our room, screaming for Pa. Ma was sitting straight up in bed, shaking with fear, Pa holding her tight in his arms.

The gruff voice, when it came, sounded very close, from beside the door or maybe at a window. "This is a warning, Tom Files. If we have to come here again, there's going to be bloodshed. Next time we will get you. All of you."

The voice told Pa to get his self into town and sign up to fight for the Southern cause.

After that there was just the crunch of gravel under the hooves of departing horses, letting us know the attack was over. The only remaining sounds was our muffled sobs.

The morning sun broke through the gray winter clouds, letting us see the damage done to our house. None of the windows was broke. Their aim had been deliberate. They'd not intended to do us real harm. It was a warning, just like the voice said. It wasn't the first time the Home Guard had paid us a call, but they'd never been that violent before.

That is how came to be that Pa and six or eight other men from around here left on the third day of the New Year in 1863. They was going to fight for the Union, with the First Alabama Cavalry, United States Volunteers. He was going to sign on for one year, so we should expect him back home about the same time the next year.

I marked that down in my mind. January, 1864. I'd be counting the days.

Pa left just before my thirteenth birthday. It was the worst day of my life, and it lasted near about three years. Longer than that, truth be told, because it still comes back in my sleep, leaving me weak to the stomach.

Pa's words that day still ring clear as a bell in my mind:

"My grandpa and his daddy fought to make this Union back in '76, and I can't sit by and let these Secesh[1] take it apart without putting up a fight. We're Patriots, and we ain't taking any part with this rebellion against the United States of America."

The trip to Camp Davies, Mississippi would take three or four days if they was lucky, travelling through the rough hill country of northwest Alabama. If snow came, or if they had to hide out from the Home Guard or Confederate conscription officers along the way, it might take a week or more. Pa figured they'd be safer traveling by night and resting up by day. If the Rebels caught them, they'd either shoot them dead on the spot or else make them sign up with the Confederacy.

"I'm sorry, Mattie, but I have to take the work mule with me," he said. "The army says volunteers like me should bring a pack animal if we have one, and old Rabbit will do just fine.

---

[1] Secesh refers to the Secessionists, those who favored departure from the United States to form the Confederate States of America.

He's near about as big as a horse and stronger than most, so he'll be easy for me to ride. You're going to need the horse for sure, and it will be here for you until one side or the other comes and takes it from you. I suppose we've just been lucky none of the scavengers have taken them both off before now anyway."

Ma was crying all the while. He took her in his arms, and they held each other tight, rocking together gently as the sun sank below the trees. Penny and me cried, too, holding on to the both of them. Then he mounted old Rabbit and headed off down the lane to meet the others. I recognized Mr. John Shaw and Mr. Jasper Whitley in the bunch, and there was some more I didn't know.

At the end of the lane Pa looked back and gave us a final goodbye wave, then turned and rode away. Ma stood, her body rocking back and forth, arms crossed tightly against her breast. She stayed there looking after him until there was nothing left to see but a faint trail of dust. When the last hint of the trail disappeared in the wind she sank down into a chair, her arm around my waist, rocking Penny in her lap. Her soft blue eyes had gone still and blank as she stared, unseeing, into the darkening winter sky.

A terrible thought came over me. We was alone.

That night I found a familiar book open on my bed. It was called *Household Tales* by two brothers named Grimm. Pa liked it because his own Pa had read it with him, and we'd been reading from it most nights before I went to sleep. It was open right at the place where we left off. I reckoned it was his way of telling me he'd still be thinking of me every night, and that made me feel some better. Still, none of us slept much that night. I could hear Ma crying softly near about all night long.

In the morning, I told her about the book. There was tears in her eyes as she told me he'd left one for her, too. Hers was a book of poems he'd given her when they was first married, called sonnets from someplace far away, by Elizabeth somebody.

That was nigh onto three years ago, when Penny was nearly five and little Peggy was not even born yet. I stopped marking down the days at the end of February in 1864, more than a month past the time he promised he'd come back. Now all I had was a deep, empty hurt where my heart was supposed to be. Pa had always kept his promises. Always. Until now.

The war and its terror finally came to an end in the spring of 1865. The news brought joy, but also sadness and despair. There was thousands of men who had not come home. Pa was among them. Who would not. Would my Pa be one of them?

In a way, spring had been a hopeful time for it to end. We'd been able to put in a good garden, knowing no soldiers would be coming around carrying off everything. Maybe we'd not go hungry like we did last year, and the year before, and the year before that. Working in the garden gave me time to think on all we'd been through.

Now came harvest time. The early fall air already had a bit of a nip to it, though winter wouldn't arrive for two or three months. We'd already dug the onions and the Irish 'taters and put them in the root cellar. Ma'd put up the tomato harvest in big Mason jars stored safely away, along with green beans, pickled okra and several kinds of peas. I helped Ma make us a good batch of sauerkraut from the early cabbages. Bunches of rosemary, thyme, sage and red peppers hung from the rafters to dry, filling the cellar with their fresh fragrances. We had apples sliced and laid out in the sun to dry, which would be the makings of pies for winter, as well as dried plums for hot pudding when the evenings turned cold.

We even managed to raise a little corn. Corn was one thing both armies had needed as much of as they could get their thieving hands on. They had their horses and mules to feed, as well as the troops. Never mind about us and what we needed. I'd been surprised that Ma had held back enough for seed. Turned out she had sealed some in a Mason jar and buried it behind the outhouse. None of the scavengers looked for it there.

Ma was fixing to make hominy with some of it, and grind some for corn meal. We'd not had any cornbread for quite a while. Not much of anything, truth be told, with the endless stream of Rebel and Union soldiers coming along. Thank God, this year the garden would be for us to use, and the thought of that made me work even harder.

There'd still be fresh turnip greens and radishes even after frost. Pumpkins soon would be ready to pick. We had the rutabagas and the rest of the cabbages to work. Then the gardening jobs would be done until time to till the soil and get it ready for spring planting. Surely Pa would be home afore then. I sure hoped so anyway. But what's the good of hoping? If you hope too much, it just makes you sad and disappointed.

That's what occupied my mind while I sacked up the sweet 'taters as Ma dug them. Peggy was too little to help with the chores. She played happily in the sandy red soil at Ma's feet. Penny helped me. I was about ready to tote another sack to the root cellar when Ma looked up and wiped her brow. Though her bonnet shaded her eyes, I could see a shadow of panic cloud her face. Her bright blue eyes turned dark and hard as she dropped her spade and grabbed Peggy.

Ma motioned at Penny and me and spoke quietly but firmly, the echo of fear filling her voice.

"There's a man coming up the lane. You girls get up to the house. Get inside and shut the door. I'm coming directly. Y'all run quick now. Run, girls! Now!"

With Peggy in her arms, Ma ran, too, with Penny scurrying along behind.

I was determined to get that sack of 'taters to a safe place. If this was another of them Rebels straggling home, he sure wouldn't get his hands on these new-dug 'taters. Not if I could help it.

Struggling with my sack, I looked up to see how close he was getting. He limped along right slow like, none too steady on his feet, leaning on a rough wooden staff. All ragged, with shaggy hair and a wild full beard, he was so skinny his tattered old jacket hung loose and flapped in the breeze. Now I could see that, sure enough, it was the fragment of a uniform.

I looked again, shading my eyes from the setting sun. His old uniform still showed its Union blue through the dirt and grime. This was no Rebel. This was a Union man, a Patriot like us.

Ma screamed at me from the porch for me to get myself up there. The other two peered out the front window, wide-eyed with fear and curiosity. Ma held the hunting rifle she always kept beside the front the door. It had come in handy more than once when rowdy Secesh ruffians had come to harass us. She knew how to use it, too, as several Rebs had learned the hard way.

It hadn't been easy for Ma, being a woman with three girls out here with no near neighbors. We'd been harassed at all hours of the day and night by Rebels angry because we'd taken the Union side. Bullet holes pocked the front of the house where we'd been shot at in the dead of night. We'd learned to be ready for most anything, especially when a strange man came along. Awhile back a rough band of Secesh had come up on Ma out in the barn alone. They'd beat her up pretty bad. She was all bruised and sore, but she wouldn't talk to us girls about it.

"Fannie, just leave those 'taters there and come on, right now. You run fast, you hear me!"

Dumb-struck, I stared at the old man limping up the lane. He didn't look to be in any shape to hurt anybody. He could hardly hold himself up. I knew I could out-run him.

He'd gotten right close and I realized he wasn't an old man at all. Just that long dirty beard made me think he was. When he heard Ma calling to me he turned and looked straight at me. A twinkle came into his black eyes and he commenced laughing. It was a weak rasping sound, but I could swear it was a voice I knew.

"Fannie? Mary Frances? Is that you, child?"

"Pa? Is that you, Pa?"

Tears of joy welled up in my eyes. I ran to him, near about knocking him over as I threw my arms around him, all the while calling out "Look, Ma. It's Pa! It's Pa!"

She took a step off the porch, the gun still leveled at him. He'd stopped a few paces away. As she stared into his face her eyes changed again. Their soft blue returned. Her voice took on a nice soft sound I'd not heard in a long, long time.

"Tom? Lardy mercy. Is that you Tom Files under all that grime and hair?"

"Yes, Martha Jane. It's me, Mattie. It's me."

The gun slipped from her grip. She moved slowly toward him as he shuffled toward her. Both of them held their arms spread wide, tears of joy streaming down their cheeks. She buried her face in his shoulder as he folded her into his arms. It seemed like a big heavy load came off of her shoulders as she relaxed against him. They stood there saying nothing, swaying gently in each other's arms. Penny and me joined in, hugging them both at once, but little Peggy hung back from this stranger, hiding her face in Ma's skirts.

"Tom, oh Tom, we thought you must be dead. We been looking for you for almost two year now since your time was supposed to be up. I tried to keep hope alive. We prayed for you every single day. Every night I dreamed of you. I saw you getting blowed to pieces off somewhere all by yourself. We thought you was dead. Where you been, Tom? I'm so glad you're home."

"Yes, Mattie. It's been a terrible long time, and there's a tale to be told. If you'll give me time to think on how to tell it, you'll hear it all. But right now could we just go in and sit down? I been walking near about three weeks and been sick along the way. I've not had but very little to eat since day before yesterday and not much for a week. Is there anything here to eat?"

As we walked toward the porch, Pa reached down and picked up the baby. Tears filled his eyes as he looked into Peggy's round little face for the first time. She started to whimper in the arms of this strange and dirty man, but Ma patted her on the shoulder.

"It's all right, Peg. This is your Pa come home."

Peggy reached out to touch his shaggy beard.

"Pa?" she said.

"Yes, Peggy, I'm your Pa," he said. She giggled as he gently pinched her cheek and planted a kiss on her nose.

As soon as we got in the house, Ma set about fixing something for him to eat. He sat at the kitchen table, hardly able to stay upright in the chair. Ma started in chattering away like she always does when she's upset or scared. Or excited.

"I'm afraid there's not much food to be had, Tom. I've got some turnip greens and sweet 'taters left over. We got them fresh out of the garden this morning. They'll be warm for you in a few minutes. I can fry you up some of these here apples. We ate all the rabbit I shot last night. We've not had much meat to speak of in a long, long while. Scavengers cleared out the smokehouse right off. The chickens, cattle and hogs went quick. That happened soon after you left. We was able to hide one of the milk cows right up to the end, and then a company of Rebels came through at just the wrong time. They took her right as Fannie was milking her. They even ran off with the milk, pail and all, so we didn't even get that. All the milk we've had since has been what little the neighbors could spare, the Shaws and the Cooners. Near 'bout everybody out here on Wolf Creek been in the same boat as us. All the men folks been gone, just womenfolk left to make out as best we could, and Johnny Reb making life as hard as could be for us. But we got good neighbors. We all looked out after each other anyway we could. Mahalia Cooner's been especially good. You know her man, Carroll, didn't get signed up 'til last year. He'd been hiding out from the Secesh up in the hills. He kept one of their milk cows with him out there. He'd slip back home to help with the chores when he could, most of the time of a night. Having a man around now and then was a comfort to all of us, but he had to be real careful not to get caught. I don't suppose you heard about what happened to him? You know that old rascal Bill Hewlett over at Jasper? He got to be some kind of colonel or something in the Rebel army. Well, he had some men come over and conscript Carroll Cooner into the Confederate army. But the way Mahalia told it, he got away and went hid over at that cave they call 'The Big House.' Quick as he could, he and some others worked their way up to Huntsville and signed on with the First Alabama same as you. They sent him off to Rome, Georgia, helping out with that General Sherman's move over toward Atlanta. But Carroll came back and stayed all that fall and winter, suffering from a sun-stroke or something of the kind. Then he went back in over around Huntsville and did another turn right at the end of the war. He's been back home for a while now. You wasn't over there with Sherman, was you? Did you run into Cooner or any of the men from here abouts?"

Ma turned to give him his food. He was sound asleep, cradling his head in his arms on the table.

"Well, I be swiggered," she said, with a twinkle in her eye. "Tom Files, ain't heard a word I been saying!"

She put the plate down beside him and let him sleep a bit, then she shook him awake.

"Tom, your food's probably cold by now but why don't you eat it anyway. Then go on down to the creek and wash off some of that traveling grime and dirt afore bed time. After that, if you feel up to it, we can talk a bit about where you been and what happened to you."

Pa rubbed his eyes. With a yawn, he leaned back in his chair and ran his hand through his ragged beard. As he finished supper he said he especially enjoyed the fried apples. He'd not had any such as that since he left here.

"Mattie, I'll sure tell you all about what's happened these near three years. Telling it will take some time, and for a truth there's a whole lot of it that's not fit for little ears to hear. Just be patient and I'll tell it all to you."

The two younger ones had gotten right sleepy. While Ma put them down, Pa went out to the creek to wash off the worst of the travel grime. I stirred up the fire in the sitting room so it would be warm for him when he came in from the creek. With sundown, the air had turned crisp and cool, so he hurried right along. Thunder promised rain, with heavy clouds moving in from the west. I thought to myself how it was a good thing we got most of them 'taters dug today. With the ground wet we'd not be able to dig any more for a day or two..

Pa's bath refreshed him a right smart. As he settled into his big rocker he noticed his little collection of books was missing from the shelf under the window. I had to tell him how the raiders took them off and threw them in the creek down behind the house – all but the Bible. They left that for us.

"Oh, wait, Pa. There's one more. I was reading it in bed the day before they came and I hid it under my bed in case they came back."

I went and fetched it. It was called *A Modern Geography*. His face was filled with pleasure to have it in his hands.

"This was your favorite, Fannie. Especially the pictures."

He opened it to the page with a team of dogs called malamutes pulling a sled through the snow in a far off place called Siberia.

"You always laughed at that funny sounding word, 'malamutes'."

I told him how we'd tried our best to dry out some of the books we found in the creek, especially the world history books he liked, but they was too far gone by the time we got to them. He shook his head in anger and disbelief.

"No call for such as that," he said. "Nothing but pure meanness in it." He let out a big sigh and sat quiet for a time. "But, then, I reckon both sides had plenty of that."

His face lit up, though, when I told him they didn't find the books he'd left for Ma and me. We'd them put away in our special places.

He commenced to rock gently, enjoying the warmth of the fire after his cold water bath. Ma always called that rocker "Pa's chair," even when he wasn't here to sit in it. She wouldn't let us play with it or even sit there.

"It's just for Pa, waiting for him to come home," she always said.

His favorite lap cover, washed and ironed, stayed neatly folded over the chair back. Sometimes when she didn't know I was near I'd seen her standing there beside that chair, gently rocking it back and forth with her fingers, staring longingly out the window down the lane toward the road.

While we waited on Ma to join us, I climbed up in Pa's lap the way I used to. I'd gotten way too big to do this now, though, especially with him all wasted away like he was. His shaggy beard tickled my face, but it felt good to have his familiar arms around me. It felt like it used to be when he'd to read to me from one of his books or from the big family Bible.

"How old are you now, Fannie?" he asked.

"I turned fifteen on my birthday."

"Fifteen years old? My, oh, my. You're a young woman already. I've missed a whole lot of your growing up time, haven't I! I'll just have to do the best I can to make that up to you. Problem is, I don't know just how to do that. When time passes, it's gone, isn't it? No use crying over spilt milk, though. The best we can do is use the time we have to the best advantage. I'm going to try to do that for you, Fannie. I'm really going to try."

After a few minutes I moved to sit on my stool and drew it up close enough so we could hold hands. I liked how his big strong hands wrapped around mine. I enjoyed being able to touch him again and to hear his deep voice, even if it wasn't a strong as it once was. We sat there staring into the fire, quietly enjoying each other's company. When I looked up, he had nodded off the sleep right there in his rocker. Ma saw it, too, as she came to join us. She touched his arm.

"Tom, you'd best go on to bed," she said gently. "You need your rest, what with all you been through. We can talk tomorrow."

Ma tucked us three girls in and stayed with us while we said our prayers. Pa made his way to their room. By the time she joined him, I could hear his steady breathing. He was already asleep.

Chapter 2

It was nigh on toward noon by the time Pa woke up. He was stretching and yawning as he joined us in the kitchen, and a smile lit up his face.

"That was the best sleep I've had in about three years."

Ma came over and kissed the top of his head. He took her hands in his.

"It sure helped a bunch knowing I was not going to get pulled out of bed before daylight to fight somewhere, and not having to worry about being attacked in my sleep. Of course, sleeping on my own bed instead of the hard ground in the rain or snow helped a right smart, too."

As he finished breakfast he said he wanted to go down to the creek and finish the bath he started hurriedly the night before. Ma objected.

"No, Tom, we're going to give you a proper bath. I'm going to scrub you down good with warm water and lye soap. Then I'm going to trim that shaggy beard and hair. I want to get you looking like the Thomas Benton Files I married once upon a time."

She sent Penny and me down to the creek to bring back pails of water, and she put some on the stove to heat. When it was hot she poured it in the big zinc tub that stayed behind the cook stove, where we all had our Saturday baths. It was the first sure enough bath he'd had in two or three months. From the looks of it, his hair had not been trimmed that often, either.

Ma laid out some clean clothes for him and sent me outside to burn his grimy old uniform. She told me to save the brass buttons, though. They had an American eagle on them. She would use them again.

After his bath and haircut he looked more like the Pa I remembered. Unfortunately, none of his clothes fit very well. Ma found an old pair of gallusses she'd knitted for him back before the war. They held his britches up sure enough, but I still had to laugh. It looked like I could near about get in there with him. Ma allowed as how she'd have to have to work on fattening him up again.

"That sounds like a right fine idea to me," he said, and laughed as he gave Ma a hug.

"But at least they are clean and pressed," he chuckled as he looked at himself in the looking glass. With a smile in his eyes, he said "I can't remember the last time me and my clothes were clean at the same time."

We passed the day walking over the farm with him, looking over the effects of damage and neglect. He noted the fences that needed mending, the land that needed clearing, the barn and smokehouse requiring repair. He spent a good bit of the day, too, sitting on the porch or napping in his rocking chair in the sitting room. During those times, Ma kept us children busy with chores and make-work so we'd not bother him.

That evening, while Ma was getting the younger girls to

bed, Pa and I sat together again by the fire. My head was full of questions and doubts.

"Pa, why did you have to go away like that?" My voice broke and the tears welled up. "I know you said it was to help save our Union, but I didn't know exactly what that meant. We was scared, being here by ourselves. We all was. Ma tried not to let us know she was, but I knew. I saw it in her face when those rough men came around, shooting up the place and talking about killing us all. I saw her hands trembling while she held the gun on them. I heard her voice shake when she told them to get on away from here and leave us be. She was strong, and she took good care of us best she could. But we needed you here with us."

He sat, rocking gently and staring into the fire like he was lost and trying to find his way back. I could see his eyes mist over. When he spoke, his voice came almost as a whisper.

"Well, Mary Francis, I didn't want to go off and leave you. But I had to go. I hope you are old enough now to begin to understand."

He ran his fingers through my hair and let his hand come to rest gently on my shoulder. "Maybe the best way I know to explain it is to tell you a story. I hope it will help you make some sense of it, Fannie. Do you understand what a Patriot is?"

"No, not really. I know you're a Patriot. The day you left you called us Patriots. Ma and the neighbor folks called those bad people who came after us 'Rebels.' So I reckon they must not be Patriots. But, some of the children at school called us traitors and said their families was patriots. So how could they be Rebels and patriots, and how could we be traitors and Patriots? I've thought about that a lot. I wouldn't ask Ma, though.

27

She had enough to think on, keeping us safe as best she could. I just puzzled on it lying awake at night."

"My goodness, Fannie. That's a whole lot of very big questions for a young mind to puzzle over. You've been thinking on all this for quite awhile, haven't you?"

He rubbed his hand over his neatly trimmed beard and stared out the window. It seemed like his thoughts must be away off down there somewhere and he had to go looking for them.

Ma'd gotten the little ones down. She picked up her knitting and came to sit quietly in her rocker beside Pa. It made me happy for us to be together like this. I'd been afraid this wasn't ever going to happen again. Ma smiled, looking over at the two of us sitting there, still holding hands. There'd not been very many smiles around here. The only sound she made was the click-click-click of her knitting needles as her fingers pushed the yarn back and forth from one needle to the other. She was making herself a new shawl.

"This is a story I heard first when I was just about your age, sitting by the fire with my grandpa. It's about his daddy, Captain John Files and his three sons. They were the first Patriots in our family that I know about."

Pa's tale had its beginning more than a hundred years before in the wilderness of the new state of West Virginia. We'd talked about West Virginia in school. The teacher told about how it broke away from Virginia because the folks over there didn't want to leave the Union when Virginia did. Before Pa left home I'd heard him talking about how our part of North Alabama wanted to do something like that. He'd called it "The Free State of Winston." Part of Tennessee and Georgia and a little bit of Mississippi had wanted to do the same thing.

Way back then, it was part a of Virginia where no white folks had ever lived. Just Indians lived there. Two white families had moved there together. Their names was David and Elizabeth Tygart, and Robert and Elizabeth Files and their family. Elizabeth Tygart was Robert's oldest daughter, named for her mother. It was early springtime when they arrived to make their new home in the wilderness. Each family had put up a log house as their homestead, a mile or two apart.

Elizabeth and Robert Files had seven children at home, including a son named John who Pa thought must have been about a year or two older than me. One day John went hunting to see if he could get a deer or maybe a turkey for the family's dinner, but he had no luck. Starting homeward, he heard a huge ruckus off in the direction of his family's cabin.

Sneaking up close where he could see but not be seen, he came upon something awful. A band of Shawnee warriors returning from battle with a neighboring tribe came upon this cabin that had been built while they was gone. They killed the all the family that was at home and burned the cabin to the ground. In horror, John almost cried out, but swallowed the sound. Clearly there wasn't anything he could do to save his family. They was all dead, laying there in the yard.

Thinking about his sister, Elizabeth, and her family, he ran as fast as he could through the woods to warn the Tygarts. He was near tears with relief when he found everyone safe. The Tygarts and the young John Files got away from there real quick like and went back to where they had come from.

"Pa, is this true? Did it really happen or are you making this up just to scare me?"

"No, dear. This story my Grandpa told me is about his own grandpa, that young John Files. Everything really happened just this way. Today, a hundred years later, there is a river in West Virginia called the Tygart River and a creek that runs into it called Files Creek."

"This is exciting." I didn't know there was any such tragic adventures in our family. "Tell me the rest of the story. What happened after they got away from those Indians?"

Pa stroked his long wild beard and cleared his throat.

"John Files grew up and got married up there in Virginia. When his children got big enough to make such long a trip the family struck out on an adventure of their own. They moved down to South Carolina."

"I know about South Carolina," I said. "Teacher said that's where this civil war started, when the Rebels attacked some fort."

"You mean Fort Sumter?"

"Yes. Fort Sumter."

"South Carolina is where John and Catherine Files were living in 1775 when the thirteen American colonies rebelled against English rule. John Files and his three sons signed up to fight in our country's War of Independence. He served as a Captain in the South Carolina Militia."

Pa said Captain John Files fought in the Battle of Cowpens, which took place not far from where he lived. He and his son Jeremiah both was wounded. The Battle of Cowpens wasn't a really big fight, but the Brits was weakened by the loss of so many of their soldiers. Turned out, this became a turning point in the whole War of Independence.

"Captain John was seriously wounded. They took him to his house over near Abbeville so his wife could help care for him. Lying there abed, he was attacked and killed right there in his own house. And do you know who did the killing? It was a group of British soldiers, helped out by some of their allies from the Cherokee Nation. So Indians helped to kill John Files after all.

"Can you believe such a thing, Fannie? As a youth of fifteen or sixteen he had escaped from those Shawnee warriors up on Files Creek. In the end, he died at the hands of the Brits and their Cherokee supporters." He went on to explain that not all the Indians in the area supported the British loyalists. A few tribes was friendly to the American side. Most, though, figured that an independent United States would gobble up too much of their territory. That was why they favored the English side in that war.

"After the war, my Grandpa Jeremiah Files and his brother Adam moved down here into Alabama. Their oldest brother, whose name was John after his Pa, moved up North and settled in the State of Illinois."

"So I guess some of my Files cousins around here must be kin to this Adam Files?" I had always wondered about that, us having the same name and all.

"Yes, they come from the same line of Patriots as you do, going back to Captain John. You may have noticed that ain't none of them Secesh, either."

"Now, Pa, there's part of this story that I don't understand about. Back then, who was the Patriots and who was the rebels? Was Captain John a Patriot or was he a rebel?"

"That is a very good question, and it's right smart of you to think of it. I've not thought of it that way before. That's something for us to ponder on.

"I hope this helps you understand why I had to go off and fight. Lots of folks shed their blood to help put this country of ours together in the first place. This Union had held together going on up toward ninety years, and I just couldn't sit by and let these Secessionists take it apart without putting up a fight. We are citizens of the United States of America. That is who we are.

"Fannie, I think that is what it means to be a Patriot. Somebody who loves their country and is willing to stand up for it. That's what my Grandpa taught me when he first told me this story. He told it to me over and over again. That is why I remember it so well after all these years. And I'll probably tell it to you a few times more.

"When I got to be a bit older, Grandpa Files wanted to be sure I understood just why this was important. To help me, he wrote out some words from Mr. Samuel Adams, a famous American who helped create our nation. Grandpa made me memorize those words so I could repeat them to him again and again. I would like for you to learn them, too."

The look on Pa's face told me he was reaching deep into his brain somewhere to find those words. He recited them to me, the way we have to recite our lessons at school.

"The liberties of our country are worth defending at all hazards; and it is our duty to defend them against all attacks. It will bring an everlasting mark of infamy on the present generation, enlightened as it is, if we should suffer them to be wrested from us by violence without a struggle, or to be cheated out of them by the artifices of false and designing men."

I didn't know what some words meant. Pa took the time to explain them to me so I would understand what Mr. Samuel Adams was trying to get across. He told me again how important this was to him. "When folks ask you why your Pa went off to fight for the Union you can tell them that is why."

Pa found a scrap of paper and a pencil and wrote down the words of Mr. Adams. I put the paper under my pillow and slept on those words. Next morning I put it away in my special safe place so I could keep it always.

Chapter 3

Pa 'woke with the sun, the way he used to before the war. When he spoke I was happy that his voice sounded stronger, almost like it used to.

"Now that I'm more presentable, I'm going into town and see if I can get us some farm animals and things like we lost in the war. Would you rather have some chickens or some hogs first, Mattie?"

"Chickens, I guess, Tom. They will give us eggs and meat. But what I really wish we had is a milk cow. We can't keep on taking from the neighbors now, with you at home."

He went to the shed and found the old wagon Rabbit used to pull. He picked up the tongues and began pulling it his own self, headed off toward town. We all laughed right out loud at the sight of my Pa pulling the wagon like he was a mule or something. I noticed how he was limping, though, and thought how this must be mighty hard work for him. We watched until he turned off onto the road toward town, then Ma and me went to work in the garden. We managed to get in the rest of the sweet 'taters and cut some of the cabbages.

It was near sundown when here Pa came riding in the wagon, pulled by a broken-down old mule, a skinny excuse for a milk cow tethered behind. In the wagon, he had a dozen chickens, legs tied to keep them from flopping around. The rooster in the bunch was protesting loudly at being confined, demanding to be released immediately.

Ma could hardly believe her eyes. "Land sakes, Tom, how did you pay for all those critters? They must have cost way yonder more than the money you got home with."

"I paid out some of the cash money I got home with, and I bartered for the balance. I ran into John Shaw on the road. Haven't seen him since our time together at Camp Davies. We got to talking and he said he could spare me this mule and cow. He has her calf and another heifer, so they'll have plenty of milk now with their children all growed up. We will give him some of those 'taters you and the girls were digging yesterday. He appreciated getting them in trade. He will be along tomorrow or the next day to get them. Come spring I'll go over and help him with plowing and things. I'm going to pay him for the mule whenever the army pays me for old Rabbit. I suppose that might be awhile coming, but it suits him to wait. He said we could bring the cow over in the spring and mate her with his bull, so we could start to build up a herd."

Ma smiled, remembering some of the ways she and Mrs. Shaw had helped each other when the men folk was gone. "They've always been mighty fine neighbors."

So that is how we began putting our little farm back together again, but it would be a long, up-hill pull. During the war one side or the other had taken off most everything we had. We had lost a whole lot, including our one good horse and ten or twelve head of cattle, forty or fifty head of hogs and several hundred bushels of corn. They even took off Ma's spinning wheel, and threw all Pa's books in the creek. It was the same with all of our neighbors and everyone we knew. Some lost everything they had, so on balance I reckon we came out right lucky that away.

Pa decided he wanted to name our new mule Rabbit, too, just like the one he took to war. "He's a sorry excuse for mule, nothing like our big, strong old Rabbit, but he's ours and he needs a name. 'Rabbit' will do as well as any."

At least now we had us a mule to pull the plow in the spring. Ma wouldn't have to do that herself the way she had for the past three years, with me guiding as best I could. And we will be able to go around in the wagon and not have to walk everywhere.

Pa put the cow out in the back pasture to graze. The little bit of corn we had managed to raise might help fatten her up so she would give more milk. Milking the cow would be my job again, like it used to be. Soon as the rooster gained his freedom, he commenced to strut all around the chicken coop, loudly declaring his independence.

The next morning, I went out to do the milking and brought in half a pail of fresh milk. I think that was the best milk I ever drank before or since. Ma allowed as how she'd be glad when that old cow could be milked twice a day. She was looking forward to having cream and churning some butter to cook with. Talk of churning brought to mind the taste of fresh buttermilk, and I was looking forward to having some of that with corn-bread and turnip greens for our supper. All the while, Ma was busy frying us up some fresh eggs for breakfast, the first of those we'd had in more than two years.

We passed the day with garden work and tending to the new critters. Pa went to see what shape the springhouse was in. Now we had a cow, we'd have to have a way to keep the milk and butter cool, and wasn't a thing better for that than the cool water of our spring. When he'd finished there, he found places where the fences needed mending lest the cow get out of the pasture. Truth was, Pa didn't have his strength built up yet, so everything he did took longer than it once did.

After supper, I cleared the table and helped Ma get the younger ones in bed. Then the three of us took our places beside the fire again. I sat on my stool at Pa's knee and asked him to tell us more about where he had been and what he had done.

Pa looked down at me and chuckled.

"Fannie, I think you've done outgrown that little stool you're sitting on. I made it for you when you were smaller than Penny. You're not a little girl anymore, are you? I need to see about getting you a chair of your own. Would you like to have a rocker like Ma's?"

"Pa, I been wishing for a rocking chair. I sure would like that."

"Well," he said, "I'll try to make a start on that." He smiled and nodded, then took a deep breath and went searching for his thoughts once more, staring down the lane and out toward the road.

"First off, I need to explain why I didn't come right on home after my year was up. That's the hardest decision I ever made, except for the one to go off and leave y'all to begin with."

This is what we really had been waiting to hear. What had happened to keep him from coming home when we thought he would?

"The simple answer is that I was scared. It isn't really that simple and I'm sure not proud to say it, but that's the truth of it. We were hearing all kinds of stories about the Home Guard and the Secesh mobs. They were lynching Union men like me when we came home. I'm sorry you have to hear about all of this, Fannie, but this is how it was for men like me, some of them was people I knew right well. Now, Mary Francis, this is going to be bad to tell and hard to hear. It's all true, but you sure don't have to listen to it if you don't want to."

I told him I really wanted to hear the whole story, so he went on with it.

"One fellow from the First Alabama told about his brother-in-law who came home when his term was up. He was badly mistreated before they strung up him from a tree in his own yard. They doused him with turpentine and set him afire while his family had to watch. George Curtis came home on leave and the Home Guard killed him right in his yard while his wife and three children looked on. The Home Guard arrested Henry Tucker at his home over in Marion County. They tied him to a tree before they gouged out his eyes and cut out his tongue. Then they literally skinned him alive. Others were ambushed. A whole lot of men were kidnapped and conscripted into the Confederate army. Union families have been tormented, harassed and killed.

"There was a family over in Jones County Mississippi whose man was shot, everything they owned trashed, burned or stolen away. That woman and her five children had nothing left to their name but the empty shell of a house. No food, no clothes, nothing. Not even a cup or a plate to drink or eat from. I thought if I came back, it would put all of us in more danger than we were in already. I was plumb scared, and that's the truth of it."

Tears formed in the corners of his eyes and slowly made their way into his newly clipped beard, then came like a flood. His whole body began to quiver and shake. I'd never seen my Pa cry like this before. When he got settled again he cleared his throat like he was going to go on talking, but Ma stopped him, taking his hand in hers. When I looked over at her I could see she was crying, too.

"Tom, this is a right painful part of the story for all of us," Ma said softly. "Why don't we let it wait a bit. We can talk more about this another time." That seemed to set his mind at ease a bit. "There is something else I want to know. You walk with a limp you didn't have when you left. You run out of breath pretty quick. What kind of injuries have you had, and where did you get them?"

"Ah, yes, Mattie. That came about during a skirmish at a place called Yellow Creek near Burnsville, Mississippi not far out from our headquarters camp. It happened on the fourth day of July 1863, our country's Independence Day. We were under the command of a Sergeant Major Dunn. I remember him because he was from Illinois and one of the nicest Yankees I ever served under. We had gone to scout out some Confederate locations and to see if we could get any pack animals or food for the regiment. When we stopped to water our horses at the creek, Johnny Reb came upon us all of a sudden like. We jumped up and scattered, looking for shelter or a way to get away.

"I managed to mount up and was looking around for Sergeant Major when my horse shied from the gun fire and confusion. He threw me, and I landed face down square on a big tree stump. Knocked the breath clean out of me right off, put my shoulder out of joint and broke my wrist. The horse stumbled on my leg and twisted it pretty bad. That's where I got my limp.

"Medics took me to Corinth where the docs said my lung was bruised up pretty bad. Never heard of such a thing, but I could hardly breathe any at all. My leg was pulled out of joint, but I sure was glad it wasn't broke. If it had been, one of them sawbones at the field hospital would have wanted to take it off for sure. I'd seen what that was like. There was pile of arms and legs stacked three or four feet high out behind the operating area, waiting to be hauled off and buried in a trench on the far side of the camp."

That made me and Ma cry just thinking that such a thing might have happened to him. She reached over and gently touched his arm as she wiped away her silent tears.

"All in all," he continued, "it took me 'til September to get so as I could move about. I guess I was pretty lucky at that, but I've not been really good for much since. Get winded pretty fast. I reckon I'll have this limp for the rest of my life, but it don't pain me as bad as it used to except when the weather turns off cold or I try doing too much. I'm just glad to be alive and back home in one piece. Thousands and thousands and thousands of men on both sides didn't make it home at all, lots of them our friends and neighbors from around here.

"We had several wounded bad at Yellow Creek, including my friend Private Murphy from over around Saragossa. He'd signed up at the same time I did, and we did a right smart amount of scouting duty together." There was a bit of a pause, his thoughts taking him away from us again as he stared into the fire. "He was a good man," Pa said quietly, gently nodding his head. "I never learned whatever happened to him after the medics took him away."

He sat looking deep into the fire, slowly rocking back and forth. Suddenly, he shook his head like he was erasing something from his thoughts. When he looked at Ma and me there was a hint of a smile on his face, but his eyes wasn't smiling.

"I spent about two months in the hospital. Wasn't much entertainment to be had. We played cards or checkers and sat around talking and singing songs. There was a soldier's song that was sung by one fellow. He sang it all the time, day and night, but I didn't care for it. It made some of us real sad, especially after a skirmish where men got killed or wounded bad. I remember some of it right well, and can even hear the tune playing in my head. Still makes me sad to recollect it:

> *'Farewell, Mother, you may never press me to your breast again;*
> *But, oh, you'll not forget me, Mother, if I'm numbered with the slain.'*

I knowed it wasn't just about mothers. It was about wives and children, too. It was one of the saddest songs I ever heard.

"When I came back in September, they bumped me up to First Sergeant in Company A. I never quite understood why they did that, but it sure made life easier on me. They say First Sergeant is one of the most honorable positions a common soldier can have. That made me feel right proud, me not being Regular Army and all. My job was to keep up with a whole lot of the records and paper work for the company. Truth is, couldn't many beside me read and write and do their numbers.

"Being First Sergeant kept me out of some of the more dangerous situations. It also let me have my own tent instead of being quartered with a bunch of folks. When I had a rough night breathing or when my leg or wrist pained me, I liked being in a tent of my own. But I still liked going out and sitting with the men, singing soldier songs around the camp fires. Some of the men had their harmonicas and played a long way into the night. Such a soulful sound that was. Made me wish I had my fiddle with me."

"Well, Tom, about the very same time you was on the mend is when our little Peggy was born," Ma said. "Did you know that? I had me a real hard time of it. When I knowed the baby was coming, I sent Fannie running over toward the Cooners to see if Mahalia could come help, but it's a right good piece over there. She didn't make it in time. Our baby girl was born right here on this floor, and me all by myself. 'Halie got here in time to help clean up the baby and get me in the bed. But it was a real hard time."

The tears came back up in Pa's eyes again. Ma moved over and put her arms around his shoulders as he slumped over, his head in his hands. We sat there quiet for a long time. After awhile we all got up and went off to bed. Ma came and tucked me in like she always does.

I didn't sleep much that night. I kept thinking about Pa hurt off over there in Mississippi all by himself and we didn't know, and Ma laying here on the floor giving birth to baby Peggy all by herself and he didn't know.

Chapter 4

Several days passed before any of us wanted to hear any more of Pa's stories, or for him to want to talk about them. He and Ma busied themselves getting the farm back into shape. He repaired some of the fences. I helped him make a better pen for the hogs he wanted to trade for. He patched the barn roof to stop the worst of the leaks, and replaced some barn siding the Rebs had taken for firewood. He talked about how lucky we was they'd not taken down the whole barn, bad as they needed wood for camp fires and one thing or another. He told how he and some of our soldiers had done just that on some farms where he'd been.

"We did some terrible things to folks," he said, while I held a board for him to saw. "It wasn't all the Rebels who did such things; we did, too. I feel bad for those folks we took animals from and whose food we stole. Of course, we didn't call it stealing. We called it confiscating, but it was stealing just the same. They did it and we did it. There are thousands and thousands of folks just like you and Ma who paid an awful price for this war. That makes me sad now that I'm here looking back on it."

We worked quietly together for a good while, sawing the boards he needed. Then, as he nailed them in place he chuckled, and a twinkle came in his eyes. It was the first time I'd heard Pa really laugh since he'd come home. He said that for all the tragedy and pain of the war, there was also some funny times. Sometimes you just couldn't help but laugh, even if you knew they wasn't funny in the end.

"Something happened before I got hurt at Yellow Creek. We were with Colonel Abel Streight. We were with him over around Town Creek and Courtland, just out from Decatur, scouring the countryside for the horses and mules. Some of us First Alabama men was split off from the rest and sent with General Dodge to help out with some secret campaign Colonel Streight would be leading. That's about all they told us. The rest was to be a big secret.

"That other bunch of First Alabama men went up around Nashville with Colonel Streight to meet up with some Regular Army. They were to come down from Tennessee to Mississippi and then fight their way across Alabama and over toward Rome, Georgia. Their aim was to destroy a railroad that the Confederates used to bring in supplies and fresh troops. The Colonel had about seventeen hundred men, Regular Army Cavalry and our Alabama Volunteers. But the thing is, they didn't have enough horses to accommodate such a crowd. So can you guess what they went off riding? They were mounted on the most rambunctious and contrary bunch of mules you ever saw."

Pa and me had a good laugh at the notion of an army riding off to war on them mules.

He went searching for the next nail in the pocket of his overalls. Finding it, he went on. "It was sure enough a sight to behold, those soldiers riding along with their feet near about dragging on the ground. My regiment, still under Dodge, set out for Tuscumbia while the others were coming down the Tennessee River."

"The Tennessee River, Pa?" That puzzled me. "I thought you said they was going to Mississippi and Alabama on this raid."

"That river starts way over east in the far end of the State of Tennessee, but it dips down into northern Alabama, then flows westward to a place called Eastport, Mississippi. It forms a little bit of the border between Alabama and Mississippi. Then it loops back up into Tennessee and goes on to Kentucky where it joins up with the Ohio River, which goes into the Mississippi River."

He promised that when we got inside he would get down the geography book and show it to me on a map. "That all figures into my story a bit later on."

He stopped and ran his hand over his nice neat beard. Clearing his throat, he took a deep breath while he was looking for his place in his story.

"It took the Colonel and his troops about nine or ten days to get over to Eastport, coming down river on flat boats. Now, I don't know if you know this or not, Mary Frances, but God didn't make mules fit to ride on a boat. Those mules didn't like that any at all.

"Soon as they got over to Eastport, Colonel Streight had to come directly over to our encampment to talk to General Dodge about the plans for his big adventure across Alabama. They confabbed until way past midnight. Over at Eastport, it was left to his troops to get those mules and all their provisions off the boats and get them settled down. And that's when the fun started."

He handed me a dipper of water from the pail he kept

nearby when he was working, and took a drink himself. Then he motioned for us to take a break, and we went to sit on the woodpile just outside the barn door. He took his red bandana from his back pocket and wiped his face.

"I want you to try to make a picture of this in your mind, Fannie. These Yankees didn't know a blamed thing about mules. And besides that, they didn't know the Rebel General Nathan Bedford Forrest had some secret scouts keeping an eye on this whole kit and caboodle. That old General Forrest was always plotting surprises for our folks. This time, though, he didn't have to do a thing but sit by and watch the comedy play itself out.

"It was early in the morning and still dark when they got those ornery critters off the flat boats, more than seven hundred of them all told. When those mules got their feet on solid ground for the first time in nine days, they set about celebrating like only a bunch of mules can do. They commenced to braying and honking, jumping around and running about and making such a fuss as you can't hardly imagine. A crazy bunch of them even ran into the river and drowned. More of them set out running across the fields and into the nearby hill country. They made enough of a fuss to wake the devil himself.

"It took several hundred men three days to round up such of them as could be found. Only a couple of hundred of the animals was rounded up, out of the seven hundred they started out with. General Forrest and his men could hear this whole sorry business. Now don't you know they laughed all the night through, watching those silly Yankees and their mule brigade?"

Pa and me enjoyed a laugh, too, just thinking about it. But then Pa turned serious. He said what happened after that wasn't

48

funny at all. All that business with the mules running off had set Colonel Streight's plan back near a week and deprived his men of the mounts they needed. These men was cavalry, not infantry and they wasn't used to walking. Of course, they wasn't used to riding on a stubborn old mule neither, which caused them a whole bunch of trouble from then on. Their adventure came to be called "Streight's Raid of the Mule Brigade." Pa said the rest of it turned into a very sad story, one he couldn't tell because he didn't see it. His units went with General Dodge back to camp over in Mississippi, while the "mule brigade" started their unfortunate run across Alabama.

Break time was over, and we went back to nailing the new boards on the barn. It took the rest of the afternoon, and by the time we finished the old barn was looking right sturdy again.

Before we went in for supper Pa said he had something to show me. There was some chestnut boards on his workbench at the far end of the barn.

"This is what I'm thinking to use to make your rocking chair. Chestnut is a good stout wood. I think this will make you a nice chair. I'll try to get on with it in a few days." That pleased me. I gave him a big hug and told him how nice it would feel for me to have a real chair of my own. He smiled down at me, his dark eyes warm and tender. "And it will be your own, Fannie. When the time comes for you to marry and set up housekeeping, it can go with you."

The thought of getting married made me giggle. For some reason, the face of Johnny Hinesley flitted through my mind. That was silly, for me to think of him right then.

That evening, we sat on the porch and enjoyed the breeze. With the sun down, the night air had more of a nip in it, but it felt good after a long day's work. Ma did some mending while we talked, and I worked on a crochet project she was helping me with. We talked about what we'd done and what we had yet to get done. We talked about the weather and hoped it would hold out a bit longer. We also talked about whether we'd go off to church the next day. We decided since this would be Pa's first Sunday back in church, maybe we'd go.

The sunset turned pale blue in the fading evening light, as we listened to the night sounds. A sly grin came over Pa's face. "Fannie, when I was about your age, I stayed up all night thinking I might see where the sun went of a night. I got real sleepy and may have nodded off. Then it dawned on me."

It took a minute for me to catch on to Pa's funny, but figured it out and nearly bent over laughing.

The had air turned crisp. so we got up and moved in to sit by the fire.

"Tom, I think it's time for us to get back to hearing where you been almost two years since you got out of the army," Ma said. "I know about you being afraid to come back here, and I sort of understand that now. But where and how did you spend all that time?"

This time Pa began to talk about it freely, without tears or sighing. He just talked kind of matter of fact like, almost as if it'd happened to somebody else and not to him.

"Well, first off, you need to understand that the First Alabama Cavalry was not on its own. We wasn't what they call Regular Army. We were just volunteers, kind of like added on to the ordinary troops. Troops came from all over these United States. I was with soldiers from Illinois, Ohio, Indiana, Michigan and all such places. There were volunteers like us from other southern states, too. They came from Tennessee, Georgia, Virginia, Florida and all over the South. One of our commanders told me there were volunteers like us from every state in that rebellious Confederacy except South Carolina. That made me feel real proud. I liked knowing that there were all these Southern Patriots fighting for our United States of America and not against it."

He stopped to catch his breath and gather his thoughts.

"I made friends with these people from all over. When my time was up, I got to thinking on that. If I couldn't come on home to you, maybe I could learn something about these United States. At the very least, maybe I could depend on these friends to help me stay safe until I could get home. I hoped maybe that would end up being of some benefit to all of us down the line.

"One of the men I met was a Major Cramer from the Fifth Kentucky Cavalry. I heard he was taken prisoner later in the war but got away and played a part in General Sherman's campaign from Atlanta all the way over into the Carolinas. Major Cramer introduced me to three privates whose time was up and who were headed back home up in Kentucky. They were named Mason, Alexander and Burdick. They invited me to travel along with them just to see that part of the country. I had never heard of the place in Kentucky where they were going. They said it was called Paducah, on the Ohio River near where it goes into the Mississippi River."

"The Mississippi River?" That got my attention. I remember when we talked about the Mississippi River at school. It is the very biggest river in the whole United States of America, isn't it, Pa? Did you get to see it?"

"Well, yes, I did see it, but you're getting way ahead of the story. I haven't gotten us out of Camp Davies yet. I thought on this idea of traveling with these men and decided it might be all right if I went along with them for a spell.

"We left camp along about the middle of January 1864, and started north across the western apart of Tennessee. We had to sleep in whatever kind of shelter we could find or make, or none at all. The weather was awful, rain and sleet and snow a good part of the time, freezing cold day and night. Most of the folks in those parts had strong feelings for the Confederacy. That meant we couldn't count on much help along the way. There was no fighting going on right then, but we knew that General Nathan Bedford Forrest had been in the area recently and might still be around. You remember him, Fannie? He's the same one who got such a laugh out of all those mules over at Eastport."

"You saw quite a lot of him, didn't you?" Ma said. "He must have been everywhere." I wondered how one man could be in so many places. Seemed like he moved fast.

"Well, as things would turn out, I saw and heard a whole lot more of General Forrest that I ever wanted to see, and none of it very pleasant."

Pa got that thoughtful, faraway look in his eyes as he stroked his beard. "So, there we were, nearly freezing to death in hostile Rebel territory. We decided it might be safer and more comfortable for us to travel by night. We could rest up during the day while we had the sun to warm us as we tried to sleep. Moving around would keep us warmer at night. As it turned out, that decision brought us some mighty good luck."

A small but warm smile brightened his face. I reached over

and took hold of his hand. "I guess you needed some good luck about then, didn't you, Pa?"

"Yes, and it came in the form of a candle burning in the window of a farm house. The house sat back off the road a ways in a copse of oak. Pin oak, I'd guess, because they still held their brown leaves even in the dead of winter. Its small flickering light shining in the darkness caught our eye.

"Private Mason knew something of the territory. When he saw that light in the window, he stopped dead in his tracks and pointed that way. He said, 'Fellows, I think we just came upon a bit of luck. If that is what I think it is, that house over there belongs to a family of Quakers. They be good folks who don't take any side in this war we been fighting.'

"That puzzled the rest of us. We had never heard tell of any folks called Quakers. What Mason said about them sounded like music to our ears. He said he knew some Quakers up around where he was from. They would keep a candle in their window of a night as a sign to passing strangers that they would be welcome at that house. That sounded very good to us. We had not slept in anything like a real shelter since we left the camp, and the prospect of doing so was most attractive to us."

"But wasn't you afraid of those strangers?" I asked. I still had bad dreams about the strangers who'd come to our house in the dark. They was not nice people.

"I understand that, Fannie. But these people put that candle in the window as a way to let travelers they would be welcome. We thought they must be pretty good folks. When Mason knocked on the door, it opened right quick, almost like they were expecting us. The man standing there wasn't as big as a minute. Not a whole lot taller than your Ma and skinny as

53

a rail, dressed in plain gray pants and shirt to match. A neat trimmed gray beard spanned his face from ear to ear, set off by pleasant blue eyes that twinkled as a smile lit up his face. His words were as plain as his dress. 'We make you most kindly welcome, friends. Thought you might be coming by afore the night had past. Come on in and get yourselves warm.'"

Ma's mouth opened in disbelief. "You mean they was expecting you, Tom? How could that be? Did they know who you was?"

"No, Mattie, we were perfect strangers to them and them to us. But he and his wife took us in like we were kin. The warmth of the welcome and of the room about overwhelmed us. We could smell the welcome in the air. There was the rich odor of stew cooking over the fire, and the sweet fragrance of fresh baked bread set out to cool on the sideboard. None of us had smelled, much less eaten such as that in a year or more. They were Mr. and Mrs. Yoder. They took us right in, fed us real good and let us sleep that night on the big stacks of fresh hay in their barn. Can you imagine such a thing?"

"But how come they was expecting you, Tom? Did this Mr. Yoder explain that to you?"

"Yes. He had been out hunting that afternoon and came upon our camp while we slept. Said he'd seen such a sight before with this war on. He could tell we didn't have much to eat and little to keep us warm. Folks like us had come to his door right regular."

Before heading to the barn for bed, Pa said they sat by the fire and visited awhile. Two of the bunch, the ones named Alexander and Burdick, was still uncomfortable being taken in like this. After all, they was out there in mostly Rebel territory. Burdick and Alexander feared it might be a trick to capture them. So Burdick asked Mr. Yoder straight out if he sided with the Union or the secession.

Mr. Yoder gave them another of his kind smiles, but with a firm set to his jaw and in his eyes. He explained that Quakers don't cotton to dividing people up in any such way as that. They don't give allegiance to a flag of any stripe. They just honor the Lord God Almighty who made us all. He said everybody is a child of God and that's all there is to that. Quakers don't believe in people shooting at each other. They'll not take up arms against anybody.

I'd never heard of any such before, and would have to think on that. If that's the way it is, then is there's not really any such thing as dividing folks up into "Patriots" and "Rebels." And what would Pa say to such a notion? I didn't think I would ask him about that just yet.

Pa, Mason, Alexander and Burdick ended up staying with the Yoders for about two weeks or more. He said their sleeping room out in the barn was as snug as a bug in a rug. The creek was convenient for bathing when the warm sun made that possible. Mrs. Yoder gave each of them a nice wool blanket. The four men helped each other keep their hair and beards trimmed properly, the way Mr. Yoder did. All told, they enjoyed the most comfort any of them'd had since before they joined the army.

They took pleasure from the exercise of helping Mr. Yoder around the farm. They fixed some fences that had got tore down by soldiers from one side or the other. The barn roof needed patching and there was plenty other chores to be done.

One day they was cutting brush down by the creek on the backside of the farm. Mr. Yoder wanted to make a pasture back there for some cattle he planned on getting, now that there wasn't so much scavenging going on in those parts. He'd come along to show them what to do, and insisted that they not take any guns with them.

The next part was one of the most interesting bits of Pa's story. He told how Burdick heard something in a nearby thicket. They moved carefully in that direction and right off came on a colored man and woman huddled behind a tree. From the looks of them, Mr. Yoder whispered, they probably was runaway slaves trying to get to freedom in up Illinois or Indiana. They was relatively clean, apparently having just washed in the creek, but they was dressed in little more than rags. Taking it all in, Mr. Yoder reached out both his hands to them. With what sounded like a smile in his voice, he spoke the same words he'd said to Pa and his friends: "We make you most kindly welcome, friends."

It amazed Pa what a difference those seven little words made to these poor people huddled together there in the woods. Pa said both of them commenced to trembling all over. Tears of relief and joy came streaming down their brown cheeks. They both took Mr. Yoder by the hands and went down on their knees in front of him. They were saying, almost singing, over and over again, "Glory hallelujah. Thank you, Jesus. Thank you, kind sir. Thank you, Massa."

Mr. Yoder lifted them to their feet and told them firmly that they was not to call him "Massa," because no man was their master now. They was not to call anybody master but Jesus. They had been created in God's own image and that meant they belong to God, and they should bend their knee to God alone.

I really liked the sound of those words. They sounded a lot

like some things Reverend McAdoo had said in some of his sermons. I heard one of the elders tell the reverend he better be careful with that kind of talk. I didn't understand why. It just sounded like God's truth to me. I think I would like to meet this Mr. Yoder. If I get to go see that big Mississippi River, maybe I can find Mr. and Mrs. Yoder and shake their hands myself.

When they got to the house, Pa said Mrs. Yoder fed the new arrivals. While they ate, she went digging in a trunk to find clean warm clothes for them. The newcomers introduced themselves as Paul and Dossie. They had, indeed, run off from a Tennessee plantation off to the east.

Mr. Yoder asked why they was running and so afraid. Didn't they know that President Lincoln had freed the slaves in the rebellious states, including Tennessee? That had happened a full year before. Paul explained that their "Massa" didn't recognize Mr. Lincoln's Emancipation Proclamation on his plantation.

"Ain't none of Massa's slaves gonna be freed," Paul said. "He say Mr. Abraham Lincoln don't be he President. Mr. Jefferson Davis be he President. He say if Mr. Abraham Lincoln want he slaves be free then he best come down to Tennessee and pay a fair price for us; then he do as he please if we be he property. He mean it, too. We done seen how he beat them as tried to get free, and how they be shackled and tied up like dogs. It took us a long while to work it out in our heads, but first good chance we get, we run. The good Lord done be with us and brung us here to you kind folks."

"Thank you, Jesus!" Dossie exclaimed, hands raised and eyes lifted heavenward.

At nightfall, Pa and his friends prepared to go out to the barn to sleep as usual, expecting Paul and Dossie to go with them. But Mrs. Yoder shook her head, saying "No," because it wouldn't be safe for them to stay out there. It would be too easy for them to be found by bounty hunters. By now several bands of them would be roaming the countryside looking for these two. Bounty hunters would get paid a pretty good bonus for taking Paul and Dossie back to the plantation.

She moved a hand-woven rag rug that covered the floor in front of the fireplace, revealing a trap door. A rough ladder led down into a concealed room under the house. She explained that it had only a dirt floor, but that the room was clean and safe. There was some rough but clean and comfortable beds down there. Pa remembered Mrs. Yoder telling "if the slave hunters come around, you will be able to hear them up here. Just you be quiet." With a warm smile she assured them "we will keep your secret if you will keep ours.".

"Yes, m'am Miz Yoder, we won't tell nobody," Dossie replied, "except maybe send word to some others who might be 'following the drinking gourd' over this away? Would that be all right?'

Pa recalled that Mrs. Yoder nodded, with a bright smile lighting up her round face. "Anybody who is following the drinking gourd will find a welcome here," she said.

"Pa, what does that mean, 'following the drinking gourd'?" I asked. We had some hollowed out gourds to drink from, but I didn't understand how a body could follow one.

"Dossie explained that to us that night. There's a song about it, passed around among slaves who wanted to escape to freedom. The drinking gourd in the song is really talking about the Big Dipper up in the sky. The handle of the Big Dipper pointed them in the right direction toward freedom in the North. Dossie and Mrs. Yoder sang part of it for us."

Paul and Dossie stayed the next day until near nightfall, when a young man came to the back door. Pa remembered that he had a beard much like Mr. Yoder's, except his was dark black, and his eyes were a piercing green. Mr. Yoder introduced him to Dossie and Paul as Eric and explained that Eric would see them on the way to the next safe house on their journey.

Dossie and Paul were not expecting that. "Oh, lands sake," Paul said with a smile, "You 'uns must be part of what I hear called a 'underground railroad, ain't you?" Mrs. Yoder confirmed it with a quiet nod of her head and a warm smile. "I reckon that be why you-uns made that room underground," chuckled Dossie. Pa said they all got a bit of a laugh about that before Eric, Paul and Dossie slipped out into the dark night.

When Pa finished telling us about his new friends, the runaway slaves, we started getting cleaned up for church the next day. We all took baths in the big zinc tub behind the cook stove where it was cozy and warm. Ma went first and washed her hair. Then Pa did the same, then the three of us. Penny complained the most about having her hair scrubbed. Washed and brushed, her long blond curls made her look like a big baby doll. I always wanted hair like hers. Mine was dark brown, almost black like Pa's and very straight. Peggy still had her light brown baby curls that had a red shine when you saw them in the sunlight.

I lay awake a long time that night thinking about those Quaker people. I liked what they said about everybody being God's children. I liked not wanting to divide folks up into enemies and friends. I especially liked the part about folks not shooting at one another. Our country had already seen way too much of that. I went off to sleep dreaming about a world where there wasn't any Patriots or Rebels, but just people who got along and lived together in peace. What would it be like around here if everybody made everybody "most kindly welcome?"

Chapter 5

Sunday morning we was up early to get the cow milked, the eggs gathered and the farm chores done so we could get off to church. Ma had laid out some Sunday go-to-meeting clothes that Pa'd not worn in near about three years. He'd put on a little bit of weight in the short time since he got home but his pants and coat still hung on him like rags on a scarecrow. His old gallusses was all he had to hold his pants up.

"Well, there's nothing to be done for it," Ma sighed. "Maybe this week I can take the britches up a bit, but I don't think I can do anything for that coat."

"That's all right, Mattie. It is what it is. It will be just fine. I'm not too proud to go to church dressed this way. Folks will understand the way it's been for us. Anyway, if they don't like the way I look, they just don't have to look at me. Ain't that right?" Ma reckoned he was right about that.

Our little church wasn't big enough for us to have a regular preacher all our own. Besides that, we had all kinds of folks in our church. There was Baptists, Methodists and Presbyterians, and even a few folks who didn't hold to any particular allegiance. Several different preachers took turn about holding services. No matter what the religious preference, though, we was all Union folks in this church. The Secesh left us when the war broke out and started up their own church on the other side of the creek. They even put up a sign saying they was called "Southern Baptist." We didn't have any sign at our church, maybe because nobody could figure out what to put on it. We was just a church, and that was plain to see by looking at it. That's what I thought anyway.

We hitched Rabbit to the farm wagon and headed off to the little white church house down the road. It used to be white, anyway. Now it needed painting right bad. Everything did. There hadn't been much upkeep done to anything since before the war. The little cemetery out back had been kept up, though. It looked real nice. The best thing was that now with the war past there was not so many fresh graves to be seen. There had been far too many buryings around here and everywhere in these hard times. I sure hoped we wouldn't have any more of those for a time.

As we turned into the churchyard, Pa asked, "Who is going to be doing the preaching today, Mattie? Do you remember whose Sunday it is?"

"Yes, I had to study that out because with one thing and another we haven't been here the last few Sundays either. I believe it's time for the Presbyterians."

Pa smiled. "I'm right glad of that for my first Sunday back. I like that Presbyterian preacher. Rev. McAdoo gives a mighty good talk, and he doesn't yell and carry on like some of them others."

Penny said she liked to listen to him talk. She thought his thick Scottish accent sounded nice and soothing. I thought he was nice enough, but he looked a bit too stern for me to say

I really liked him. With his bright red hair, his long thin face and those wire-framed spectacles perched on his sharp pointy nose, I didn't know whether to be afeared of him or to laugh.

We had no more than stopped the wagon in the churchyard than folks commenced gathering around. The men folk wanted to shake Pa's hand and say howdy. Most didn't know he'd gotten home, and they was surprised and pleased to see him. Nobody asked him anything about where he'd been, though. Such talk as that could wait awhile, even if it had been going on at the Ladies Aid Society for two years already.

I spied Johnny Hinesley standing off to the side. Johnny usually sat behind me at school when we had one. He was always real nice to me, and I enjoyed being around him. He gave me a big bright smile and a shy wave of his hand. I smiled back and quickly turned away. I hoped nobody saw me blush, especially not Ma or Pa.

When we got home, Pa set to skinning and cleaning a brace of rabbits he'd shot. Soon Ma had them cut up and frying slowly on the back of the cook stove. She had a big pot of fresh cut collard greens on to boil while sweet 'taters and cornbread baked in the oven. There was a fresh apple pie ready to go in the oven soon as the 'taters and cornbread came out. What a feast we had for Pa's first Sunday at home. We all sat around the kitchen table eating and talking and laughing, just like it used to be. I don't know when I had been so happy.

After dinner we sat on the porch and talked until Ma and Pa decided it was time for a Sunday afternoon nap. Penny and I took Peggy and went down by the creek to play. We sat on the bank and played a game of seeing who could spy the most interesting critters. We saw minnows, tadpoles, bream and crayfish. I even spotted a baby snapping turtle sunning on a rock on the far side. We couldn't see him, but we heard a bull frog off in the weeds saying, "Harrumph. Harrumph." Peggy liked to splash her hand in the water and cry, "Fishy, fishy," but that scared the minnows and tadpoles away.

After a while Ma and Pa came to see about us. They brought a picnic snack. It was cold milk and the apple pie left over from dinner. Penny and me remembered how we used to do this before the war, but this was Peggy's first picnic. She thought it was fun for us to be eating beside the creek.

Ma looked up in a pine tree and pointed to a robin perched on on a limb. She put her finger to her lips, telling us to be quiet, the she whispered, "Listen to his song. What is he singing?" We listened and listened, the Penny said, "He's singing 'pretty, pretty; pretty, pretty!" We all thought that was just right. When the robin flew away, Pa taught us a rhyme he learned when he was a boy:

> Little Robin Red breast,
> Sitting on a rail,
> Niddle-noddle went his head.
> Wiggle-waggle went his tail.

I liked being a family doing things together again.

When we got back to the house Pa got out his old fiddle. I'd almost forgotten about how he used play it on a Sunday afternoon. Sometimes Ma would sing along, and they taught me some of the songs. One of my favorites was a song that was new not long before Pa went away, written by a fellow named Stephen Collins Foster. Pa had ordered a copy of it in the mail, and he and Ma learned it. That was back when Pa had money to spend on such things. It was called "Beautiful Dreamer." I thought that song must have been the most beautiful song I ever heard. I asked them to sing it, and they did. I especially loved to hear Ma sing it of an evening just before bed time:

> *"Beautiful dreamer, wake unto me,*
> *Starlight and dewdrops are waiting for thee;*
> *Sounds of the rude world, heard in the day,*
> *Lull'd by the moonlight have all pass'd away!"*

I hummed the tune in my head as I was going to sleep, and dreamed beautiful dreams for the first time in a long time. They was interrupted, though, when a terrible storm came up. Wind-driven rain tapped steadily on the window and pounded the tin roof all night long.

The next morning we went out and found that some shingles was ripped off the roof and that the barn was damaged. Limbs and leaves from the trees left a mess everywhere. It took us working together as hard as we could all week to set things to right again.

Pa cut down some cedar trees and split the wood into shingles to repair the barn roof. He said it would be best if they could cure awhile before we put them on, so he figured out a way to make temporary repairs to keep the rain out until the new shingles was ready. While he was at it he decided to make up a supply of extras in case such a thing happened again.

When that was done, we set out to make the pig sty bigger. Pa wanted to see about getting us another pig or two. He thought maybe he should get us a sow so we could have some piglets to raise. Then we'd have a supply of pork to enjoy and could sell or trade some hogs for other things we needed.

Next day, Pa hitched the mule to the plow and set out to break up the ground in the old corn field out beyond the garden. Ma'd not been able to plant but just a little bit of it in corn last year. Most of the field had all growed up in weeds, some of it even taken over with pine saplings. I watched as he struggled to guide the plow through the hard soil. He had a rough time of it, given his bad leg, breathing problems and all. When he came in of an evening, he just wanted to wash up, have supper and go right to bed. This was not at all like the strong man I remembered from before the war.

In the night Peggy woke everybody up screaming, crying and carrying on, all doubled up in her crib with a mighty bad tummy ache. I'd never had the colic, but Pa had seen some of it in the army. Their doctors treated it with a heavy dose of Castor oil mixed with a little turpentine and honey. They'd give a dose of it about every three or four hours until the pain stopped. After two doses, Peg was resting easy and sound asleep. The rest of us was not settled so easily. After being awake so much of the night, even Pa slept until well past sun up.

It was the end of the week before we was to hear about what happened after Paul and Dossie left the Yoder's house. Pa thought he and his friends stayed there about another week. It was toward the end of February or early in March when they set out again. By then the weather had moderated a right smart. Mrs. Yoder made sure they had provisions enough for several days. She even insisted they take along the warm blankets they had used out in the barn.

"Those goodbyes came hard," Pa remembered. "That

Quaker couple had been real good to us as well as to Dossie and Paul. We couldn't help but think we might never meet up with them again in this world."

The men agreed it would be best to travel at night, the way they did before. They ate a good supper together and enjoyed pleasant talk around the fire until after sunset. Then, with handshakes all around, the men set out again, with a Quaker blessing fresh on their ears:

> *The Lord bless thee and keep thee.*
> *The Lord make His face to shine upon thee, and be gracious unto thee.*
> *The Lord lift up His countenance upon thee, and give thee peace.*

Pa's eyes grew sad and his brow furrowed with deep wrinkles as he sat motionless. "But there would be very little of peace in it." It sounded almost like a moan.

"We got a good two or three days along the way. Of a sudden the relentless sounds of gunshot pierced the morning air. The deep, familiar rumble of canon fire shook the ground under our feet, mixed with the tat-tat-tat of small arms fire. The light breeze coming at us from the west became heavy with the sharp acrid smell of battle.

"The war. Here we were, being drawn back into the horror of it. We had almost forgotten the gut wrenching terror of it during those weeks of living with Quaker tranquility. But there it was again. The sound, the feel, the smell of death and destruction came over us like a blanket of doom. Exactly where it was we didn't know; that it was fairly close was as sure as sure could be. There would not be much rest that day."

He fell silent. Ma reached over and touched his hand. When she did, his whole body began to tremble and jerk. Beads of sweat broke out on his forehead. His face contorted like he was in some terrible pain. His mouth stretched open, crooked and wide in a voiceless scream. Ma fell to her knees and took him in her arms. He began rocking back and forth, moaning like a baby. I commenced to cry and call to him, but he didn't seem to hear. Whatever tortured world he had gone to in his mind, we couldn't go there.

"Fannie, help me get him to the bed." Ma had him in her arms, trying to lift him from the chair. "Go turn back the covers. Then it will be best for all of us to go the bed. I think he will be all right in the morning. He's just been working too hard. When he's had some rest, everything will be better."

It felt to me like the war had started up all over again in Pa's head. It worried me how this war didn't seem to want to be over. When I tried to talk to Ma about that, she just said I was too young to be worrying my head over such things. Why did she keep on treating me like I was still a little girl? Couldn't she see that I was growing up and thinking grown-up thoughts?

Ma was wrong. Pa was not better. He stayed in bed far later than any of us had ever known him to stay abed. He just lay there, not moving, not speaking, his bedclothes wet with sweat. His glassy dark eyes was open wide without seeing anything the rest of us could see. Sometimes he blinked furiously and his body trembled like he was crying, but there was no tears. Now and again his mouth would open as if he was about to scream, but no sound came.

Ma told Penny and me to take Peggy outside and play. She would sit there and keep him company. She wiped his face and arms with a wet cool cloth, humming to him very softly. I thought I recognized a song from church, but I couldn't recollect the words.

We went outdoors but we didn't feel like playing. We found a place where we could look in through the window without Ma catching us. We wanted to keep our eyes on Pa, too. We was afraid, even Peggy. She couldn't understand about it but she sensed our fear. Penny kept whispering to me, "Pa's not going to die is he?" I told her I didn't know, but I didn't think so. He had lived through all that fighting. I didn't think he would die now, being safe at home and all.

About midday we saw him move. He said something to Ma and then put his feet off the side of the bed. He sat there for several minutes talking to Ma. We moved up closer to the window to try and hear, but his voice was weak and wobbly and hard to understand. We got only a few words. He said "war" and he said "Forrest" and he said "horrible." He said "blood" and he said "murder" and he said "escape." When he said "Forrest" I knew he must be talking about that Rebel General Nathan Bedford Forrest again. After a few minutes Ma helped him stand up, and they moved off toward the kitchen.

We decided to go look in at the kitchen door. When we thought we could get on with it we'd go running inside and give him a hug. That's what we did, and it made him smile for the first time since this fit came on him.

"There's my girls," he said. His voice was soft but not as weak as I expected it to be. "I been wondering where you had gone."

The more he talked the more his voice sounded just the way it should. His dark eyes even had a little bit of a sparkle in them again. Ma put water on to make him some coffee. Of course, it wasn't real coffee. She'd not been able to get any of that since right after the start of the war. She concocted this drink from roasted dandelion root that she dug herself, dried and chopped up into little pieces. She said it made a pretty good kind of coffee if you didn't work too hard at remembering what real coffee tasted like. Anyway, she thought it was better than some of what other things folks around here used. She didn't like to use chicory, burnt corn or dark roasted peas. She also set about frying up some eggs while I sliced some of the fresh bread I'd baked before Pa got bad.

Pa picked Peggy up and sat her on his knee, bouncing her up and down and singing her an old song his Pa sang for him and he had sung to Penny and me.

> Ride a cock-horse
> To Banbury Cross,
> To see what a penny can buy.
> A ring on her finger,
> A bonnet of straw,
> The strangest old lady
> That ever you saw.

She giggled and giggled. Whenever he stopped she squealed "Do it again, Pa," so he did it again and again until Ma put our food on the table.

After we finished eating he said, "I think I'll go over toward town today and see if I can get us that sow we fixed the sty for.

Or maybe I'll get us a drift of piglets to raise. If we got a gilt or two, we could build up our stock faster. Anybody want to go with me?" He glanced over toward us and smiled. Penny jumped up and down and raised her hand with excitement, squealing "I want to go, Pa! Can we? Can we""

I was just as excited as Penny was, but I wasn't about to jump up and down like a seven-year-old. "Yes, Pa, we want to go, please." I smiled. We'd not been anywhere with Pa since he got home except to church on Sunday.

Ma thought it best for her to stay home and keep Peg. They might go out and see what needed doing in the garden. She'd seen where some pecans had fallen and thought maybe Peggy could help her pick up a sack full. She might even make a pecan pie for supper.

"And that reminds me, Tom. Yesterday I saw a dead tree trunk over beyond the garden. It looks to have a good-sized bee hive in it. Do you suppose you remember how to rob the honey out of it? I sure would like to have some of that honey to cook with." I chimed in that I wanted a piece of the comb to chew. Pa looked doubtful, but said he would think on it.

He hitched the mule to the wagon and we climbed in. We got to sit on the front bench with Pa, one on each side. We even got to hold the reins and take turns driving the mule. He taught us how to "gee" and "haw." We learned that "gee" means go right and "haw" means go left. I couldn't help but wonder how that dumb old mule knew that. Didn't seem very likely that his own Pa might have taught him any such as that.

When we got to town Pa stopped off at the general store. He wanted to talk to one of the men who was sitting on the porch whittling on a piece of pine. When the wagon drew up, several of them said, "Howdy, Tom." They allowed as how they was right proud to see him home safe from the war. All but one of them, that is. He never said a word. In a minute, he hurried off like he had an errand that took him somewhere else.

Once more didn't anybody ask where he had been and why he stayed gone so long. Seemed nobody wanted to talk to him about that. Pa went over and sat down to talk to the whittler. I had seen him around, maybe at church, but didn't know his name. Pa gave Penny and me a penny each and told us to go inside and see if they had any hard candy in there.

We was delighted. We'd not had any candy in an awful long time. Ma always said she didn't have any money for such foolishness. She said she had enough problems just keeping food on the table for us. And I reckon she was sure enough right about that.

Us children had never been allowed to go in the store all by ourselves before. I felt like a grown-up. I knew just where they kept the candy, in a big glass case near the front wall. I remembered when it had been filled up with more kinds of candy than you ever could imagine. Now they had just a few peppermint sticks, lollipops, jelly beans and some hard drops of horehound and sassafras. They was three for a penny. Penny pressed her nose against the glass so she could get a good look at everything. I chose one sassafras and two peppermint sticks. Penny just got three peppermints. She'd never had any of the other kinds but knew the peppermint was good.

A kindly lady with gray hair done up in a bun on the back of her head got the candy for us. She wrapped it up in bits of brown paper and asked in a very nice voice if that would be all for us today. I said, "Yes, thank you," just the way I had heard

Ma say it. I felt like a real grown-up when I slid my penny across the counter to pay her. I think Pen did, too. When the lady said, "Thank you very much. Please come again," I couldn't help but giggle.

As we turned to leave, I noticed Johnny Hinesley standing at the back of the store with his Pa. I slowed down and looked his way, but I don't think he saw me, so we hurried on out. How come seeing Johnny always made my face go red?

Pa and the whittler was waiting for us by the wagon. As we all got in, Pa said we was going out to Mr. Swindle's farm to look at those piglets. He and Mr. Swindle sat up front this time. We had to sit on the floor in the back of the wagon. Pa looked back to be sure we was all right. He smiled and said as how he might look into putting another bench back there for us to sit on. I sure liked that idea. Bouncing around on those rough boards hurt my bottom. And anyway, I was getting too big to sit like that.

It wasn't far out to Mr. Swindle's place. He had lots of pigs of all kinds and sizes. Pa said that was about all he raised. The stink was awful. Penny and I held our breath nearly all the time we was there. I didn't understand how a body could stand to live around that smell all the time. Maybe they got used to it, but I didn't think I ever could.

Pa and Mr. Swindle agreed on a pair of gilts and a couple of boars. In return, Pa would come over in the early spring and help Mr. Swindle do some repairs to his barn and fences. It was a good trade for both of them. Mr. Swindle tied the feet of the pigs together to keep them from running around or jumping out of the wagon. They squealed and fussed about it, but soon settled down.

Penny and I was real glad we could sit up on the front bench with Pa again. We didn't like the idea of sharing the back of the wagon with those pigs. We offered to share our candy with Pa, but he said that was a special treat just for us. When we got home we helped Pa take the little pigs out to the sty with the old sow. She seemed quite pleased to have these young'uns for company. They went right to the trough and began eating like they'd not been fed in a month of Sundays. When Pa was satisfied that they was settled in, we went in to clean up for supper. While we ate, Pa told Ma he'd remembered how to rob the bee hive. He said he'd do that as soon as the weather turned cold.

"Matter of fact I was talking to one of the fellows at the store about that. He reminded me of how to go about it without getting bad stung. Besides that, he said he would trade me a jar of blackstrap molasses for a jar of honey with the comb in it, and we shook on it." That pleasured Ma quite a bit. She allowed as how she liked cooking with blackstrap.

Pa never said a word about what had happened the night before. Neither did any of us. Some things was better left alone.

Chapter 6

The weather began to feel more like winter, with the winds turning from the north. Pa commented that the heavy coats on the wooly worms was foretelling hard cold weather to come. I didn't understand how any old worm could tell about such things as that. He said he sure didn't know how they did it, either, but his Grandpa had taught him how to look for the signs. He said, when the brown bands on the woolly worms are narrow when the fall is coming on, that means a harsh winter coming. If the brown bands are wide, you can look for a mild winter. We turned over some leaf litter until we found one of the little critters. Sure enough, it had a narrow brown stripe around its middle.

I still didn't understand how they knew. Anyway, we commenced to work extra hard building up a good supply of kindling and firewood, just in case those little woolies was right.

Pa said we really didn't want to use pine unless it was all that was to be had. Oak wood was the best. When I asked why, he said, "You sure are full of questions these days, aren't you!" I told him my teacher at school said asking questions was the best way to learn about things. Pa nodded and smiled. "Yes, I guess that's right. Well, when you burn pine wood it puts out a kind of tar that sticks to the inside of the chimney. The heat from the fireplace can start the tar to burning, and maybe set the house afire." After that, I didn't pick up a single piece of pine.

Later that winter, the McDade's house up on the ridge above where we live caught afire. It burned plumb down to the ground. From our front porch we could see the bright yellow and red light from the flickering flames lighting up the night sky. I wondered if burning pine wood in their fireplace was what caused that fire. Wasn't anybody hurt, but they lost everything they had. Everybody for miles around came to help. They pitched in to raise a cabin to get the McDades through until spring, when they could build something better. Even some of the Secesh came and worked alongside Union folks to help out. Ma took Mrs. McDade a patchwork quilt she'd made. Others brought more things to help them get back on their feet.

Seeing how all these folks pitched in to help made me feel real good about our neighbors. It made me think on what those Quaker folks said to Pa about how people ought to treat each other. Still, I sure hoped we wouldn't ever need any such help as the McDade's got.

After supper that night we sat by the fire the way we did of most evenings. The last several nights Ma had sung us some songs or Pa read from the family Bible. Some nights Penny would stay up a spell, now that she was getting older. Tonight, though, it was just the three of us, the way it was most of the time.

Pa reminded us of what he'd told Ma the very first night he was back home, about how some of what he had to tell it wasn't fit for little ears to hear.

"And that's the truth if ever it's been told under heaven," he said. "But Mary Francis is right grown up. Maybe it is just as well she hear some of what terrible things we human beings can do to one another. So, if you want to, Fannie, you can stay and listen. But what I'm about to tell is pretty bad. If you decide you don't want to hear it, you can just go on off the bed whenever you want to."

I told Pa that with us four being here all by ourselves through most of the war, I'd already seen and heard some pretty awful things. I told him about the time I was near about late for school and took a short cut through the woods. About half way to the school house, I came across a dead body hanging from the limb of a big oak tree.

"It looked like he might've been a colored man." I looked to see how Pa was taking what I was telling him. "I couldn't hardly tell for sure because he'd been set afire hanging there by the neck. The sight and smell of that made me sick to my stomach. I ran away from it as fast as I could. I went on to school, but I didn't tell anybody about it. When I got home I told Ma. She said what I'd seen was called a lynching. It was the way some white people treated some of the colored. Ma told me sometime the Secesh even did that to white men like you who took to the Union cause. So you see, Pa, the war wasn't just way off yonder where you was. It was right here where we've been, too. I reckon maybe I've seen and heard more bad things than you've known about."

Pa's eyes filled up with tears. Seemed to me like he did that right often now. Far as I know, he never used to. I reckon the war must have hurt him more than just in the leg and lung. He sighed one of those really deep sighs like he did when he was sad or worried. I was afraid what I'd told him might set off another of his bad spells, but he just stroked his beard, caught his breath and went on.

Then he told the most awful story I ever heard.

He and his traveling companions had been gone from the Yoder's place about three or four days and was getting pretty close to the Mississippi River.

"Fannie, you've been asking if I got to see it. We had gotten near a place called Henning, a bit east of the town of Memphis that was right on the banks of the river. That's what the four of us were talking about when the sun broke through the twilight. Our immediate task had to be finding a place to rest up until nightfall.

"The land off to the west of the track they was on was nothing but marsh and swamp, so they stayed to the east where the land was higher. There was a thick copse of beech and oak on a rise that would provide us a good place to stop. Mason went exploring and found there was a small cave in a pine thicket at the far side of the grove. That cave was the best camping spot we had found in our travels. Burdick discovered a small spring back up in our little cave, and brought water to make us some coffee, such as it was. For some time we had been hearing very familiar sounds of battle coming from off to the west. About the middle of the morning, maybe around ten o'clock, an awful ruckus came crackling through the air.

"Burdick was the first one to say anything. The rest of us were too surprised that of a sudden we could be so close to the war again. That dreadful sound does strange things to a body, makes the heart pound like it might bust. I wonder if that fear will ever die away, or does it just keep on eating at a man 'til he can't stand it anymore? That still comes to my mind of a night when I hear a strange noise off in the distance. Especially if it's a gunshot, even if I know it's just a hunter in the woods.

"We'd not seen any sign of war since before we got to the Yoder's place, though we'd heard that General Nathan Bedford Forrest had been hanging around those parts."

Burdick knew there was a Union Army outpost over north of Memphis where one of his cousins had been stationed at a place called Fort Pillow. I wondered why the army would name a fort after a comfortable place to lay your head. Pa assured me there sure wasn't anything comfortable about it, certainly not with what they was hearing going on over in that direction.

"At first we talked about going exploring to see what we could see, but the more we thought on it, the less we thought it was a good idea. We had seen about all the shooting and killing we ever wanted to see in our lifetimes. We agreed it would be best for us to stay put for as long as need be until we could figure out the lay of the land, even if it delayed us for a day or two. Maybe we could figure out what the ruckus was about without going over there and sticking our noses in it. We broke out the food left from what Mrs. Yoder had fixed for us and ate the last of it for our midday meal. Then we stretched out to get some rest."

There was no sign that Pa was having any problem talking about all of this. In fact, he sounded kind of removed from it like as if he'd not been there himself but had just heard somebody telling about it.

"Well, whatever kind of battle was going on over there, it was a sure 'nough big one. Along about middle of the afternoon, there was a bit of a lag, with just some sporadic light arms fire. Alexander reckoned as how that meant one side or the other was looking for a truce or surrender, and I agreed. But that didn't last long and then everything started up again, but more ferocious than ever, if that be possible. The Rebels were really pounding them hard, sending a thick gray haze across the horizon, and the foul smell of fire-and-brimstone gunpowder.

"Late in the day the sounds changed again. Now we could hear voices screaming and shouting, along with the crackling of small arms fire. Alexander said, 'Oh, that don't sound good. I'd say they're down to hand-to-hand combat now. The Rebs must be whipping them pretty bad.' Everything fell silent except for occasional gunfire. What we called the 'cleaning up' operation was probably underway, but believe me there's not anything clean about it. The infantry is going through the field, looking for people bad wounded but not dead yet and putting them out of their misery with a shot to the head."

Pa broke out into a heavy sweat, droplets running down his face into his beard and staining the collar of his shirt. But his eyes, his voice and his mind was clear. He paused to mop his face with his bandana and catch his breath.

"As the sun was going down, things fell deathly quiet. This had been the time of day we usually started out traveling. Mason rekindled the fire and pretty soon the cave became downright cozy. We didn't even need the blankets Mrs. Yoder had sent with us, except they made right good pillows for our heads. Burdick went out to see what he could find for us to eat and came back with a clutch of doves. Not much meat on them, but we roasted them over the fire and let that be our supper. Having eaten, the other three dozed off, and I stood guard on the first watch.

"About midnight, Mason came to relieve me at the watch. As I started into the cave, we heard movement in the underbrush off to our right. On full alert, we aimed our rifles in that direction and waited. A voice, weak as could be, called out for help, coming from nearby. 'Is there anybody here can help me?' A young man, not more than twenty or twenty-one I'd say, came crawling through the brush."

Pa sat, head turned so he could gaze out the window down the lane, like what he was going to tell was coming to him from down there and he had to wait for it to get here.

"That young fellow wore the tattered uniform of a sergeant in the 13th Tennessee Cavalry, United States Army, a Southern Patriot like us. His chest was covered in blood, his hands and feet battered and bruised, and he was covered with mud and slime from head to toe, like he'd been traveling through a swamp. The legs of his trousers were worn away as were the sleeves of his coat, leaving his knees and elbows scraped and skinned pretty bad. He must have crawled like that a right good distance.

"None of us knowed any medicine, but Alexander said he had helped out some as an orderly in one of the hospitals in Corinth when they was short- handed. He had seen some of what they did, and helped with the doing when there wasn't anybody else to pitch in. He tore the cloth away from where the wound seemed to be and we saw he had a gunshot to the shoulder. The bullet was still in it. We didn't have anything to clean it with except water, but Alexander said we had to get that lead out of him or he would die from the infection for sure.

"His name was Jeffrey Thompson from near Paducah. When we told him that was just where we were intending to go, he

81

shook his head and said 'Don't go there. Not safe.' Alexander was heating the blade of his Bowie knife in the campfire. Alexander told him he was sorry but this was sure to hurt a lot. Thompson nodded that he understood. Burdick found a sturdy stick and had him bite down on it to help endure the pain. Alexander poured some warm water over the wound to wash away the blood and dirt, and then used the heated point of his Bowie knife to pull the bullet from the wound. Fortunately it came out right easy like, without any cutting, but Thompson still passed out from the pain. We all thought he was a brave young man. We washed the wound again as best we could, but we had no clean cloth to make a bandage. It would just have to be what it was."

During the night, Pa said, three more Union soldiers found their way to the little camp in the woods. All but one had minor injuries, but all were wet and covered in mud. The one that was hurt bad died almost as quick as he got there. They decided they'd have to bury him nearby, but that would have to wait 'til they was sure it was safe to leave their hiding place. All these men were Patriots from the 13th Tennessee. The ones who was able to talk told how they had been deep inside the fort and had escaped through a gate in the wall backing onto the Mississippi River. The only way out was through the swamp land to the east of the fort. That accounted for the shape they were in when they found us.

"Well, Fannie, now comes the really bad part, so if you would rather not hear it you better go on to bed now." Pa looked at me real serious like. But I didn't want to go. I wanted to hear it to the end, no matter how bad it got

Pa paused and shook his head. He said he could see the

fear and horror still in the face of one of the young soldiers as he told of hearing the Confeds coming around shooting people. He just knew he was done for. He played dead as best he could, and Johnny Reb passed him by.

The others told that it was like that for them, too. What they told about was a terrible killing. One of them recalled seeing his best friend leaning against the wall of a building, with a bloody mass that looked like snakes spilling out of his belly. Pa said they all called what was happening around them a "massacre." I didn't think I'd ever heard that word before, but I knew I was glad I never had to see one.

Over the next few hours, the soldiers gave Pa and his friends the details of what had happened at Fort Pillow. Pa told their story in a low but strong voice.

"It seemed like they really needed to talk about it. They had heard that General Forrest was headed their way. He wanted to capture the horses and stores of ammunition they had at Fort Pillow, and he had the advantage. After all, this was his home territory. Burdick allowed as how Forrest had been mayor of Memphis and was a wealthy slave trader before the war. Seems there were only about six hundred Union troops at the fort. All of them were Southern Patriots, colored and white, and General Forrest was known to hate all of them. He had brought some two thousand against them, so it wasn't a fair fight at all. But that's the way it is in war. Ain't much fair about it most times.

"About half the Union men were from the Second Colored Light Infantry. I had run into some of them when I was scouting out Rebel locations and strength north of Corinth up into Tennessee. Back then I think they were called by a different name, something like Light Infantry of African Descent.

"It was hard to keep up with which of these soldiers was telling what. Sometime several were talking all at once. What they told was an awful story of bloody warfare at its worst. Best we could understand, Forrest attacked the fort sometime in the early morning. The Union men were under the command of a Major Booth, who was shot and killed by one of Forrest's sharpshooters early on in the fight. Jeffrey Thompson told as how he saw the major killed; said his head exploded like a melon when the shell hit him. After Booth was shot, a Major Bradford took charge. In his judgment, Major Bradford was not the sharpest knife in the box. In a short time, the Confederates over-ran the barracks that were on the south end of the fort.

"That surprised us. The commander should have ordered them burned down when they saw the attack was coming. As it was, those buildings gave the enemy a clear shot right down into the fort itself, leaving the troops exposed like sitting ducks.

"The fighting went on for a long time. The fellow called Jimmy thought it might have been five or six hours. Forrest sent a messenger under a white flag, bringing a demand for the fort to surrender. Major Bradford requested an hour to discuss the matter with his officers, but the general demanded an immediate answer and gave him just twenty minutes to think on it. The major replied he could not meet such a demand without time to consult with his officers. General Forrest considered that a refusal to surrender."

Pa sat still, shaking his head like he could hardly bring himself to go on with the story.

"All three of the soldiers jumped into the telling at that point. The Confederate assault was worse than ever. Mason and Burdick both remembered hearing a great increase in the noise of battle sometime in the middle of the afternoon. That was when the infantry got right into the fort and started going at it hand-to-hand with the Union men. The fort was supposed to get support from some Union gunboat in the river on the back side of the fort near where these three men said they were. But the gunfire was so fierce that the boat had to close up its gun ports to keep their powder from being shot into and set on fire. After a time, the boat gave up the fight and started to move toward the north, away from the fort. So the Union troops didn't get the expected support from that quarter.

"After that," Pa said, "the whole fort just turned into a slaughter field. The attackers, with bayonets drawn, ran into the Union soldiers crying out, 'Give no quarter! No quarter!'"

"What did that mean, Pa? 'Give no quarter?'"

"Ah, Mary Francis, that means that no one would be spared. No mercy was to be shown. Many of the Union men were trying to surrender. They threw down their weapons and raised their hands. But that stopped nothing. The slaughter went on and on, especially the killing of the colored troops. It seemed to the men talking to us that the colored were being marked especially for killing. Jimmy said it looked to him like there was no more than a handful of them left to be taken prisoner. It was pretty much of a mass lynching. He saw some of the Negroes go on their knees unarmed to beg the Rebels for mercy only to be shot down on the spot.

"Two of the men who had escaped down by the river told how they saw a hundred or more of the colored troops throw themselves into the Mississippi trying to get away. They said every one of them either drowned or was picked off by the sharpshooters until the river ran red with blood as far down stream as they could see."

Pa's face was red, with sweat running from his brow. I couldn't imagine why or how folks could or would do such things. Didn't they know every one of those boys had a momma and daddy, maybe sisters and brothers, maybe wives and children back home waiting for them just the way we was waiting for Pa? But Pa said that is the way it gets sometime in battle. Blood thirst just takes over. The killing takes on a life of its own. Nobody is thinking about it anymore. They just go on killing 'til there's nobody left to kill."

My mind went to all the graves of soldiers I'd seen being dug in our church burying ground. It made me wonder how they buried all the men that was kilt at Fort Pillow. When I asked Pa about it, he got real still.

"Well, Fannie, there's more to the awful story Jeffrey Thompson told me. He said General Forrest set some of the captured colored troops to digging a big, deep ditch. Then he ordered them to commence tossing the bodies of their dead comrades into it, colored and white together. Quick as they filled one up, he had them digging another one. I don't reckon anybody knows how many graves like that there was.

"Next day, when General Forrest was ready to order his troops out of Fort Pillow, he just had them set fire to all the buildings still standing in the place. Some of them was where the Rebs had put men who stood some chance of living, but Jeffrey Thompson didn't know just what happened to all of them. We could see the smoke and fire all the way to where we was camped. But that wasn't the worst of it. Near sundown, the wind shifted out of the west and blew the smoke right our way.

There was so much of it, it made us all sick. And it wasn't just the smoke, Fannie. It was the smell. The smell of burning flesh. That devil of a general must have been burning up the bodies of some of our soldiers. We were hoping and praying they were all dead before they were set on fire."

That made me sick to my stomach just thinking on it. I didn't want to hear anything more about Fort Pillow. But I told him I did want to know what happened to those three soldiers who was with them in that cave. I know they was headed toward Paducah, Kentucky, but that one young sergeant had told them it was dangerous to go there. Lots of questions swirled round and round in my head, but now wasn't the time. We was all ready to head off to bed.

I didn't sleep much that night after hearing about all of that killing. Ma and Pa didn't either. I heard them talking together way into the night, and I think Pa was crying part of the time. After all the bad things he'd seen and heard about, I'd still be crying about it, too. A body can take only so much of such terror and suffering until the mind and soul can't stand any more. That's what I thought, anyway.

Fall weather set in and we went about getting the pumpkins out of the garden and cutting the collards and turnip greens. The three of us girls had fun toting the pumpkins to the shed, even Penny. Ma and Pa laughed at the sight of their littlest daughter struggling to tote the biggest pumpkins she could get her little arms around. When this was all finished, Pa thought he might as well hitch old Rabbit to the plow and turn the soil over so as to be ready for the spring planting.

A light snow was falling as we went off to church on the Sunday before Thanksgiving. Pa had made that bench he promised so us girls had a good place to sit in the wagon. Instead of looking forward like we usually did, we turned around to look out the back. It was fun watching the wagon wheels leaving tracks in the fresh snow, with the mule's hoof prints in the middle. In the cold morning air we could see our breath, and Penny thought that was funny. Seemed to me even Rabbit was happier pulling the wagon in the cool weather.

Rev. McAdoo was our preacher again and that made Pa glad to be there. Everybody was surprised to see him, though, because this was supposed to be the Baptist preacher's time. Before getting the service started, Rev. McAdoo announced that Brother Womble had moved up to Ohio. There was a church up there that wanted him to come to be just their pastor, so he wouldn't be sharing his time with any other church. Our elders would be trying to find somebody to replace Brother Womble, but for the time being, Rev. McAdoo and Parson Wainwright would be taking turn about.

The preacher said he had brought something special for us. It was a message from our new President, Mr. Andrew Johnson. I knew we had gotten a new President after Mr. Lincoln was shot and killed, but I didn't remember his name. That was one of the saddest things that had ever happened to our country except for that awful war. I was interested to hear what President Johnson had to say. Rev. McAdoo read us the President's Thanksgiving Proclamation, dated October 28, 1865, from The White House. I didn't rightly know what a proclamation was, but if President Johnson had sent it to Rev. McAdoo to read to us I knew it had to be something important.

President Johnson wrote that we should thank God because, "it has pleased Almighty God during the year which is now coming to an end to relieve our beloved country from the fearful scourge of civil war and to permit us to secure the blessings of peace, unity, and harmony, with a great enlargement of civil liberty."

When I heard those words I said "Amen," right out loud, much to the surprise and embarrassment of my parents. Both of them turned to "shush" me at the same time. The people sitting near us snickered, but I didn't see anything funny about it. I meant that "Amen" as much as I have meant any word I ever spoke in my whole life.

After church was over I asked Mr. McAdoo if he'd please read those words to me again so I could remember them. He very kindly sat down with me on the front pew and showed them to me so I could follow along while he read them. When he saw how interested I was, he gave the paper to me to keep for my very own. After that, I was quite sure Mr. McAdoo must be the very best preacher in the whole wide world, and from that day to this, I have always said I was a Presbyterian, no matter what kind of church I was in.

When we got home I sat down to read Mr. Johnson's words again. I also got out the paper Pa'd given me with the words of Mr. Samuel Adams on it, and I read those words again, too. I kind of liked how the words of Mr. Johnson and Mr. Adams went together and reminded me of what my Pa had done to help save our United States, and what his Grandpa had done to help make us a country. I felt really good about having Patriots in our family from a long time ago and now.

Ma spent most of the days before Thanksgiving thinking on what she'd fix for Pa's first Thanksgiving dinner back home with us. She said this would be the finest time of sure enough thanksgiving our little family had ever had. I thought as how that would be true of near everybody except those families whose men folks had not come back to them. And there was a whole lot of folks like that on both sides in the war. I thought on the children I knew who didn't have a Pa anymore. And what about the Secesh? Would they be giving thanks this year? What would they be thinking about what Mr. Andrew Johnson said? I wondered if their preacher read his words at their church.

Pa went hunting to see if he could get us a deer so we could have a venison roast, but we knew that wasn't very likely to happen. "I've seen nary a sign of a deer anywhere in these woods for more than a year," Ma told him. "And believe me, I have gone looking, as hungry for meat as we was."

He went anyway, hoping maybe he would have special good luck. He came back with a passel of pigeons. "I never saw a sign of a deer anywhere in the woods, and I went a long way looking. I really had my mouth all set to have venison for Thanksgiving dinner, but I guess it just wasn't to be." Ma was sure the pigeons would make us a fine meal.

When we sat down to eat, it was for sure the best dinner we'd had since before the war. Ma had roasted the pigeons seasoned with fresh parsley, sage and a little thyme, and cut up Irish 'taters to cook with them. There was boiled cabbage cooked with a little fatback Mahalia Cooner had sent over to us because she knew we didn't have a hog to slaughter yet. There was squash, turnip greens, black eyed peas and baked sweet 'taters. I had helped Ma make two pies for dessert, one out of pumpkin and one out of pecans.

I couldn't decide which to have so she let me have a little piece of each one. "After all," she said "this is a special Thanksgiving Day for our family." I said another "amen" just like I did in church, but this time didn't anybody try to 'shush' me. They all joined in.

Chapter 7

A couple of weeks after Thanksgiving, there came the awfulest snow-storm seen around these parts in many a winter. It was near a foot deep in our yard, and that wasn't counting where it had drifted up against the porch. That made me powerful glad of all that good firewood we'd laid in back in the fall.

The weather kept us indoors nearly all the time except to go milk the cow, gather the eggs and feed the critters. The pigs didn't like the cold. It's a good thing Pa had built a shed for them so they didn't have to get out in the snow very much. The chickens stayed on the roost, all huddled up together to keep warm. We spent a lot of time sitting around the fire and playing games.

Ma and Pa and me played Dominoes, but Penny didn't like Dominoes. She played with the cloth doll Ma'd made her. Sometimes we played "Give Us a Clue," where each of us would act out a word or something and the others had to guess what it was. All of us except Peggy liked to play that game. It was my favorite, because I liked words and what they meant. Ma would usually sit and knit, darn our stockings or work on a sewing project while she played. Seems she most always needed to be doing something with her hands while she doing other things with her mouth and mind.

Being inside gave plenty of time for Pa to tell us what happened with those Union soldiers who managed to escape from General Forrest's massacre at Fort Pillow. The three healthy men took over caring for the Sergeant. When it was safe, Burdick and Mason took the body of the young man who died and found a clearing where they buried him. They marked the grave good with some stones in the hope that someday they'd be able to tell his family where he was so they might could visit his grave or maybe even move him to a better burying place.

"We all stayed there for near onto a week. Mason, Alexander, Burdick and me decided we needed to move on. When we told them we were headed up toward Paducah, they all said we ought to think on that a bit afore we went. General Forrest had left the town in pretty bad shape.

"We didn't know just where Forrest went or what he was doing when he finished up at Fort Pillow. We knew we couldn't stay where we were though, so we decided to start northward and see what we could learn along the way. That turned out to be a pretty good decision."

"So, Pa, are you ever going to see that big river I been wanting to hear about?" It was taking an awful long time to get to that part of the story. I was sure enough interested in knowing about the Mississippi River, and I was afraid he might forget to tell me about it with all this talk about war and battles and people dying.

"Just you be patient, Fannie. I'll tell you all about the Mississippi River directly.

"On our way northward, we came upon a bunch of fellows

from Illinois headed home from back east somewhere. They were camping in a wooded area near where we were thinking of stopping. Most of them were right friendly like, for being Yankees and all, and some of them invited us to camp with them. Right off one of them, though, commenced commenting on my Southern accent, and being right rude about it. He wondered aloud if I was a Rebel spy and made it plain he didn't much cotton to having us camping with them. That made me mad, but I tried to hold back my temper. I told him about my Grandpa and his Pa and the Battle of Cowpens. Then I told him just why it was I had joined up to fight for the Union. Once more, I was the first Southern Union man this Yankee had run into. Like so many others I met, he didn't really know there were any such. I took pleasure in telling him that there were Union men like me from near about every one of the rebellious Confederate states. His jaw dropped at that because it was news to him, as it was to most of the others of them. After that, they all were lots more friendly like. We ended up staying with them for three or four days.

"When they finally were able to trust me, we picked up a right smart amount of information about what had been going on with the army and the country while we had been traveling by ourselves. We learned that a few weeks earlier, Lt. General U. S. Grant had been given command of all the armies of the United States. At that news, we gave up three cheers. General William Tecumseh Sherman replaced Grant as commander of the army in the western territories. They also said they had heard that General Hood was now in charge of the Rebel army in these parts around Tennessee, so that put Hood and Sherman right up against each other head to head. And they let us in on what that old fox Nathan Bedford Forrest was up to.

"Seems when he left Fort Pillow, he headed out for Memphis, but for some reason changed his mind and went off down toward Mississippi where we had just come from. That news was right disconcerting and caused us to fear for our friends we'd left down there. But at least we now knew we didn't need to worry about running into him if we decided to go on up toward Paducah. But they also confirmed that everything was right bad tore up thereabouts. Old Forrest had done quite a number on the place.

"Well, that news pretty well tore up my three friends who were from up that way. Burdick especially was near tears with worry about his ma and pa. He said they lived all by their selves, two old people alone right smack dab in the middle of the town. Mason and Alexander were concerned, too, but not as tore up as he was. This talk set their minds for sure on going directly up to Paducah to see about their kin. I wanted some time to think on it and figure out what would be the best for me to do.

"Next night just at sundown the three Paducah men set out north. We said our goodbyes and promised we would stay in touch somehow. I told them I might come up there, too, but wasn't ready to decide just yet."

"So Tom, that left you there all by yourself with these Yankees who was not sure they wanted you there?" Ma was right concerned for him. "Wasn't you afeared of that? I sure wouldn't like the idea of taking up with people who didn't want me about."

Pa stopped to catch his breath before answering. It seemed to me his breathing problem from that lung injury was worse off in the cold weather. I had seen how when he was outside he would have to stop right often to let his breathing catch up.

"Well, Mattie, there was a funny thing about that fellow who made me so mad. He and I went out hunting, looking for some kind of game for our supper. We scared up a whole warren of rabbits, enough to feed us pretty good that night. We got to talking and he said he was real interested in what I had said about my grandpa and great-grandpa Files being at Cowpens. Turns out his great grandpa and great uncle were there, too. He had heard the old folks telling stories about a Captain John Files and how he got murdered after being wounded in that fight. And that isn't all there was to it, Mattie. He had met up with some folks with some kind of a Files connection when he went to trade cattle a year or so before the war. Best we can figure, that must be some kind of kin to John Files, Jr., son of Captain John. I recollect hearing Grandpa talk about his uncle going off up North. But none of us down here had heard hide or hair about any of those folks in many and many a year.

"Well, that set my mind straight. I asked this fellow, Jeremiah Conway was his name, if he cared if I went up to Illinois with him. He thought on it and while we were eating our rabbit stew he told me he reckoned it would be all right for me to go on with him. So that is what I did.

"I asked Jeremiah if we were going up to Paducah and cross over the Ohio River there. He allowed as how it would be better for us not to go that away, especially with all the havoc General Forrest had made of Paducah. Our best route would be to go west of there a piece to a place called Wickliffe, Kentucky. It was right where the Ohio River joined up with the Mississippi."

"Oh, Pa," I cried. "Is that where you got to see the great big river?"

"That's right, Fannie. And that's not the most of it. As that river comes down from the north, it keeps getting bigger and bigger. When it gets right there where the Ohio River joins in, that is where it becomes the really big, mighty Mississippi River you keep asking about."

I was really excited now. "I sure do wish I could have been there with you to see that sight, Pa. Maybe someday I'll go up there to White Cliff, Kentucky, and see it for myself."

"I hope you can do that, Fannie. But before you start out for it you better remember the name of the place you are going to. It's not White Cliff. It is Wickliffe. The town itself is not much to see, but that mighty Mississippi River sure is."

That night I dreamed of going through the wilderness up to Wickliffe, Kentucky and seeing for myself the sight of the Mississippi River turning into the mighty Mississippi River.

Chapter 8

It snowed again just before Christmas. I asked Pa if we could have us a Christmas tree this year. We'd always decorated the house with ivy and holly with red berries, and sometimes with mistletoe if we could get it down from high up in the big oak trees, but a Christmas tree was a new idea to him. He'd never seen any such, and wanted to know what it was and where I got the idea.

I told him how I'd seen my very first Christmas tree at a house down in town last Christmas Eve. It was sitting on a table before a window of one of the big fancy houses on Front Street. It was so beautiful that I just had to know what it was. I went up and knocked on the door. I was so excited I was not afraid at all about going up to that strange house.

"A girl just my age came to the door, and she was very happy to tell me about their Christmas tree. I told her my name was Mary Francis and she said hers was Mary Jane. 'So we are both named Mary, just like the mother of the baby Jesus,' she smiled. She was very nice. She opened the door wide and asked if I'd like to come in and get a good look at the tree. Oh, it was even more beautiful as I stood there beside it. It was a little cedar tree almost as tall as me, and it was decorated with all kinds of beautiful things. Mary Jane said she and her mother had made the decorations out of colored paper, scrapes of cloth from her mother's sewing box, and popcorn strung on thread, and small pine cones they had painted red and blue. On top there was a star made out of heavy paper painted red.

"Mary Jane's mother found out about the Christmas tree from a piece in *Harper's Weekly*. She went and got the magazine so I could see it for myself. There was drawings of trees decorated with all kinds of pretty things. It said this was a tradition in other places in the world, but it had started up in the United States just a few years ago. It said that since the war, people needed something bright and special to cheer them up, so more Americans had started putting them up in their houses. I knew right then that when we could, I wanted us to have a Christmas tree in our house.

"And now with you home with us for this Christmas, we can celebrate this special Christmas with a tree. Can we, Pa?"

"Ask your Ma about that, Fannie. If she says we can, I'm sure we can find a cedar tree the right size. But the decorating of it would be something you and your Ma would have to see to."

"Can we, Ma? Please, can we? Penny and me can work on making the decorations, and maybe even Peggy can help. It'd be something we could do around the fire at night. May we please, Ma?" I knew from the twinkle that came in her eyes that the answer would be yes.

"Oh, thank you, Ma. Can we go cut the tree, Pa? Can Penny and Peggy and me go with you to do it?"

"Yes, you girls can go along to find the tree. But wouldn't it be best to wait to cut the tree until closer to Christmas? Y'all can start making the flub dubs to decorate it with any time Ma says, though."

Our house came alive with exciting things to do. Ma found some scraps of red and blue and green cloth. She helped us cut some of them into stars and other shapes. Some long thin pieces, she sewed together to make garlands. Ma showed us how to mix up some paste with flour and water, so we could make a garland out of pieces of paper glued into loops and put together like a chain.

Penny and Peggy went out and picked up an egg basket full of pinecones just the right size. We didn't have anything to paint them with, but we all thought they looked beautiful just the way God made them. One night, Pa got some corn and popped it over the fire for us, and we all set to stringing pieces of the corn on thread until we figured it was long enough to wrap around and around a small tree.

Christmas Eve finally came. At last we could go out and find our very first Christmas tree. Pa had to keep reminding us that it needed to be a small one, little enough to sit on the table in the front window. Peggy kept pointing to trees and saying "Cut that one, Pa. Cut that one." But the ones she chose was all way too big.

"Peg, that tree would fill up our whole house. We need to find a small one. How about this one?" Pa pointed to one that was just about as tall as Penny. We all agreed that it would be just right, so Pa cut it. We each took turns helping tote it back to the barn.

Pa found two boards left from repairing the barn and nailed them together in a kind of a cross. Then he nailed that to the cut end of the little tree and stood it up on his workbench. It was just perfect.

"Now, let's leave it here to dry, and then we'll take it inside and you girls can put your fancy do-dads on it."

Decorating the tree was our family entertainment that night. Even Pa helped. When we finished, Pa got his fiddle down and we sang Christmas songs, "Joy to the World," and "Silent Night." Ma suggested we sit around the tree while Pa read the Christmas story to us from the Bible.

It was just too exciting! We had our very own Christmas tree. That night in my dreams there was lots and lots of beautifully decorated Christmas trees. I thought that maybe next year we could make a fancy one, like the one I saw in town.

Christmas Day was crisp and cold. When we got up, we had to go take care of the farm critters first. When we finished, Ma said "Lands alivin' children, lookie here what I see. Seems like old Santy Claus must have come to our house this year." We went running to see the Christmas tree, and sure enough there was a new Sunday dress for me, and a cloth doll for Penny. Peggy had a nice wooden pull toy. Each of us also had an apple, a little packet of pecans and some molasses taffy candy.

"Do you girls like all the things Santy Clause brought you?" Ma wondered. The three of us giggled and said we did.

I didn't let on what I really thought. I'd noticed that my dress and the one Penny's doll wore was pretty much like some of the cloth decorations on our Christmas tree. And Peggy's pull toy looked a whole lot like the one I'd seen under some rags on Pa's work bench out in the barn. But that was all just for me to think on and for nobody else to know about.

"Martha Jane, there's something missing. I'm pretty sure old

Santa brung something special for you and Fannie, but I don't see them here by the tree. I think we ought to go looking about and see if he might have left them somewhere else by mistake."

He took Ma by the hand, and we went looking all through the house. We looked in every room. Wasn't anything there. Pa looked right puzzled.

"You don't suppose he might have put it out in the barn, do you?" We went to look, and right there in the barn was what we was looking for. Santa had brought Ma a spinning wheel like the one them Rebels had took off from her.

She squealed with delight, clapping both hands to her face and all the while jumping up and down for joy. I hadn't ever seen my Ma act in any such way as that before.

"Oh, Tom! Lardy mercy! I can't believe my eyes. Now if I can get me some cotton to card, I can go to spinning again. I sure have missed having my own yarn to use."

"Well, Mattie, it looks like old Santa Claus might have thought of just about everything." He nodded toward a sack sitting on the edge of his work bench nearby. "Why don't you look and see what's in that poke." It was half full of cotton bolls, ready for Ma to go to work on. The brightness in her eyes and voice told us she was as pleased as punch.

"But wait just a minute, Fannie." A bright twinkle came in Pa's eyes. "There's something else we've not found yet. We better keep looking."

We found it hidden behind the wagon, toward the back of the barn. It was the rocking chair Pa had promised to build for me. He explained what I already knew. "Didn't Santa bring this though," he said through a smile.

I gave him a big hug. I was so happy I couldn't hardly talk.

I had a real chair of my own, made of beautiful, honey-colored chestnut that was polished to a bright high shine. I was sure it was the most beautiful chair in the whole wide world.

When we got inside, I gave Penny the stool Pa had made for me when I was about her size. She gave her little one to Peggy, so we all had comfortable places of our own to sit, lined up together in the sitting room.

The days between Christmas and the start of the new year of 1866 was cold and damp. I reckon maybe that little wooly worm was right after all. We didn't have any more snow, but nobody wanted to be outside except when we needed to be to take care of the farm. Pa sat by the fire planning the garden we would plant in the spring. He said it was going to be the finest garden anybody around here ever saw.

Ma found her carding combs and went to work preparing the cotton Santy had brought her. The spinning wheel stood in its familiar place in the corner near the window where the light was good, ready to start turning cotton strands into knitting yarn. My chair took its place near the fireplace. Peggy was all over the house pulling her new toy about. We all kept busy with this and that, wishing for warm weather to hurry along so we could be outside. I didn't like milking the cow in this cold weather. I don't think the cow liked it very much, either.

New Year's Eve being a Sunday and all, we started out to go to Sunday meeting but we didn't get very far when sleet commenced to fall. Pa decided it wouldn't be safe for us to go farther. He turned the wagon around and took us back home.

Just before we got to our lane, Ma squealed and pointed to the hillside across the road from our house. "Look over there! Look, quick before it's gone." There before our eyes was a deer, a young doe standing all alone, the only one we'd seen in these parts in near about two years.

When we got in the house, Ma put a kettle of apple cider on the stove to warm. She even put a bit of cinnamon in it, and soon the sweet odor filled the whole house. Ma poured a cup for each of us. As she handed one to Pa she said, "Tom, I hope you enjoy your first cider of the New Year, because it is also the last we'll have anytime soon with cinnamon in it. I knowed how much you like it so I put this bit away and saved it for when you got home. But this is the end of it, so enjoy." It was a rare treat, and the sweetness and warmth soon had us all in good spirits.

Ma called all three of us girls to come sit beside her.

"Since this is a time of celebrating for us, I have got some good news to tell you. Come sometime in the summer, y'all going to become big sisters to a new little'un at our house."

We all burst out with excited giggles and questions. "Is it going to be another girl or will it be a boy?" Penny said she really wanted a little brother. Ma laughed and said we'd have to see when the time came. I could hardly wait to hold that new little baby. Like Penny, I hoped for a brother, but I really wouldn't mind so much having another little sister.

It wasn't planned, but we fell into talking about Pa's journey in Tennessee. Penny and Peggy had got warm and cozy after the chill of the wagon ride, and had fallen asleep. Pa'd always tried to tell about his adventures when the young'uns was in bed, because he thought they was too little to hear some of the bad parts. What he didn't know was that I'd been telling Penny about some of it, but not that part about Fort Pillow. Now what he had to tell wouldn't be so hard for them to hear. Even if they woke up during the telling, it'd be all right.

He and Jeremiah headed out for Wickliffe, Kentucky, and the mighty Mississippi River. I couldn't hardly wait for them to get there so he could tell me about that river. As they was traveling along, this Conway fellow showed considerable interest in where he had come from and what his life was like. Pa told him about our farm, and about Ma and me and Penny back home waiting for him, and that there was a new young-'un he hadn't seen yet.

Jeremiah asked how many slaves our family had. The question took Pa aback. It hadn't ever occurred to him that anybody would ever think he was a slaver.

"I told that Yankee, 'Heck, no, our family never had any slaves. That was for rich plantation folks. Where I live, up in the hill country of North Alabama, hardly anybody had slaves.' He got a real peculiar expression on his face. It was like he thought most everybody down South had slaves. I reckoned as how, as much time as he spent soldiering among them, he must not have talked to many ordinary folks who lived there. He allowed as how that was true."

Pa told him flat out that he didn't hold to the notion of any human being owning other human beings like they was property.

"Just to be plain about it, that part of it wasn't my war. That part of it was the rich man's war. The bad thing of it, though, is that the rich folks sent the poor folks off to do the fighting for them. But that slavery business had nothing to do with me. Seems to me that any man, colored or white, could run his own life better than having somebody else running it for him. This is supposed to be a free country, and seems to me that if everybody's not free, not any of us is free. That's what I think, anyway.

"I signed up for this fight because my kin folks, and yours, too, from what you told me back there at the camp, fought and lots of them died to make this United States of America for us. Now, that's worth fighting for in my book. To preserve the Union those folks made for us back in 1776. Now, since you asked a plain question, that's the plain answer. That's how come I am here, and that's all there be to it."

Pa said Jeremiah got right quiet. With a real thoughtful look, he stopped and looked Pa straight in the eye. Sticking out his hand, he said, "Sergeant Files, I want to shake your hand. You are about as fine a Patriot as I ever came across in my life, and I am proud to call you friend. What you just said makes all we been through these past four years seem worthwhile. You ought to go around the country giving that talk for everybody to hear. I want you to tell it just that way when we get up here with my family and friends."

Pa's face glowed with pleasure as he told us about that.

He asked Jeremiah about the country they was headed for. "Is there any Rebel action that you know about?"

"Jeremiah hesitated like there was something he had started to say and changed his mind. He went on to explain that earlier in the war the Union and Confederate forces had contested the area a right smart, mostly because of military and commercial access to the river. Seems there was a railroad line that ran from up in Ohio all the way down to Mobile, Alabama on the Gulf of Mexico. It had been real important as a supply route for both sides, so this area had changed hands right often back in the early days of the fighting, but that rail line had been pretty much tore up in recent years and was not of much use to anybody."

Jeremiah went on to tell him an amazing story about something that happened over on the river, a ways west from the path they was on.

"The Rebels came up with a right crafty idea. There was a place over there called Columbus, Kentucky, built on a low bluff overlooking the Mississippi. Jeremiah asked if I had ever heard tell of the Confederate General Leonidas Polk. I told him yes, I had heard talk about him. He had been down in Corinth, Mississippi for a spell before I got there.

"Well, it seems this General Polk was the one who thought up this special project. He built a fort over at Columbus. It was named Fort DeRussey, but everybody called it 'The Gibraltar of the West.' Apparently, General Polk himself was the one who started calling it that. Polk devised a plan to put a great big chain clear across the Mississippi River. That chain was big and strong enough to put a stop to boat traffic from getting by, north or south"

I could hardly belief my ears. "A chain clear across that big river, Pa? How ever did they do that? That must have been powerful big to be able to stop a riverboat. Did you see it?"

"No, Mary Francis, we didn't go over there to look at it. We were afraid there might still be some Rebel soldiers stationed over there, though Jeremiah thought the fort had not been very important for awhile now."

"So that isn't where you went to see the river?"

"No, that came a little while later. Jeremiah said that chain was more than a mile long. It was anchored on the other end across in the State of Missouri at a place called Belmont. Do you know how long a mile is, Fannie?""Not exactly. Ma said we walk almost a mile to school. I can't hardly imagine a chain that long, Pa. When I grow up and go to see the Mississippi River, maybe I can see that big chain, too."

As we went off to bed, the house was still filled with the sweet smell of Ma's cider and the happiness of being a whole family again.

Chapter 9

One afternoon in late January, Pa came back from town with good news for Penny and me. Folks had gotten up enough money to fix up and reopen our school. A new teacher had been hired, and she'd be here to commence teaching in about two weeks. Some of the men was going over to the school in a day or two and put in a supply of wood to heat the little one room building. Pa said there was some problems with the roof, and he'd be taking some of the cedar shakes he'd saved from doing the work on our house back in the fall, and help fix the school roof. Some of the benches was too broke up to fix and somebody would need to build some new ones. He'd help out with that, too.

Unfortunately, somebody had stole away the heat stove. Somehow they'd have to find a way to get another one. Stoves was right hard to come by, but not nearly as hard to come by as the hard money it would take to pay for it. Some fellow had told him there was a bunch of people called Shakers who lived up north of here over in Tennessee. They made really fine stoves that gave off more heat with less wood. That was a long way to go just to get one, and nobody knew how much it'd cost to buy one from them. He wondered if one of the smithies in the neighborhood could figure out how to build one.

The idea of school starting up made me real happy. I'd missed learning things and seeing my friends. I liked learning new words and learning about geography and history. Reading was my very favorite thing to do. I didn't like doing my numbers, though. I didn't really understand them. What I didn't like the most was having to get my chores finished in time to get there. Ma said it was almost a mile to where my school was. I didn't mind that. I liked to walk when the weather was nice.

Our new teacher was named Miss Camellia Throckmorton. Her family lived in Athens, up north of here. She told us she'd learned about teaching school at what she called "a fine Methodist school." Then she added, with some emphasis, that the school was part of "the Methodist Episcopal Church, South." I didn't know just what that meant, but when I told Pa what she'd said, that seemed to have bothered him right smart. I wondered why.

"Miss Throckmorton is from a well-known slaver family over in Limestone County," he said. "There was not a whole lot of slave holding in Limestone, and there was a right smart of Union sympathizers in those parts, but all her folks were Secesh during the war."

Now with emancipation done and the war over, her family was plumb broke. Pa reckoned she had to take up teaching to help take care of her own Ma and Pa.

There was still plenty of bad blood betwixt the Secesh and us Union folks, and getting to be more so. Pa wasn't happy that we was being taught by someone with that kind of background. He'd lots rather we had a teacher who was a Patriot like us.

We all knew, though, that there was a bunch of Confederate sympathizers in the school, too. I wondered how all of this was going to work out. Would differences like these ever go away or would they always be part of life in these parts?

School took up in the middle of February, so the mornings was still right cold and would be for another month or two. Some snow lingered on the ground now and then. That's when I really hated that long walk. Penny did too. With her short legs, she had trouble keeping up. I would have to go slow or stop and wait for her. Some days we got there after Miss Throckmorton had started the reciting. She didn't like that very much. She made us both stay inside during recess and read some more pages in our *McGuffey's Reader.*

On the Saturday after the start of school, the whole family went into town. They had started having something they called a "Trade Day," and Pa wanted to see how such a thing worked. He said it sounded to him like if people had something they didn't need no more, they could bring it there and see if somebody else wanted it. They might trade for it, or maybe even buy it for cash money if they had any. He took along a bunch of old tools and things he had a mind to trade or sell, if he could find anybody who cared for them.

When we got there, I found out why he really wanted to go to town. He wanted to find out more about Miss Camellia Throckmorton. I'd brought my McGuffey's Reader along and sat in the wagon pretending to be reading up for school. Actually, I listened to Pa talking to some of the men on the porch at the general store. There was lots I didn't understand, but all of them seemed to be real upset about something they was calling "Reconstruction." I'd heard talk about it before, but I didn't

113

know just what it was. It seemed to be something about re-building everything now the war was over. There certainly was plenty of that to be done! I figured I couldn't ask Pa about it, though, because then he'd know I'd been listening in on what they'd been saying. This Reconstruction thing must be real important, the way everybody was talking about it. But what did that have to do with Miss Camellia Throckmorton? I'd have to think on that some more.

After a time, Ma came to get me, and us three girls went in the store with her to look around. We didn't come to buy. We just wanted to see what there was to be seen. Right away, I spied Johnny Hinesley at the far end of the store. He was helping bring in some sacks of flour from the back room. When he caught sight of me, he took on a sheepish grin and gave me one of his shy little waves like he always did. I smiled and waved back to him, but my face flashed hot and I know it must have turned pink. Why did seeing Johnny always do that to me? I sure hoped Ma didn't notice. If she did, she didn't say anything about it, but I noticed there was a little bit of a smile on her face. I wondered what that was all about.

Pa'd been able to trade two of his tools for some garden seed we would need in a few weeks. Ma was very pleased to hear talk about the garden. She'd saved some seed over, but we'd need more if we was to have the kind of garden she hoped for this year. Pa had already turned the soil; planting time would be here before too long. I liked working in the garden alongside my Ma. Having Pa to help us with it this year would be special nice.

Back when we didn't have school, Ma and Pa had let us stay up to hear about Pa's travels. Now, though, we had to be in bed right early. Ma said we needed to let our brains rest up so they'd be ready for the learning we had to do the next day. At school I listened real careful like, hoping Miss Throckmorton would tell us something about that Reconstruction business, but she said nary a word about it all that week. I wondered if I should ask about it, but decided this might not be the time for that.

We didn't get to hear any more about Pa's travels until Friday night. I asked if he'd been telling things to Ma without us being there, and he said he had been, but that it was all grown-up talk that we wouldn't care about anyway. He promised he'd wait to tell about the good things until we could hear, too.

On Friday night he started up again telling the part about getting to see the mighty Mississippi River. This is the part I'd been hankering for from the very first. Before school had closed down last year, our teacher had showed us a map of the United States of America. Teacher showed us with her finger where the Confederate States of America was, but when she talked about this big river I found that the most interesting part of it.

"Now, Fannie, I know this is what you've been awaiting for." Pa smiled. "I was excited about seeing it, too. There came a time when we could hear the sound of it before we caught sight of it. It was the sound of mighty water flowing along at a pretty fast clip. We came up over this little rise, and there it was all laid out there before us. Mary Frances, it was maybe the most wonderful sight these eyes of mine have ever beheld. When we first saw it, I would have sworn it was three rivers we were seeing all at once. The smallest one coming down toward us from the north and another great big one coming at us from the east."

Pa reached for the geography book and found the map that

showed what he was telling me. Pointing, he said "That one is the Ohio River. It is bigger than the Mississippi. Those two rivers joined together right there." He put his finger on the spot. "The one it made, flowing on down toward the south, is the mighty Mississippi River you've been talking about."

My eyes was near about popping out of my head. My heart was just racing with excitement. My, how I wanted to see that for myself.

"When we got to Wickliffe, I could see that it wasn't really much of a 'there,' there. Looked to me like it was just a few houses and a store or two perched on the bank of the Ohio, but amid some of the prettiest country in all of God's creation. Jeremiah pointed off across the river. That was Illinois we were looking at. He lived just a few miles north.

"Problem was, as best we could see, there was no ferry boat right there. Jeremiah was sure there had been, but it wasn't there now. So we would have to figure out how to get over there to the State of Illinois."

They stopped at the general store and asked if there was a hotel or a boarding house thereabouts where they could stay the night. Somebody pointed them to a house down by the river. There was a widow lady lived there who had a room she would rent out to men who worked on the river. Sometimes she let folks passing through stay there for a night or two. He said she enjoyed the reputation of being a more than passably good cook. If they stayed with her, it was likely they'd eat right well that night.

"Her name was Mrs. Johansen, and she gave us a warm welcome. I took her to be near about the age of my own Ma. She had neat gray hair all pulled back and made up into a bun on the back of her head. I liked her right off. She showed us the room she had and said the fare was seventy-five cents for the night, with dinner thrown in, and coffee and eggs for breakfast. We asked if that was for the both of us and she said it was. So I slept in a real bed and ate real food for the first time since leaving the Yoders. She even showed us a place down by the river where we could go to bathe without being disturbed. Cold as it was, we decided to put it to use. When we came back to the house, Jeremiah got out his straight razor. He trimmed my hair and beard, and then I did his, so we looked much more presentable than when we arrived. We thought we had done died and gone to heaven."

"So how did you get across over to the Illinois side of the river, Tom?" Ma wondered. "If two of those rivers were as big as you say, this must have been quite a chore." Ma knew her husband was good at solving such problems. She wanted to hear how he had worked it out.

They asked Mrs. Johansen if the towns' people ever made that crossing. She said a few did now and again. She confirmed that there once had been a ferryboat, but the Confederates had sunk it to keep them Illinois Yankees from getting over to this side. She pointed up the Ohio River a ways to a little shack that sat right down at the water. An old man lived there who had a skiff. If he was amind to, he might agree to take them over.

"But she warned us he could be a right ornery old cuss. He might decide to run us off with his shotgun instead of talking to us about it. She advised us to get within shouting distance and call out to him instead of just walking up and taking him off his guard. And if we had our firearms with us, we should

117

put them down on the ground before he saw us, so he wouldn't feel threatened. His name was George Smith.

"So we did just what she said. And she was sure enough right about his orneriness. He answered our call by coming out cussing and carrying on, shotgun in hand. In a gruff voice, he wanted to know what we meant coming around calling out to him for all the world to hear. He looked to be about as old as Methuselah, with wild white hair and a beard down to where his belt buckle would have been if he'd had one. His worn out brown pants were held up by a bit of dirty rope tied around his waist. When he saw we had disarmed ourselves and looked harmless enough, he growled, 'Whatever it is you want, state your business.' Jeremiah asked if he would ferry us across the river. He wanted to know, 'What you want to go over there for? It ain't good enough for you on this side?'"

Jeremiah explained that they was just soldiers come back from the war, and he was trying to get home. They sure would appreciate the accommodation if Mr. Smith could see his way clear to oblige them. Next thing they knew this old man let out a string of cuss words that Pa wouldn't say in front of Ma and us girls.

Pa could see that Mr. George Smith didn't like that war very much. He wanted to know what side of the war they had been fighting for. Now, that question worried both of them. They didn't know which side this Smith fellow had taken. They figured the answer they gave would decide the answer they would get, but there was nothing to be done for it but just say it straight out. They both stood at attention and Jeremiah spoke for the both of them.

"Sir, we are proud to say we fought under the stars and stripes of the United States of America."

They was relieved and happy when he broke into a great big toothless grin, laid his shotgun aside and exclaimed, "Well, why didn't you say so in the first place? Come on in, boys, and rest your feet a spell. Tell me where you been and what you been up to."

The day was getting on toward the late afternoon by the time they finished this confab. Smith had one more question. "Well, now who are your folks over there in Illinois? How far you got to go when you get across the river?"

Jeremiah identified himself as a Conway from up south of Pulaski. The old man surprised them again when he asked, "You be any kin to Jeremiah Conway?" In astonishment, Conway answered that he was Jeremiah Conway, and so was his grandpa.

"That old man was full of surprises for us."

Pa stopped to clear his throat and take another deep breath. He was having bad breathing trouble again.

He said that old Mr. Smith's face lit up like a house afire. He reached over to shake Jeremiah's hand. He said he'd fought in what he called "the second war of our revolution" back in 1812, and that he'd served with Corporal Jeremiah Conway. They were together with Andrew Jackson in the Battle of New Orleans. Clearly pleased to meet this young Jeremiah Conway, he wanted to know what rank he held in the United States Army. When he found out Jeremiah, too, had held the rank of corporal, Mr. Smith glowed with satisfaction.

"Smith turned his attention to me and wanted to know my rank and what unit I was in. I told him I was First Sergeant with the First Alabama Cavalry of the United States Volunteers. His face got right dark. 'Alabama, you say? Ain't no Yankee soldiers from down in Alabama. Ain't they all just Rebels down there?'

"He was just like one of them Yankees who didn't know about us Southern Patriots. Jeremiah jumped right in to my defense. He told Smith all I had told him about why I had taken the Union side in the war. When he heard about what Jeremiah had to say, his mouth opened wide with another toothless smile, and he broke into the strangest sounding laugh I ever heard. It was more like a cackle than what fellow would call a laugh. He did just what Jeremiah had done back there on the trail. He came right over to shake my hand. He said he was right proud to make the acquaintance of the only Southern Patriot he had ever heard tell of. Then he allowed as how it was time to be getting into the boat and starting across the river. We needed to get that trip done before dark fell.

"As Smith pushed the little skiff away from the bank, the moon broke out across the water, rippling on the river like candles reflecting on the current. It took two to row, so Jeremiah and I took the oars while Smith pointed the way. Even so, it was clear that the swift current of the Ohio was taking us further downstream than we expected. Jeremiah chuckled that the Ohio must be in a powerful hurry to join up with the Mississippi. Mr. Smith pointed toward the northwest and told us about where we would likely put in to shore. Clearly he had made this trip many times before. He pointed out some landmarks that would help us get our bearings as we started toward Pulaski and the Conway place.

"That is when we realized what a great sacrifice this old man was making to help us out. When he started back, he would be rowing alone and going against a very strong current, so he was bound to hit landfall a long way west of his place. He then would have to haul his little boat all the way back home. Even so, he wouldn't take any money from us. He said he couldn't take money from a couple of Patriot boys on their way back from the war.

"And, frankly, it's a good thing because the truth of it was that we had precious little money between us. We'd paid Mrs. Johansen most of what we had for our room and board."

Chapter 10

Springtime makes me so very happy. Always has. It is the most wonderful time of the year, and it was coming. The birds was singing and building their nests in all the trees. The grass was starting to grow lush and green. The redbud and dogwood was beginning to paint the woods with splashes of red and white. Purple and white violets was peeking through on the meadow. In the shade down by the creek, the trillium was prettier than it had been in several years. It was time for Pa and me to be out fishing for bluegill and largemouth bass. Time for him to go hunting, hoping for young turkey and maybe even a deer, now that we knew there was at least one doe in our woods. Time to be splashing in the creek. Time for sitting on the porch of an evening with Pa playing his fiddle and all of us singing the songs we loved.

It was time to be putting in the garden. I was excited to see how many different kinds of seeds Pa had got for our garden at Trade Day. He'd broke up the soil back in the winter, so now it was easy work making the furrows. Penny and me hurried home as soon as we could when we got out of school. Even little Peggy did what she could.

We put in several rows of cabbages and beets. We planted

lettuce and onions and, of course, three or four rows of Irish 'taters. Ma and Pa set out to plant as much corn as they could get seed for. Pa prepared the soil for more than two acres of a cornfield. They figured they would be able to plant most of the field this year. That'd be very good, if we got enough rain, but not too much.

It'd be yet another month or so before time to plant some of the other things. In good time, we'd have beans, peas, onions, squash and tomatoes. And sweet 'taters. What would we do without those nice, orange sweet 'taters in the winter?

When Saturday came Pa hitched Rabbit to the wagon, which was loaded down with some more old tools and things he was going to take to Trade Day. It was too full for there to be room for us.

Ma needed Penny and me to help her at home. With her belly getting so big, she needed a lot of help getting her chores done. Today was washday and Pa didn't want her to be doing any heavy lifting. He gave Penny and me the job of toting water up from the spring to fill the washtubs.

After we waved goodbye, Penny and me got the water buckets from the shed. We filled the big black iron wash pot suspended from a metal frame in the back yard. Then we set about making the fire under them. Penny brought kindling and sticks from the wood pile and arranged them under the pot. Ma fetched the little box where she kept her flint stones, gathered a little pile of dry leaves and small sticks, and struck the flints together. When the spark took, she carefully blew up a suitable flame. Soon the fire was burning bright.

While we waited for the water to get hot, we brought water to fill the other tubs with rinse water. Then we went to help Ma gather up the dirty clothes. Peggy went to find the big wooden paddle we'd need to stir and lift the hot clothes, and she brought the bar of lye soap Ma kept near our bathing tub.

By the time we'd gathered everything together, the water was getting pretty warm. Ma scraped a generous amount of lye soap into the water and put the clothes in it. As the water boiled, Ma stirred and stirred the clothes in the soapy water. Holding each item up to drain, she put it in the first rinse tub to soak. My job was to be sure the soap was well rinsed in two rinse waters, and then carefully hang each garment on the porch railing and shrubs to dry.

The sun soon had everything dry and ready for ironing. Penny and I helped Ma fold the clothes and take them into the kitchen. The heavy black iron sat on the cook stove getting hot. Ma went to work pressing the wrinkles out of my Sunday dress and all the other things. It was a long hot chore, but when it was finished, we had clothes ready to wear to church on Sunday. I liked the smell of my dress when it was clean and fresh pressed.

We had just emptied the last of the water out of the pots when we heard Pa's wagon coming along. He waved to us from down the lane, a great big smile on his whole face. Ma whispered that must mean things had gone well for him at Trade Day.

Indeed, they had. He had been able to trade everything he took for other things he needed.

"But the best news of all," he said, beaming from ear to ear, "is that two of my old tools sold for cash money. And I didn't take any of that old no good Confederate paper money either.

"You'd be surprised, Mattie, how many folks are still trying

125

to use that worthless paper. I reckon it is all most folks have. One old fellow offered me $1,000 of it for that rusty posthole auger I had. I just laughed at him. I told him that $1,000 wasn't worth two cents. That didn't please him at all. He looked me right in the eye very serious like and said, 'Tom Files, you're still that same no good fool who went off fighting against your own homeland. You should have knowed better then, and you should know better now. You put this $1,000 away and keep it for awhile. Don't you know the South's going to rise up again and this money is going to be better than ever?'

"I told him if he thought that money would be so great he should just take it back home and stick it back under his mattress and leave it there 'til it turns into something good. Maybe it would make him rich again like he used to be."

"Who was that old fool, Tom?" Ma was curious. "Is he anybody we know?'

"I couldn't say as how we really know him as such. It was that old coot George Maynard Hall. He lives in that big old house way up on the hill out the other side of town. You remember the one? It's the one with the big white columns and all."

"Land sakes, Tom. You've not been out that way in a while, have you? Why, Union soldiers set fire to that place a good two years ago. There might still be a room or two in it where he can live, but it's nothing but a burned out shell. Before Lincoln set the slaves free, he had a whole bunch of them on that place. He was might near the biggest slaver anywhere near these parts and richer than King Solomon. Now I doubt if he's got a mattress left to stash his money under."

"Well, anyway, I didn't take his $1,000. What I've got instead is good American silver money." He took some shiny silver coins from his pocket and held them out for us to see. Right on them was the words "United States of America."

Ma was so happy. "Except for what you brought home with you, Tom, that's the first hard money I've seen since they started up with all this 'Confederate' tomfoolery. The way things be, I can't think who around here could get their hands on any such money. But it sure is a sight for sore eyes. This will help pay off what you owe for them critters you got for us back in the fall."

Pa reckoned as how she was right about that. "I'm set up to work off the rest of what we owe mending fences, doing some plowing and helping out with other chores. In a week or two, we'll have all our debts settled up with everybody, and I hope we have some of this cash money left." He was plumb pleased with himself.

"But that's not all to be told yet." His eyes was sparking. "You girls come sit over here on the stoop, and let me show you something."

We ran and found a place to sit. He sat between us and reached deep into his pocket. His hand came out holding a fist full of some kind of long, fat nuts. We had never seen such thing as these before.

"What are they, Pa?" The three of us talked all at the same time.

"They are called 'Goober peas,'" he said. "Folks who live way south of us and over in Georgia have them all the time. Some of our Confederate prisoners of war told about boiled Goober peas being all the grub they had to eat, sometime for days on end. But this is the first of them I ever had in my hands.

These are seed for us to plant. By fall, we will have a right good supply of them and can find out what they are like."

Ma looked puzzled. "What do you do with them, Tom? Do you eat them raw, or are they to be cooked somehow?"

Pa said all he had ever heard about was boiling them in the shell with some salt, but with salt so precious folks roasted them over the fire. He had gotten these from one of the Freedmen in town. That fellow told him the colored folks knew all about them. Some had even heard tell of them from their grandparents, who remembered them all the way from Africa.

We went out to the garden and planted two hills of Pa's Goober peas. As we put them in the ground, he explained that the peas grew underground.

"We will dig them up in the fall, the way we do our 'taters."

I could hardly wait for them to start to grow so I could see what they would be like.

After supper, we asked Pa if he'd take up with the story of this journey up to Illinois. It'd been quite a while since we'd heard about his adventure. He reckoned he could do that. He was in a pretty good mood after his good luck at Trade Day.

Pa and Jeremiah was relieved to be across the Ohio River. Pa'd never been in a Yankee state before. In fact, before this trip he'd just been in Alabama, Mississippi, and Tennessee. I thought on how exciting it would be to go out into the world and see all these strange places. I'd studied on them at school, but didn't know anything much about them. The farthest from home I'd ever been was to the schoolhouse, to church and into town with Ma and Pa. Because of what Pa was telling us, I was learning about a big, wonderful world full of interesting people and places. Until now, these was things I'd only learned about in books.

They was on the last leg of their journey up to the Conway farm, which was situated a little ways east of the little Mississippi River. There was some rolling hills sloping down toward the river, and the soil was real good. They could see folks beginning to plant their crops, mostly corn from what Pa could see. There was also some wheat. He saw herds of brown and black cows and flocks of snow white sheep grazing on hillsides off in the distance.

"As we got closer, I could tell that Jeremiah was getting right nervous. He kept looking back over his shoulder, and his eyes were darting from one side to the other. He had not been anything like this until we got across the river. I asked what the matter was. That is when he told me that this area had been somewhat divided between the North and the South, with a right smart of Confederate sympathy here abouts. Turned out some Union soldiers had been killed not far from there. He said there were a few bands of Confederate sympathizers who roamed the area, shooting and beating up on Union supporters."

This news reminded Pa of the Home Guard and other rogues like them that attacked us in our home just before he left for the war.

"I asked him how such as this could be? Where did these folks way up there in Illinois get such notions? Turns out a whole bunch of his neighbors came from down South, from Tennessee and Mississippi and over in the Carolinas. They brung their outlooks with them. That was why he had been so surprised when I had told him so firmly that we were not

129

slavers. The folks he knew up there came from that kind of background.

"That disturbed me mightily. Up 'til right then Jeremiah had been making out like a real, sure enough Yankee with unwavering Union loyalty. Now he was telling me that was not true of everybody up there where he was taking me. There were Rebels up there. I was not happy.

"He assured me of his loyalties and those of his own family, but he couldn't say the same for some of his neighbors. Looked like I was about to find myself in a hot bed of northern Secesh attachments, almost as if I was back in Alabama. I might as well have come home. I sure did wish he would have told me all of this afore we made that long trip."

Pa stopped to wipe his brow. He ran his hand through the stubble of his beard and fell quiet for a while. We could tell he was still real upset about this development. It brought tears to Ma's eyes. She couldn't help it. Us down here all alone and Pa off up in Illinois, both surrounded by Confederates. She reckoned he was in near about as much danger way up there as we was way down here.

"Confederate supporters in those parts were called 'Copperheads.' I reckoned as how that was a right appropriate name for such poisonous snakes in the grass. Jeremiah agreed. He went on to say, though, that it was kind of like the opposite of Patriots like us living amid a majority of Secesh down in Alabama. They were in the minority, but they could make a heap of trouble if they were amind to. I had to cogitate on that a bit. I decided maybe he had a point.

"As we approached the homestead, I could see that it was a right prosperous holding, a whole sight better than our place down here in the hill country of North Alabama. A whole lot of this had once been river bottom, rich soil that would grow a powerful good crop of wheat or corn. Conway said his folks mostly raised corn and cattle.

"I asked about the corn up there. Where did they have to take it to sell? He said that was one of the reasons some of his neighbors didn't support the war. They used to send their corn down the river to markets in New Orleans, but they lost the southern markets for their crops when commercial traffic on the Mississippi River was closed down by the Federals.

"I had no idea the war made any such problems as that for farmers way up there. But I had a lot more to learn about this. Nearly all the Illinois banks had issued paper money based on Confederate government bonds, and a bunch of them went broke. Jeremiah's family lost a right smart of their savings when their bank failed. There were only a few solid banks left in the whole state of Illinois.

All of this swirled around in Pa's head as he and Jeremiah turned into the lane leading up to the Conway place. Jeremiah's Ma spied them coming. She dropped her broom right there on the porch and came running toward them, calling his name and crying at the same time. "Jerry! Jerry!" She was all flustered at seeing her son for the first time in about two years. It sounded to me a whole lot like the way we welcomed Pa home, except there wasn't any little ones there.

"Jeremiah looked around to see who else might be there. Seeing no one, he asked about the rest of family. She said they were out in the field getting the corn planted. Everybody was in a rush because they thought it might be going to rain soon.

"It was pretty clear they weren't expecting us. She said they

131

had just been talking about him over supper the night before, wondering where he was and when he would be home. 'Last letter we had from you said you would be getting out soon. But we didn't hear anything more about when you might get here.'"

Ma dropped her knitting and jumped up, hands on her hips. She looked Pa straight in the eye. "Now you just wait a dad gum minute, Tom Files. There is something about this I don't understand. I been puzzling on this for more than two years. What you just said brings it fresh to mind. I reckon we might just as well get it out now. This Jeremiah fellow was writing letters back home, telling his family where he was and what he was doing. So, how come you couldn't have done that? How come we had to sit here all this time worrying ourselves sick over you? Not knowing if you was alive or dead. Dreaming and hoping and worrying ourselves sick day and night, and nary a word from you. If Jeremiah Conway could be writing home, how come you couldn't do it, too?"

I hadn't seen Ma this upset anytime since Pa got back. Her cheeks had turned bright red and tears welled up in her eyes. She drew in a deep breath and held it, trying to control herself while waiting for him to reply.

"Oh, Mattie. There was a big difference between my circumstances and Jeremiah's. He was always behind Union lines. His letters were going up North into Union territory. The Confederate Post Office wasn't amind to be delivering mail from Union soldiers, no matter where we were. Jeremiah could send letters to Illinois through the United States Post Office. Union could write to Union. Confederates could write to Confederates, but there was not much of a way to get mail across those lines. Any letter I tried to send you most likely wouldn't get here. If I tried, there was a chance it might get into the wrong hands and bring more misery down on you than you already had. Don't you know my heart ached to be able to tell you where I was? How much I loved you? How much I missed you? How much I wanted to be here with you? I couldn't write to you any more than you could write to me. I just didn't know of any way to get it done."

Ma let her breath out and sagged down into her chair. Her face turned pale, all drained of color. She closed her eyes, tears still streaming down her cheeks. "I'm sorry, Tom. I guess I didn't think about all that. When I heard you talking about how the Conway family was getting letters from him, that just flew all over me. It was just so hard not hearing anything about you all that time."

We sat for a spell. It didn't seem there was anything to be said. There was just too much hurt, too much sadness. Ma picked up her knitting from the floor beside her chair and started again. Pa glanced at her, as if asking if it was all right for him to begin again. She nodded ever so slightly, and he picked up his story where he'd left off.

At first, I wasn't listening. I was thinking on how they didn't know where Jeremiah was, just the way we didn't know where Pa was. It seems his Ma was just as surprised to see him coming home as we'd been when we saw Pa coming up the lane. That made me happy and sad at the same time. I knew exactly how that felt inside, not knowing and then having him there.

"Jeremiah introduced me to his Ma. He didn't tell her my story, just that I was another soldier come to spend some time with them. Mrs. Conway smiled and bid me welcome. She took us inside and laid out some cake for us while the coffee was making, real coffee, too, Mattie. It tasted so good.

"Their house was way yonder bigger and nicer than our little clapboard place. It was neat and painted white on the outside. On the inside the walls were covered over with fancy paper with pictures of flowers and things on it."

I was excited about that. "I saw some rooms like that in the big house on Front Street where they had the Christmas tree in the window. It was so pretty. I hope we can do our walls up like that someday."

Pa allowed as how that was for rich folks. We had better ways to spend our money than on such foolishness as that. I thought to myself that when I was all growed up and married, I'd find a way to have pretty things. But I didn't say anything more about it.

"The house had two stories, with a staircase going up from a hallway by the front door. There was a sitting room, and a big kitchen and what she called a dining room on that first floor. I found out they ate their dinner of a Sunday and at special times in that room. Can you imagine such as that, Mattie?

"Mrs. Conway told Jeremiah to take me upstairs and show me to my room. There was another big hallway up there, and four bed rooms, one in each corner of the house, with big windows to catch the light and the breeze. As we went down the hallway, Jerry pointed out a room that was his parents' and another that was for his brother, Ezekiel. I didn't know until right then that he had a brother. Those were the two rooms at the front of the house.

"He pointed to a room on the left that was his. Then he opened the door to the room on the right. He told me this would be my room. I nearly fell over, Mattie. Can you imagine? I was to have a whole big room all to myself. Jerry said this was the guest room. There was a big bed so high you had to have a little footstool to get up into it. And, Fannie, that bed was near about big enough for all five of us to sleep in. I never saw any such. On the inside wall, there was a fireplace, with wood already laid for a fire. I reckon every one of those sleeping rooms had one.

"There was a beautiful tall cabinet with mirrors on both of the doors. It was to hang up all your clothes. Of course, I didn't have no clothes to hang up except one pair of britches and my coat. I opened the doors and it smelled like cedar wood inside. There was a little sideboard over in the corner. Jerry called it a washstand. It had a little mirror on it, and a real nice white and blue washbasin and pitcher. Under the bed there was something Jerry called a 'necessary pot.' It was blue and white like the basin and pitcher on the washstand. It was a whole lot nicer than the galvanized pails we have.

"The sound of doors opening and closing and of voices drifting up from downstairs announced the return of Mr. Conway and Ezekiel from the corn field. Jeremiah went bounding down to greet them. I was surprised to see that Ezekiel was a whole lot younger than Jeremiah. Maybe sixteen or seventeen. I was introduced briefly and welcomed by the others. They were nice enough, but kind of distant at the same time."

Pa said Mrs. Conway interrupted the festivities by announcing that dinner was almost ready. In light of Jerry's unexpected but welcome return, they'd be eating in that dining room.

"Candles and kerosene lamps filled the room with light." Pa's eyes glistened as he recalled the scene. "The table was set with bone white china plates, cups and saucers. The knives, forks and spoons were real silver. Mattie, you would have been pleasured by the beauty of that room. I didn't hardly know how to act with such finery. I was right nervous, being in the company of strangers and all. I sat across from Jeremiah and decided to watch him and do just what he did. That got me through."

"What did you have to eat, Pa?" I was real curious about the Conway family. "Was it all some kind of fancy food? Or was it food like we like to eat?"

"Most of it was the same kind of food like we eat when we can get it, Fannie, except there was more of it than we have ever had except like we used to have at Christmas. Baked ham was served with a juicy, dark gravy sauce. We had sweet 'taters, green beans and corn fixed with a creamy white sauce. For dessert we had a pie made from a berry I had never heard tell of. It was called a gooseberry, round green berries that were tart but sweet. There was a real sweet, chewy topping that was not like any kind of crust I ever saw. It was all real good."

I thought Mrs. Conway must've been a right good cook. I'd like to know more about those gooseberries. How did they get that name?

"When we first sat down, everybody held hands around the table and bowed their heads in a moment of silent prayer. This reminded me of what Mr. and Mrs. Yoder did at their table. Then Mr. Conway said, 'For what we are about to receive, O Father, make us truly thankful,' and everybody said 'Amen.'

"When the praying was finished I asked if this was a Quaker family. There was a puzzled look around the table. Mrs. Conway answered, 'Why, no, Mr. Files. We are Methodists. Why do you ask?' I told them about being with the Yoders and how their silent table prayer was very similar, except they didn't have that last spoken part. They looked at me kind of curious like, but no one asked me anymore about it. In fact, there was very little conversation around the table. Still, I was aware that everyone was watching me while trying not to let me catch them at it. It made me feel right uncomfortable. It was almost like I was turning purple or growing horns or something, but they were all trying not to notice. I wondered if I was doing something wrong at that fancy table, but I was doing just what Jeremiah did. I was glad when we were finished with dinner."

Pa found it strange that after dinner the men folks moved over into the sitting room by themselves while Mrs. Conway cleared the table. Mr. Conway brought out his tobacco and pipe, filled and lighted it. The tobacco gave off a sweet fragrance and soon smoke filled the room. Pa didn't like that.

"I was glad to see that neither Jeremiah nor Ezekiel smoked. Not being a smoker myself, I found it annoying and started to sneeze."

He observed that nobody seemed to notice except Jeremiah, who asked if Pa'd like to join him on the veranda to enjoy the evening breeze. Pa didn't know just what a veranda might be, but said that would be right nice. Turned out that the veranda was what we call the front porch. They sat out there for a time, and then rejoined the family when they heard Mrs. Conway asking where Jeremiah was. Pa wasn't happy when they had to go back in.

He learned that Mr. Conway's name was Amos and Mrs. Conway was called Deborah. Jeremiah told his parents about how he'd met Pa and about crossing the Ohio River with George

Smith. He brought up how Smith had fought with Grandpa Conway down in New Orleans. Amos said Grandpa'd be coming for Sunday dinner, and Jeremiah should tell him about meeting up with Smith. Jeremiah also told them about Pa's connection to the Battle of Cowpens in the Revolution. Deborah smiled and noted that her great grandpa had been there, too. Pa expressed some interest in that, but she didn't respond. He was puzzled when that was all there was to that conversation.

"It surprised me that nobody asked me anything about myself or where I came from." Pa took out his bandana and wiped his face before going on. "If we had a stranger spending their first night in our house, I'd sure enough want to know all I could find out about them. That I was a friend to their son seemed to be enough for them to know. They said nothing to discomfort me, but I was mighty uncomfortable all the same.

"Amos read a passage from the Bible, one of the Psalms, best as I remember, and we went off to bed. That was my introduction to the Conway family. My big bed was mighty comfortable, but I didn't sleep too good. I passed most of the night puzzling over this family and my welcome here that was warm and cool all at the same time.

"Now, speaking of going off to bed, I think it's time for us to do the same."

I went to sleep that night thinking on Pa's first dinner with the Conway family in that fancy dining room. I tried to conjure up what gooseberry pie might taste like. I dreamed of bountiful food and of beautiful rooms all brightly lighted up with candles and oil lamps.

Chapter 11

As I was coming back from the barn with the pail of milk, the warmth of the rising sun felt nice on my face. I looked over toward the garden. I'd not been there in a few days, though I could see where Ma'd been hoeing the weeds recently. I was right surprised to see how many of the seeds we'd planted was sprouting already. I wanted to go see if those Goobers was coming up yet, but it was near about time for Penny and me to start out for school.

It was Monday morning. Miss Throckmorton announced that school would finish up for this term on Friday. We had just four more days. In one way that made me sad, but in another I'd be glad to spend the days outside, helping Ma and Pa around the farm and playing in the creek. School had been good, and I'd miss it.

Johnny Hinesley and me had got to be friends. Most days we sat together and ate our lunch under the big Chestnut tree in the far corner of the schoolyard, away from the little kids. When I got to know him, I found he wasn't as shy as I thought. In fact, when just the two of us was together he talked quite a lot. We figured out he was almost two years older than me. That surprised me because I was just a tiny bit taller than him.

I didn't think that would matter none. We could still be friends. In fact, I thought I'd miss seeing him every day when we didn't have school. I liked how he looked at me, always right serious like and with a smile in his big blue eyes.

School would be out until September so I'd have to ask Miss Throckmorton about that Reconstruction thing soon. Come Wednesday, I got around to raising my hand just as she finished our history lesson. She looked up and asked if I had a question. I told her I did, but it didn't have to do with what she had just been telling about. I asked if she could explain to us just what "Reconstruction" was.

She came up very straight in her chair. I could hear her draw in a deep, fast breath. She stared at me for what felt like a really long time. Then she said calmly, "Mary Francis, that is not part of our lessons for this term. Perhaps you should ask you father about it." She shrugged her shoulders, her face relaxed, and she moved on to our spelling lesson.

She said nothing more about it and neither did I.

When Penny and me got home from school, Ma was out in the garden, and we went running over to join her. As we got near, I saw she was just standing there, leaning heavy on her hoe. She was holding on to her swollen belly, and she had a right pained look on her face.

Penny saw it, too.

"Ma, are you all right?" she asked. "You want to come over to that stump and sit for a spell?"

"I reckon I should, Pen. I don't feel so good. It can't be the baby coming. It ain't time for that for another three months or so. Maybe if I just sit a spell it will pass. Fannie, go and get me a dipper of water to drink, would you?"

I dashed off to the spring and got it for her. I asked her where Pa was; I didn't see him anywhere around. She pointed toward the field beyond the pigsty and told me he had gone looking for that old sow. She had gotten out of the pen and run off again. I looked that way as best I could and didn't see him anywhere. I sure hoped wasn't anything terrible wrong with Ma. I didn't know what to do to help her.

Before long, we heard Pa coming along driving that troublesome sow. She was complaining mightily about being rounded up. He'd just closed the gate to the pen when he saw us gathered around Ma.

"Mattie!" Alarm colored his voice as he hurried over to her. "What's the matter? Are you all right? Is the baby all right?"

Ma waved away his worry. "It's all right, Tom. Don't you worry none. I got to feeling a little faint, that's all. The girls came along just in time. Everything be all right. The baby is fine, and so am I now I've been sitting a spell."

He helped her back to the house. She might have said she felt better, but I noticed as how she leaned on him real heavy like. He got her to bed and soon she was sleeping.

Penny and me took the hoes and went back out to take up where she'd left off. Pa went to sit on the porch. That told me he must be mighty worried; he never sat down during the day except to eat.

As we worked, I noticed that nearly everything was starting to sprout, even the Goober peas. I could hardly wait to see what they'd be like come fall.

Toward sundown we heard Ma stirring around. When she came into the kitchen, I was just putting our supper on the table. Pa'd gone down to the creek and caught a small mess of bream, which I'd fried. There was some left-over collard greens, and I'd made fresh corn pone to go with them. We all liked turnip greens and corn pone in pot likker. Ma ate a bite or two of the fish, but she wasn't very hungry.

She wanted to sit up for awhile, so we gathered by the fire and Pa told us more about the Conways. A few days after he got there, he and Jeremiah went out to the barn to feed the horses. With nobody else around Pa told his friend how uncomfortable he was, feeling welcome in some ways and not in others.

"'I just don't understand it, Jeremiah. Nobody talks to anybody. There's no conversation going on. Nobody seems to care anything about who I am or anything like that. They take what you say or what I say, and that's all there is to it. It just don't give a body a real friendly feeling.'

"Jeremiah said he understood what I was saying. But he explained that folks up there in what he called the 'Midwest' were different from the folks he had met down South. 'We just don't talk much, and we sure don't go prying into anybody's business. We figure if there's something a body wants us to know, they will tell us; if they don't want to tell us, then it just isn't any of our business and we stay out of it.'

"Well now that plain flummoxed me. It sure was a different way of dealing with folks from the way us Southerners did. I reckoned as how I had a right smart to learn about Yankee ways.

"While it was just the two of us, I asked Jeremiah if he thought there was any way I could find some work on one of the farms there abouts. I wanted to earn my keep while I was there and I also wanted to save up enough to get me a horse.

If I had a horse, I wouldn't have to walk all that way back to Alabama when the time came I could go home.

"He said he would ask around. Problem was, the nearest neighbors were from Mississippi and didn't like it when Jeremiah went off to fight against their kinfolks. They might not take a shine to having me around. They would most likely say I was a traitor to their Southland and would not be welcome on their place. I allowed as how I wouldn't want to be working in any place like that."

"Well, Tom, it pleases me to know you was already thinking and planning on how you would get back to us." Ma was smiling. "But you didn't have no horse when you got here. How did all that work out?"

"That's too much story to tell tonight, Mattie. The long and short of it is that Amos agreed to hire me to work on his place. He paid me $14 a month, with room and board thrown in, which was right generous pay for a farm hand. I did finally get me a horse, and a right fine one at that. Amos let me stable it with his at no cost. The rest of that story gets all tangled up in what happened on my way home. Complicated as it is, I promise you will hear every bit of it in good time."

"Well, if you stayed there and worked on the Conway place, did you stay in that fancy room and take meals with them?" Ma knew most of the time farm hands had rough quarters in a barn loft or some such place.

"Yep." His face lit up with a broad smile. "In fact, they came to treat me pretty much like one of the family. But there's a bit of a tale about how that came to be, too. Maybe I can tell you about that tomorrow. Don't you think it's getting on to being your bed time now, with all you've been through?"

I went to bed that night feeling all warm inside knowing that as quick as Pa got up to Illinois he started thinking on how he could get back down here to us. I dreamed of fine horses running through a green meadow, the wind blowing in their manes and their tails held just so.

Pa insisted that Ma had to stay in bed the next day. He kept me home from school to help look after her. He told Penny she could go, but she begged to stay home, too. She promised to do all she could to help out, so Pa let her stay.

I didn't really want to stay. With just two school days left, I didn't want to miss a single one. I wondered if Miss Camellia Throckmorton would be our teacher again next year. I kind of hoped so, and I kind of didn't. I liked her all right, but I don't think she liked me so much, especially not after I asked her about Reconstruction.

When time came, I fixed us something to eat. While I like to cook, I know I ain't near as good at it as my Ma, but I fixed us some fresh greens and baked a pan of sweet 'taters. Pa had trapped two rabbits and cleaned them, and I put them on to fry. There was some cornpone left over, and that went good with the greens. I reckon it was a passable meal. Pa said he enjoyed it, but I think he just didn't want to hurt my feelings. All Ma wanted was a bit of cornpone in pot likker from the greens.

Up toward evening, Ma decided she wanted to sit up. Being out on the porch sounded right good to her, so Pa helped her. Her color was looking better, and she allowed as how she didn't hurt like she did. We sat a spell just enjoying the time together.

As darkness fell, Penny pointed down toward the cow pasture. "Look yonder," she said. "There's the biggest swarm of lightening bugs I ever did see." The whole pasture was lit up with little lights blinking off and on all over the place.

The wind came up, and it commenced getting cooler. Pa didn't want Ma to get chilled. He allowed as how it was time for her to be getting back to bed. When Ma went to bed Pa had me bring the book of stories by the Grimm brothers. He read some of my favorite tales aloud as us girls sat at his feet.

Next day the weather turned off uncommonly cold, so Ma stayed inside. After we got the chores done we all came to sit by the fire. I brought the churn into the sitting room so I could deal with our excess milk while we talked. Ma said she was curious about how things worked out after Pa had that talk with Jeremiah.

"Well, there's a story to that, too. Come Sunday we all went to preaching at the Methodist Church about two miles away. When we got there, I was right well impressed. It wasn't a plain white clapboard building like ours. It was built out of fieldstone and had colored glass windows with pictures in them."

"What kind of pictures, Pa?" I'd never seen any such windows as that.

"There was one big one up front of Jesus with children all around his feet and a little white lamb in his arms. There was another of Jesus on the cross, and one of the baby Jesus in the manger of Bethlehem, and some more but I don't rightly remember what they were. With the sun shining on them, they glowed like you can't hardly imagine and cast colored shadows on the walls. The preacher wore a long black robe. I'd never seen a preacher dressed like that before. He gave a right good talk, what of it I could understand, but it wasn't anything like what Rev. McAdoo does at our church.

"Folks crowded around Jeremiah just like they did me on my first Sunday back. Some had heard about him getting home, but most had not. He introduced me to some, and everybody was friendly and all, but it was the same kind of friendliness I got from the Conway family, warm but cool.

"Up in the afternoon, folks commenced arriving at the Conway house. As far as I know wasn't nobody expected, but they just kept on coming. They wanted to welcome 'Jerry' home. Everybody brought food of some kind. Mostly it was cakes and cookies and the like, but there were two plates of chocolate fudge candy. Now, you know how I took to that, Mattie! We'd not seen any such as that in many a year, sugar and chocolate being so precious and all."

One of the people Pa met that afternoon was Jeremiah's Grandpa. Jeremiah told the older man about meeting up with George Smith over in Kentucky. That brought quite a smile to the old man's face.

"'You mean to tell me that old coot is still kicking?' He exclaimed. 'Well, well, well. I reckon I must have done a pretty good turn, didn't I?'"

Neither Pa nor Jeremiah knew what that meant. He started into telling how he'd rescued Corporal Smith when he was wounded back in '13, but the story got interrupted by other people coming up to speak with Grandpa Conway."

I had to go take care of the butter and the buttermilk. It took quite a while to work out the butter and get it into the mold. Then I took it and a crock jar of the buttermilk out to the spring house to keep cool. While I was doing that, Ma went to rest some. Pa had some chores he needed to tend to out at the barn, and Peggy and Pen went to help him. It was evening again before we got back to hearing about the gathering at the Conway house.

Pa took up where he had left off. "The lady who had played the organ at church sat down at the piano and started playing some hymns and things. Until then, I hadn't noticed that the Conways had a piano. Everybody started to sing along. Most of them were familiar to me, and I enjoyed the singing.

"When they took a break from the music, Jeremiah got everybody's attention. 'We have a special guest in our home right now. He is a soldier I met on my way home, and I invited him to come up and stay with us for awhile. His name is Sergeant Thomas Files. Let's give him a warm welcome.' Everybody looked at me and commenced to clap, smiling and nodding to me. Nothing like that had ever happened to me before, and I didn't know how to act. I reckon my face must of turned right red.

"When Jeremiah told them I was a soldier from Alabama, things fell quiet, with dark frowns replaced the warm smiles. Jeremiah went on. 'Now you need to know that even if he is a Southerner, Sergeant Files fought on the same side as I did in this war. He served with the First Alabama Cavalry, United States Volunteers.' Whispers of disbelief filled the room. In a loud whisper one fellow commented how he had never heard tell of any Southerner fighting for the Union.

"Jeremiah raised his hand to get their attention again. 'Like most of you, I thought everybody down South were just Rebels. That is not the truth of it. As we were traveling along together Tom explained to me how such a thing could be. What Tom Files told me about himself and a lot of folks he knows was the best reason for this war I ever heard. Tom, would you please tell my friends what you told me?'

"Well, I was plumb dumbfounded. I had never made a speech to this many folks before, but they all got right interested, and one after another commenced to encourage me. So what I did is, I told them just what I had told Jeremiah back on the roadway. As best I could remember it, I said pretty much the same words. When I finished, the room was so quiet you could have heard a penny drop on that big thick rug. Somebody started the clapping and it just built up, louder and longer than before.

"The lady sitting at the piano commenced to play 'The Battle Hymn of the Republic,' and everybody started singing. They sang several more patriotic songs, winding up with that new one about seeing the American still flag flying at the end of a battle at sea. You know the one I mean, Mattie?"

"Yes I do, Tom. That's come to be one of my favorites. Some folks is saying it ought to be our national song. I especially like one part of it." She commenced singing:

"Oh, say does that star-spangled banner yet wave
O'er the land of the free and the home of the brave?"

"I tell you truly, Mattie, I got so choked up I couldn't hardly keep singing. When I looked around the room I saw tears on many a face, and it wasn't just the women. It was some of the men, too.

"As folks started leaving, every single one of them came up to shake my hand and bid me welcome to their neighborhood. Some of them asked if I would do them the honor of coming to their home and having dinner with their family. One of the oldest men of the bunch said he wanted to take me to meet his friends who were all veterans and sons of veterans of the Revolutionary War. His name was Mr. Gabe Andrews. He said those old soldiers, lots of them well past ninety, would really like to hear what I had to say about being a Patriot. I told him I wasn't no public speaker, but I would be honored to meet his friends. I would be glad to tell them what I could, but I couldn't teach a soldier of the Revolution anything about being a Patriot.

"As she prepared to leave, the organ lady commented on my singing. She said I had a right nice tenor voice and invited me to come sing in the choir. I told her we didn't have a choir at our little church, but that I'd think on it and just might like to do that. They practiced on Wednesday after folks finished their chores. So I commenced to singing in the church choir. It felt nice to be included in something.

"That gave me the notion that we might start up a little choir at our church. What do you think about that idea, Mattie? Of course, I would have to take it up with the elders."

Ma thought that'd be nice. She named off five or six folks she thought might sing in it. I asked if I could sing, and wondered if Ma'd go. She had the loveliest voice I ever heard. She thought that'd depend on the baby she was carrying, but wasn't no reason I couldn't go with Pa.

"And so, Mattie, that it how it came to be that I felt welcomed up there at last, home sick as I was. There was no end of people wanting to know all about me and about my family. They were concerned about you and the girls, wishing there was some way they could get some help down here to you. I told them it couldn't be done. Even if they could find a way, the attention it would draw might make things worse for you. They wanted to hear more about how a body could go about being a Patriot deep down in Rebel territory. I was invited to visit one family and then another all summer long."

Ma was getting pretty tuckered out again. She went to bed early and slept through the night. She woke up feeling right chipper with no discomfort. While she wouldn't be doing any garden work for a spell, she did feel up to working around the house some. I helped with the sweeping and dusting and making the beds. Then she got down her quilting frame and took to piecing a new quilt she'd started, like the one she gave to the McDades after their fire.

Pa came in with the news that it looked like two of our new pigs be giving us some piglets this summer, which was sure enough good news. If we could get our herd built up, maybe this time next year we could start having us some pork to eat. It would be good to have something beside rabbit and squirrel, and even the fish we caught now and again. We kept hoping Pa might get us some deer meat, but for as long as he'd been home we'd seen only that one doe in our woods.

Pa wanted to see what shape the old smoke house was in. It'd not been used in about four years. It'd need to be in good order so he could smoke us some ham and pork shoulder when the time came. In fact, he allowed as how he just might see about buying or trading for a hog to butcher.

"Oh, Tom, that would make me so happy," chimed in Ma. "I'd be so glad to have me some bacon to cook with. It would sure make our green beans and turnip greens taste good. And we could render some lard for me to bake with. I'd near about forgot all those good things we used to have before our hogs got taken off. My pie crusts was the best in the neighborhood, but they can't be made without lard. Lardy mercy, Tom Files, you done set my mouth to watering already."

Pa went looking for a hickory tree he could cut down. He wanted to be sure the wood would be good and dry in time to use in the smoke house.

"Why do you want hickory wood in particular?" I asked.

"The smoke from hickory is what gives ham and bacon their special taste," he explained. I didn't know that. I just knew bacon and smoked ham was mighty good eating.

He came back with the news that the smoke house was in pretty good shape. It just needed a bit of patching and a new roof. Since he already had the cedar shakes left from fixing the barn and the schoolhouse, he reckoned he could start putting them on when he got around to it.

That evening he played his fiddle for us, but Ma wasn't up to singing. After a time, Ma asked Pa to tell us more about Illinois. He said he would, but there wasn't much more to tell about until way on into the summer.

"I worked for Amos, saving up all my money so I could get me a horse. That took a right interesting turn the night I went with Mr. Gabe Andrews to meet his soldier friends. Like I said before, the veterans among them was all well over ninety years old. Those old men wanted to know everything I could tell them about the First Alabama Cavalry. Just like everybody I met, they didn't know anything about there being any Southern Patriots. They asked about my family and why come I wasn't home with y'all instead of up there in Illinois. So I told them what had happened to other Patriots and why I was afeared about going home. Being old warriors, they tried to think up some way they could get you some help. One fellow of the younger men, who was a son of one of the veterans, came up with the notion of sending a rescue party down here to get you and the children and bringing you up there. Took all I could do to keep from laughing out loud at that notion. Can you imagine what folks hereabouts would have thought if they saw a band a Yankee raiders invading Wolf Creek to fetch y'all off to Illinois?

"One of them asked about what I wanted most. I told him how I was saving up to buy me a horse so I wouldn't have to walk home when the time came. After the meeting broke up, he took me off to one side and introduced himself as Colonel Andrew Marcus. The colonel was a good size man, one of the oldest in the crowd, with sharp brown eyes and auburn hair streaked through with gray. You'd never guess he was old enough to have fought in the American Revolution. He said he had a stable full of fine horses and invited me to come see them some time. I thanked him for his kind invitation and told him I would be glad come see him just as soon as I could. About a week later I borrowed one of Amos' horses and rode over there.

"The colonel took me out to his stables where there were fifteen or twenty fine horses. He said, 'Sergeant Files, I want you to choose the horse you want out of this bunch. I don't care which one you pick. It is yours as a reward for your fine service to our country.'

"Why, Mattie, you could have knocked me over with a feather. I told him I couldn't take such a fine animal without paying for it. He insisted. He said, 'I'll be a hundred years old come next January. What am I going to do with all this horse flesh? Yes, I could sell them, but I don't need the money.

I've already got more than I can spend in whatever time I have left. My only son is gone. He and his only son both died while being held by the Confederates at Andersonville Prison down in Georgia. My two daughters don't care much about horses, and they are well fixed for life anyway. It would give this old soldier a great deal of pleasure to be able to recognize you for your service to our country.'

"I'm telling you the truth, there were some mighty nice horse flesh in that stable. The horse I chose was cream-colored, with black eyes. His mane and tail were silver white, his hair gradually becoming darker toward his feet. When I chose that one, Colonel Marcus smiled and said I had made a right good choice. He seemed real pleased. The horse's name was Jack, named after a similar animal that once belonged to General Ulysses S. Grant. That was why Colonel Marcus had bought that horse in the first place.

"Next day, Jeremiah went with me to get it. So that is how I managed to get me a horse to ride home. I still had all my money. I was right pleased with the prospect of having some cash money to bring home to you. 'Course you know that ain't exactly what happened, and I'll tell you why in due time. There's a whole lot more to this tale before it's all told."

I dropped off to sleep marveling at a man who had so many horses and so much money that he could give my Pa such a fine gift. Most of all, I was puzzled about what had happened to Jack before Pa got back to us.

When the chores was done next morning, Pa said he was going over to Mr. Swindle's place to help him repair an old barn that was near falling down. It was to pay off the last of our debt for the pigs we got from him. Instead of hitching up the wagon for that trip, he just put a bridle on the mule. Since we didn't own a saddle, he rode old Rabbit bareback. It wouldn't be too comfortable, but there wasn't far to go so Pa thought that'd be good enough.

Penny and I decided we'd go out and do our best to take care of the garden. The weeds was getting pretty bad. We'd worked hard at keeping them down, but they'd done got ahead of us. There'd been a spot of rain the day before, so the ground was easy to work. When Ma called us in for lunch we was proud to report that we had done got six or eight rows all cleared out.

It was near about sundown when we quit for the day. We'd just taken our garden tools to the barn when we heard some-body coming up the lane. It was Pa. Rabbit was just plodding along right slow like with Pa slumped over and holding on to his mane to keep from falling off. We called for Ma to come and went running to where Rabbit had stopped.

As we got near, Pa about toppled off before we could catch him. I reached out to steady him on his feet. He staggered a bit, but managed to stay standing. His face it was bloody and cut up. Blood gushed from his nose and both his eyes was all swoll up and turning black. Peggy and me commenced to scream and cry, calling out for Ma.

"Pa's hurt, Ma. Come quick! He needs help."

In her condition she couldn't come very quick. It took a few minutes for her to waddle down the steps and across the yard. Pa was leaning on me and trying to walk, but he could hardly shuffle along, putting one foot out and dragging the other.

When Ma saw him, I thought she going to faint. I couldn't give her any help and hold Pa up, too, and Peggy wasn't anywhere near big enough. Ma managed to catch herself and not fall.

"Gracious sakes, Tom. What has happened to you? Who done this to you? Are you all right?'

His words came in a bare whisper. "No, Mattie, I'm not. Maybe if I can just get up on the porch I can sit in one of them rockers."

With me on one side and Ma doing what she could on the other, we made it to the steps. The hardest part was getting him up onto the porch. Finally, he eased down into one of the rocking chairs, closed his eyes and sat there breathing hard, his chin resting on his chest.

Penny brought a wet cloth, and I went to fetch some cool water for him. Ma washed away the blood and dirt from his face and arms. She kept asking him what happened, but he didn't have the energy to answer. He tried to open his eyes, but they was too swoll up. Again he took in a deep breath and began trying to talk.

"It was a gang of them Confederate rogues, Mattie. Hiding in the woods. Come up on me right sudden. Old Rabbit couldn't run, I didn't stand any chance at all of getting away. They pulled me down and commenced to beating and kicking on me. I don't know. Might have a rib broke. Can't keep on talking. Hurts to breathe. Don't know just what it is, but it's bad, Mattie. Real bad."

We finally got him to bed. Ma helped him off with his boots and clothes. That's when she saw just how beat up he really was. We heard her sobs and his groans of pain as she tried to dress his wounds. I brought a pan of hot water and she made warm compresses to put on his worst bruises.

Ma asked if I knowed the weeping willow tree down by the spring. When I said I did she told me to go break off several good-sized young branches and bring them in. I should peel the bark off and put it to soak in a pan of boiling water. When it was done, she began giving the liquid to him one spoonful at a time. After he'd taken about half of it, he seemed to be resting a little easier. When I asked her about it, she a Cherokee woman told her that such a concoction from willow bark would help ease pain. I boiled up some more of it, then put the other girls to bed before going to sleep. Ma said she'd stay up and keep an eye on Pa.

She was napping in her chair when I woke up in the morning. Pa seemed to be sleeping. I went out to cut more bark to make a new supply of medicine. When I took it in, Pa seemed to be sleeping. Ma was awake, but put her finger to her lips for silence.

When Penny woke up, we got busy with the morning chores. It took most all morning for us to get them done by ourselves. Penny got Peggy up and we fixed breakfast, and Pen took Peggy out to play. By then, Pa was awake and sitting up in bed. Ma fed him a thin gruel we had made with corn meal. I reckon he was glad to have something he could eat without opening his mouth very wide. She gave him some more of the willow bark medicine, and soon he was asleep again. She ate a little breakfast, and I offered to sit with him so she could get some rest. She went to lay down on my bed awhile, but I don't think she ever went off to sleep.

It was like this for near a week before Pa was able to talk enough to tell us just what had happened. He was coming home from Mr. Swindle's place when a band of five or six ruffians

156

came at him from out of the woods where they was waiting to ambush him. They gave out the Rebel yell, dragged him off the mule and commenced beating and kicking him. One was carrying a frayed old Confederate battle flag and kept punching him with the blunt end of the flagpole. Another beat him with the butt of a rifle. He was afraid they was going to shoot him or maybe even lynch him. They kept cussing and calling him a "rotten Yankee-loving scalawag" and all kinds of other things. He didn't know how long this went on, but after a time they kicked him to the side of the road and took off back into the woods where they came from.

"Did you know who they was?" I needed to know the names of the evil people who would do a thing like this.

"Oh, yes, Fannie, we know all of them. We see them most every time we go into town. Two used to be in our church before they went off to be with that Secesh crowd. One of them is always sitting off by himself on the porch at the general store. You remember the one I mean?"

I knew just who he was talking about, the strange acting man who was always there, not saying anything but just glaring at us. He was a right mean looking fellow. Pa said he was the one carrying the Rebel battle flag.

This brought to mind some of the things Pa'd told us about why he'd been afeared to come home before the war wound down. Now we could see that the end of the war didn't bring an end to the meanness. We still had a whole lot to be afraid of.

Chapter 12

It was a full month before Pa could do any work at all. Them rascals had given his bad leg some special attention, leaving his limp much worse. He got winded with any exertion at all. With Ma unable to do much, most of the farm work fell to us girls or else it went undone. With summer in full swing, it seemed we might lose the benefit of that fine garden we'd worked so hard for. The ghost of hunger raised its ugly head again, bringing back awful memories of how it'd been before.

Penny, Peggy and me picked peas and beans and brought in the tomatoes as they ripened. Ma managed to put most of it up in Mason jars for the winter, while we enjoyed eating them every day. The corn was looking good, but it wasn't near ready to pick or cut for silage. There was a few roasting ears that we enjoyed.

Early of a Saturday morning, we set about doing what we could to get the mid-summer harvest in. There was a lot left to be done. Ma worked in the kitchen doing the canning as we brought things to her, but she had to stop and rest now and again, so the canning was going right slow.

Along about mid-morning we heard what sounded like

a whole passel of folks coming up our lane singing a song we knew from church:

> *"Bringing in the sheaves,*
> *Bringing in the sheaves,*
> *We shall come rejoicing,*
> *Bringing in the sheaves."*

There was three wagonloads of folks from near and far. Some we knew and some we didn't. There was even several well-known Secesh among them. They started out telling Pa how ashamed they was that some sorry trash from our community had done this to him.

Mr. Silas Townley, one of the Secesh, spoke right up. He said that with the war over, it's time for all of us to pull together and make the best we can of whatever might be coming next. He promised Pa that there was more good folks around here than there was of these ruffians. They'd do what they could to make amends and see if these scoundrels could be brought to justice. It was a right good speech he made, about how in the war everybody had done what they thought was right, but we needed to put all that behind us now. No matter where our loyalties had been placed before, we all be Americans now. As neighbors, we needed to live together in peace. I guess that had to be about as close as I ever came to hearing a Secesh sounding like a Patriot.

They'd come to help any way they could. They asked what needed doing. Ma was so overcome she could hardly talk. They set out stripping the garden of the things that was ready for picking. The women folk took over all the canning and preparing of the vegetables that was ready. The parts of the garden that'd continue to produce was cleaned of weeds.

They allowed as how the corn was looking right good. If we continued to get plenty of rain at the right time, it should make a good crop. That sure was good news because we would be needing lots of corn for the farm animals as well as for ourselves. Some of the men allowed as how they would come back at harvest time and help out with the corn if need be.

Come lunchtime, the women brought out baskets of food and spread it out on tails of the wagons. There was more good things to eat than a body could have hoped for. Everybody had plenty, with more to spare. The women told Ma to pick out what she could use, and they left it for us to have later.

Pa mentioned how he had been planning to fix the smoke house roof. A bunch of the young men got up and went to nailing the cedar shakes into place. Fences needed mending here and there. The pigsty needed to be shored up a bit where the old sow had kept rooting her way out under it. The spring needed to be cleaned out where leaves and trash had fallen in. There was two boards needed replacing on the springhouse.

By the middle of the afternoon everything had been put into tip top shape. The storage shed was filled with canned goods of every kind and description. The house had been cleaned from front to back. The garden looked good like when we first put it in.

One of the young men who'd worked in the garden said he had a question. He wanted to know what that vine was growing close down to the ground. He'd never seen anything quite like it. Pa was able to get out a good laugh. Well, more like a chuckle than a real laugh, but it was the nearest thing to a laugh we'd heard from him in a while. It was the Goober peas the fellow was asking about. Nobody there knowed about them. Pa promised that when the Goobers was ready to dig, along about September, we'd be sure to share some with anybody who wanted to try them. Just about everybody did.

One of the older women asked to talk with Ma in private. Her name was Mrs. Sheffield, and she went to our church. She explained that she'd been a midwife in her younger years. She reckoned as how Ma's baby would be born very soon. In fact, she said, if her experience was worth anything, this could happen any time now, maybe even tonight. She lived alone and had nobody depending on her. With us living way out here with no near neighbors to call on, she wondered how we'd manage. She said she'd be glad to stay for a day or two, if that would be a comfort. Ma was pretty sure she was right; the baby could come at any time.

"Why, Mrs. Sheffield that is a right generous and gracious offer. If you are sure it wouldn't be too hard on you, I would be real relieved to have you nearby." She told her about how bad it was when Peggy was born, and us out here all to ourselves.

As the others was getting into the wagons, Elder Parker from our church stood up and called for attention. He said he wanted to read a verse from the Bible, Psalm 126:6:

"He that goeth forth and weepeth, bearing precious seed, shall doubtless come again with rejoicing, bringing his sheaves with him."

Then he said a prayer of thanksgiving. The wagons headed

off down the lane with their load of tired but cheerful people. As they went they sang another church song:

> "Come, ye that love the Lord,
> And let our joys be known;
> Join in a song with sweet accord,
> Join in a song with sweet accord
> And thus surround the throne,
> And thus surround the throne."

Mrs. Sheffield had been right. Way up in the night we was woke up by the screaming of a newborn baby. Our sister Etta came into this world, welcomed on what had been a day of peace, plenty and rejoicing. I thought as how that just might be a right good sign.

Over the next few weeks Penny, Peggy and me had way too much fun playing with Etta. The garden was still doing well. Best of all, Pa was on the mend. All in all, things now looked pretty good to us.

One evening after Ma had fed the baby and gotten her down for the night, we commenced thinking about Illinois again. Pa thought he could talk enough now to tell us a bit more.

He started off with that far-away look on his face as he gazed off down the lane toward the road. He said this attack had got him to thinking about something that happened to him up there. It came not long before he started back toward home. In fact, it is what put getting out of there in his head.

"I had started to taking my new horse out for some exercise nearly every evening after the chores were done. I wanted Jack to get used to me, and I wanted to learn about his way of doing things. Jack was a right smart critter. It wasn't many days until we had each other figured out."

"What do you mean you 'had each other figured out,' Pa?" I'd never ridden a horse, but it didn't seem to me there was much to figure out. You either got on the critter and rode him or you didn't.

"Well, Fannie, there is a kind of conversation that goes on between a horse and a rider. It's almost like you need to learn each other's language. When it works right, the rider can guide the horse in very gentle ways. It might not take anything more than a slight nudge with one knee or the other to let the horse know which way you want to go. You can tell by how tense or loose his muscles are as to how the horse feels about what's going on around him. He has ways of letting you know that what he needs right now to just let loose and go for a good run. It's little things like that you have to learn about each other."

I was real interested in that. I hadn't heard about any such before. That is when I began to dream of having a horse of my own someday. At the least, I hoped our family could get a horse. And I was curious about what happened to Jack. Why didn't Pa have that horse when he got home?

"So that is what we were learning about each other on these evening rides. I would talk to Jack as we rode. I wanted him to know my voice when he heard it. Every evening, I always went the same way. We took the main road south from the Conway place and then made right turns until we got back home. That's how the roads were built up there. Jeremiah told me they followed what he called 'section lines.' The whole territory was laid out that way, in squares except where the river got in the way.

"Jack and me had been taking these rides for two or three weeks. One evening, we took the turn around one of those section lines and found a surprise waiting for us. Jack and me were drawn up short by five or six men mounted on right fine horses, lined up so as to block our path. Right off I noticed they were dressed in gray and wore identical black hats with high crowns and broad brims. They had what looked like a brown patterned hatband, and some kind of emblem on the front. The rifles they carried looked right new. I had not seen guns like them before. None of the guns were aimed at me; they all pointed up toward the sky, but I knew that could change in the blink of an eye. That meeting did not have a good feeling about it. Jack must have sensed it, too, for he skittered nervously sideways a few paces before I got him under control.

"The fellow in the middle of the line seemed to be the leader of the gang. He asked if I was 'that Sergeant Tom Files everybody around here was talking about.' He had a familiar Southern sound to his voice. I told him, yes, I was Tom Files. He glanced up and down the line at the other fellows who were with him like he was indicating their agreement as he said, 'Well, Sergeant Files, we have a message for you. No matter what these Yankees around here been saying, you are not wanted in these parts. Some of us here have kinfolks down there in Mississippi and Georgia and Alabama. They are all good, loyal Southerners. We are, too. We don't take kindly to folks who been shooting at our kin. Now that you got this fancy horse to ride, why don't you just head on back down there to where you come from? I believe you'll find the air down South a whole lot healthier for you in the long run than it is around here.' As he spoke he moved closer toward me. Now I could see what I thought was an emblem on his hat. It was a real snake's head, and the brown hatband was snake skin. Copperheads. These were some of those northern Rebels Jeremiah had told me about. Being there face to face with such men sent shivers down my spine. It took all the concentration I could muster to keep them from seeing my fear.

"After he spoke his piece, they all fired several rounds into the air, turned as one and galloped off. A bit down the road, the fellow who had done all the talking stopped and turned to snarl at me, 'Sergeant, I sincerely hope we don't have to meet like this again.' Giving me a crisp but insulting left-handed salute, with fingers pointing directly at the exposed fangs of the snake mounted on his hat, he swung around and rejoined the others."

That run-in with the Copperheads had shook Pa up. When he got back to the Conway place, he took Jack to the barn and gave him a good rubdown. But his hands shook so hard he could hardly hold the sponge. After putting Jack in his stall and giving him some oats and water, he sat there alone for near an hour. He decided not to tell the Conways about any of this. Not even Jeremiah.

"So you see, I was kind of like 'invited' to leave. The attitude of those Copperheads was not a whole lot different from the gang that beat me up down here. Both would gladly kill me. Given a choice, if I was going to die I would rather die here surrounded by my family, not off up there in a strange land. Right then and there I decided it was time for me to find a way back home. But how was I going to do that? The war was still raging. Travel was still dangerous. It was not going to be an easy matter to resolve. I would have to think on it and make me a plan."

Pa's energy was all used up, as was Ma's. They was both still mighty weak. That night I decided not to think on any of the things I'd heard and seen. Tonight, I would try counting sheep to put myself to sleep, but such sleep as I had was troubled and troublesome.

The next morning Pa said he felt up to going outside for a bit, thought he'd go and check on the pigs. He came right back in with the news that our pigs had given birth to eight piglets in the night. They all seemed to be healthy and she was letting them all suckle. This was very good news. This litter would be a good start to building up our stock. He reckoned that in two years, we would be able to start selling off or trading some pigs. He was in real good spirits thinking on the progress we had made these last few months.

Little Etta was growing a right smart. Peggy took special pleasure in playing with her. It was like she had herself a new ragdoll. It was a big help to Ma to have her looking after the baby. Ma wasn't up to any hard work yet, but she took care of some light cleaning and the cooking. Pa was getting strong enough to do some of the outside chores that didn't require heavy lifting. He took over the milking from me while I did some of the jobs that was hard for him. They was hard for me, too, but I wasn't in any pain like he was. Penny and I were pretty much keeping the weeds down in the garden after the neighbors got it cleaned up so good for us.

I wondered how we was going to handle digging all those 'taters this year. That's right hard work that took all of us working together last year. When I told Pa about this worry, he said, "What you're not thinking about, Fannie, is that we've got a mule you didn't have last year. He would be able to plow up the 'taters. The biggest job is going to be picking them up and putting them in the sack." Well, that sure made me feel better. Penny and I were real good at picking up 'taters. Besides, this year Peggy was big enough to be a help, too.

That put me to thinking about how Pa had been back with us coming up on a year in a month or two. I could hardly believe it. Almost a year, and just look at all we had got done. We've got a cow and a mule now. We've got a powerful good garden. We've had plenty of food to eat and to put up for the winter. We've got us a dozen pigs, with that new litter of piglets. Some of the hens had hatched their eggs, so there is a good flock of chickens again. Our corn is about ready to be cut. And there are those two big hills of Goober peas to dig. The barn and the smokehouse was fixed up, and we had milk and butter in the springhouse. Most of all, we've got our whole family together, including little Etta. Ma's feeling better, and Pa's on the mend. I figure this had been a right good year, all told.

We was all in a right good mood when we sat together that evening to hear Pa take up what he was telling about his plan for getting back down here to us.

"The morning after my run-in with that gang of Yankee Rebels, Jeremiah, Ezekiel and me were working together in the barn. I commenced to talking about home and family. Jeremiah asked if I was ready to head back south. I told him that was playing on my mind. I allowed as how I sure was missing my wife and young 'uns. I reminded him that I got me a new little baby I had never seen. I didn't even know if it was a boy or a girl. My eyes teared over when I told him I didn't even know if any of y'all were still there. I didn't know what the war and its meanness might have brought. I said I needed to head on home soon as I could figure out how to bring it off.

"Right then we commenced to set out a plan. Ezekiel said he had overheard Amos talking about buying some livestock from a cattle farm over to the southern part of Indiana. Jeremiah reminded me that it was the folks who had some kind of a Files connection. If Amos got serious about making such a deal, it would be taking me in the right direction.

"We went in to clean up for supper. When we walked in, I smelled some real good food cooking. Deborah smiled and said 'Can you tell what I'm making for dessert, Tom? It's your favorite.' And I knew it was one of her good gooseberry pies."

I liked that idea. "Pa, was you still eating in that fancy dining room?" I liked the idea of a room that was just for enjoying good food.

"No, Fannie. That room was set aside for special times. We took our regular meals at the kitchen table. It was plenty big for everybody and was close to Deborah's cook stove. When we got settled, Amos said he had something on his mind that needed talking about. He turned to Jeremiah and said, 'Son, remember how we have been thinking about getting us a new bull to help build up our live stock?'

"Jeremiah glanced across the table at me and allowed as how he remembered that right well. He tried to keep a straight face as Amos went on. 'Well, I think it's about time we did that. I wrote to that same fellow over in Indiana. He's still got one for sale. I want you and Ezekiel to make a trip over there and get it for us. You think you could do that before the end of the week?'

"The three of us near about fell out of our chairs. We didn't need to make any kind of a plan. Amos had already made it for us. I reckon he saw the surprise on our faces and asked if anything was the matter.

"'Oh, no sir. Nothing's the matter. We can head over that way maybe tomorrow, or no later than the next day.' Smiling over toward me, Jeremiah said, 'I think that's near Paducah, Kentucky isn't it?' Amos nodded it was.

"Ezekiel asked if it would be all right for me to go along with them. Amos thought that was a fine idea. So there it was, Mattie. The whole thing just fell right into our laps easy as falling off a log backwards.

"After dinner the three of us excused ourselves, saying we needed to give the horses some exercise. While we were riding around the far pasture, we agreed I should tell Amos and Deborah that I was leaving for good. When we got back to the house I sat down with Amos and Deborah and explained it all to them. Jeremiah let them know I was some kind of kin to the very folks they had bought those cows from. Amos and Deborah said they were sorry to see me go, but knew I needed to find my way back home.

"Deborah said if she'd knowed this was going to be our last dinner together, we would have taken it in the dining room. I said that would have been real nice, but the main thing was that we were enjoying being together. I thanked them again for taking me in like they had. I told them I wouldn't ever forget what fine people they were and how much they had helped a poor Southern boy far from home. They wished me well. Amos said a little prayer for me. We parted all friendly like. There were even a few tears shed.

"Next day, the three of us saddled up just about sun up and

started our trek east. Ezekiel and me didn't know where we were going, but Jeremiah did. He said we would be traveling about a day and a half, if all went well. I was real excited. I had Jack to ride and that sure beat walking. I had more than a hundred dollars hard money in my pocket. Best of all, this was the first step bringing me back South. Back to you. I didn't know how it was going to work out, but I was sure it would. And I reckon it did, but not just the way I thought it might. Not for Jack, not for that hundred dollars and not for any of us. But here I sit, and I reckon that's the most important part. Anyhow, that was how it started. Of course, there's a whole lot more to the working out of it than there's time to tell tonight."

I slept well that night with happy thoughts of Pa riding Jack on his way back to us, but I still wondered just what happened to that fine horse along the way.

Chapter 13

On Sunday our church had all-day singing and dinner on the grounds. Pa had got the elders to agree for us to have a choir like that Methodist church he was in up North. There was eight or nine of us in it right regular, including Pa and me. Ma didn't think she could do that just yet, but planned to start when Etta got some bigger. Johnny Hinesley came. He sat beside Pa. Pa thought Johnny was going to be singing bass as soon as he could get better control of the sound. I was glad he and Pa had this chance to get better acquainted. I sat in front of Johnny and had a good feeling listening to him sing, even when his voice broke a bit on the high notes.

The Methodist Parson Wainwright preached for us that day. He had just stood up to start talking when the door opened and five folks came walking it. We all turned to see who would be coming in so long after church time. One of the women toward the back of the church let out a startled gasp and a twitter of whispers spread through the congregation. It was one of the Secesh families who had left our church when that other one started up. I recognized the man as Mr. Townley, the man who made such a nice speech when all those neighbors came to help us after Pa got beat up.

Mr. Townley stood facing Parson Wainwright, holding his hat over his heart. Clearly he had something he wanted to say, but waited for the parson to give him permission to speak. What he said brought the whole church so quiet I could hear a mouse running around somewhere up in the rafters.

"Parson Wainwright," he said, "you and everybody here knows that me and my family left this church to go with them others who started up that new church the other side of the creek. Well, sir, I want to say to everybody here today, that wasn't right. That was about politics and hatred, it weren't about religion. After that church decided they was going over to the Baptists, I found out I had done made a big mistake.

"Me and mine have been Methodists all our lives. I came here today because I knowed you was going to be the preacher. You baptized all my babies right here in this church. I was baptized in the Methodist Church over near Townley, where my Grandpa Townley was a steward. I ain't going to make this a long talk. The long and the short of it is that that Baptist preacher wanted to take me out to the creek and dunk me, but I told him I had done been baptized already. I wouldn't have no part of that for me or mine. So they never would take us into that church. Now, I don't know the Good Book too good, but I know there's some words in it about 'one baptism,' and that's good enough for me. Far as I know, we all still be on the list right here. I sure hope that's so because we want to come back and be part of this church. I sure am sorry for all the ruckus we caused back then. Now it's time for us all to let bygones be bygones and work together to bring such good as we can out of all that meanness."

My Pa came right to his feet and, without asking permission

174

from anybody, he said, "Brother Townley, you and your folks came to my aid when Mattie and me were in real bad shape and couldn't do for ourselves. You made a right fine talk on that occasion, kind of like what you just said. Back in the war, we took opposite sides. But that is over, thank the good Lord. I'm not an elder here, and I got no right speak for anybody but myself." He moved over to stand beside Mr. Townley. Holding out his right hand, he said, "As far as I'm concerned, all there is to be said is 'Welcome home, brother. Welcome home.'"

The whole congregation stood up, clapping and whistling and saying "Amen." I never saw any such commotion as that in our church before. Everybody came around to shake Mr. Townley's hand and gave him and his family a welcome.

"Well, now," said Parson Wainwright loud enough to get attention as folks began moving back to their seats. "This here is an interesting coincidence. You didn't have any way of knowing this, Brother Townley, but the sermon I came ready to give today is about when the Prodigal son went back home. Seems to me there's no cause for me to do anything now but read that scripture from the Gospel of Luke, chapter 15. The truth is, that story just came to life right here among us. Praise the Lord! And welcome home, Brother Townley." After reading the scripture, the parson offered up a prayer, we sang a song and everybody went out to get ready for dinner.

Just as church was letting out, a wagon pulled into the churchyard, drawn by the finest pair of horses anywhere around. It was Mr. Jake Feltman. Mr. Jake was quite old, dressed in a black suit of clothes and with a very full gray beard. He never came to church, but he was a regular visitor at our dinners and spent the afternoon visiting with folks. He always brought the same thing, four roasted chickens. He told everybody it was a recipe his grandma brought over from what he called "the old country." I never knowed just what country that was.

Pa liked to tell about the time one of the ladies at church, who had very little learning, asked Mr. Jake why he didn't ever come to church. He told her he was a "Hebrew." That puzzled her a right smart, but after thinking on it she said, "Well, Mr. Jake, I don't rightly know of any other Hebrews here abouts, but there's a book in the Bible by that name so I reckon that makes you a right good man to know."

While the adults put out the food they had brought, Johnny asked if I would care to go for a little walk. The only place there was to walk was out through the graveyard. We went along looking at the graves of folks who had died during the wartime. There was too many of them, and they wasn't all soldiers. Women and even little children had been killed or died of disease or hunger. We passed one bunch of three little graves together alongside their mother, as sad a tragedy as a body could ever imagine. From somewhere in the distance I heard a Whip-poor-will singing its name over and over again like as if he was in danger of forgetting it.

We didn't really do much talking. Didn't feel any need to. We just walked along enjoying each other's company. He allowed as how he was glad Pa had got the choir going. He commented on what a nice voice I had. That made me blush again. I told him how our family would sing most evenings and Pa would play the fiddle. We fell quiet for a spell. Johnny ducked his head in his shy kind of way and darted his eyes over toward me. In a quiet voice, almost a whisper, he said both of us being in the choir meant we could be together a bit more and he was special glad of that. He reached out his hand and took hold of mine. When I looked up, his face had turned a bright shade of red. That made me smile, but I knew my face was red, too. About then we heard folks calling everybody to come for dinner.

As we turned to go back, I saw that Penny'd been following along behind us. I didn't know how long she'd been there, but I could have strangled her right then if I could have gotten my hands on her. Little sisters can be such pests sometimes.

When we went into the church for the singing, Mr. Townley and his wife came and sang with us in the choir. I couldn't help noticing how much Mrs. Townley's voice sounded like my Ma's.

On the way home I didn't have much to say. I was just thinking about taking that walk with Johnny, and how it felt for us to be holding hands. Ma and Pa was kind of looking at each other with a little smile on their faces. I wondered what that was all about. When I heard Penny giggle, I knew what that was about. I gave her a hard look, and she stuck her tongue out at me. I wanted to slap her sassy face. I would have done it, too, if Ma'd not turned to look at us just then.

When we got home Pa unhitched the mule while Ma, Penny and me unloaded the dishes and food we'd brought back from church. After awhile Pa took down his fiddle, and we sat on the porch and sang some more. Then, as often happened, we began to hear about Pa's adventures. Last we'd heard he and the Conway boys was headed over to buy that bull Amos wanted to get.

"Our travels went without incident. Along the way, Jeremiah told me about these folks we were going to meet. Their name was Scott. Mrs. Scott was the one who was some kind of kin to the Files. I was looking forward to hearing about some tie with this long lost part of our family. Jeremiah chuckled. He said he had just now remembered the name of the Scott's cattle ranch. They called it The Cow Pens. We all got a good laugh out of that connection with the Battle of Cowpens.

"We came upon the Scott place in the early afternoon of the next day. Ezekiel and Jeremiah concluded their business with Jake Scott and planned to start back home with their new bull the following morning. While we were eating dinner, Mrs. Scott and me – Catherine was her name - got to talking about our Files kin and the Battle of Cowpens. She had a painted picture of her great-grandfather, my great grand uncle, John Files, Jr. That was right interesting for me to see. He was the spittin' image of my own Grandpa, Mattie. We never had any pictures of any of our folks that I know anything about.

"I knew that John had been at Cowpens with his daddy. What I didn't know was that he had first joined up with the Virginia Militia to fight for our independence way back before that, on July 2, 1776. Catherine told me that, unbeknownst to John Files, that was the very day when the Continental Congress up in Philadelphia had voted on their resolution for independence from Britain. That means he had already been a Patriot for more than ten years when he, his brothers and his Pa were together at that battle down in South Carolina."

Ma was taking a special interest at what Pa was telling, especially about all these faraway places during those important times for our country."I'm glad you learned more about your folks in the Revolution, Tom. I've heard you talk about some of it before, but knowing all this adds to the notion that what you did in the war was the right thing to do."

"But, Mattie, Catherine's story got a whole lot more interesting than that."

Pa paused to catch his breath. Ma and me waited patiently for him to be ready to start talking again. His breathing was a bit better, but his voice was weak after all the singing we did at church and again at home. He cleared his throat and picked up where he had left off.

"In 1777, a few months after he signed up with the Virginia militia, John Files was assigned as a scout with a unit lead by a Captain Robert Cravens. You would never guess where Captain Cravens' unit was sent. They were sent to scout the Indians down in the Tygart River Valley. Can you imagine that? John Files, as a soldier of the Revolution, was sent to scout the Indians right back there to where his family was massacred all those years before.

"Catherine knew a whole lot about our family that I'd never heard before. After the war was over, the young John came up to Kentucky and then settled down in that part of Indiana for several years. Some of his adult children stayed, and they were Catherine's kinfolks. But he continued on up into Illinois somewhere. That is where he died and was buried."

Pa was grinning from ear to ear. You could tell he was right pleased with what he'd learned. I was enjoying hearing this, too. Here these kinfolks of ours had been out there wandering around in that part of the country a hundred years afore Pa ever got there. Now, there he was sitting at the dinner table with this cousin he didn't even know existed. I thought on that for a long while. It just goes to show how you might have family most anywhere you go to, if you can just figure out how to find them.

After the Conway boys left, Pa stayed with the Scott family a few days. They let him help out around their ranch. It was the first time he'd ever seen a real cattle ranch, or been around more than a few milk cows, for that matter.

He was planning to head out the next morning when something right remarkable happened. Catherine Scott got a letter in the United States Mail that evening. It was from her brother, who lived way over east, near Louisville, Kentucky. He told her how his son, who was also named John Files, had just mustered out of the 27th Indiana Regiment. He'd been fighting all over the South for three years. But here is what got Pa's attention. A buddy had come home with John and was headed back down South to join up with General Sherman, who was planning a big attack on Atlanta. That got Pa to thinking. If he could get over there and hitch up with this fellow, maybe they could travel part way back down South together. He was pretty sure they'd both be right glad for the company.

Next morning he said his farewells to Jake and Catherine Scott and started out lickety-split for Louisville, Kentucky. Time he got there, John Files' friend had done left, but there was a regiment of Ohio troops under a Captain Nash leaving out for Tennessee. Ma and me couldn't hardly imagine how Pa could have such good luck right then. Here they were, headed right down here near where he wanted to get.

Pa paused again to catch his breath. Ma allowed as how a cool drink of water might be a help to him. She said she wouldn't mind a swallow her own self. We took a break while I went to fetch fresh water from the spring. While we sipped on it, Pa picked up where he'd left off.

"When I first talked to this Captain Nash, he was downright

suspicious of me. It was clear he was afraid I might be a Confederate spy or something. When I showed him my discharge papers from the First Alabama that changed everything. He said he was plumb tickled to have me ride along with them. He thought I might come in handy as a guide or scout or something. I explained I didn't know anything about this middle part of Kentucky we would be going through. I was right good at scouting, though; that was the most part of what I had done with the First Alabama. He complimented me on my fine horse and how it would be a great advantage for my scouting assignments.

"While I was waiting for us to leave out of there, I found a right interesting newspaper called *The Louisville Union News*. It was the first paper I had seen in quite a long time, so I sat down and read every word in it. I found out that President Lincoln had declared martial law in Kentucky. He had put a General Stephen Burbridge in as military commander of the state. From what I read, Burbridge was pretty tyrannical about how he ran things. Whenever any Union sympathizer was killed, he would take four Rebel prisoners out and shoot them in public view.

"The same afternoon after I read that newspaper I decided to go for a walk just to see the place. I turned onto one of the main streets, called Broadway, and found myself face to face with four men hanging by the neck from a scaffold set up in the street. One of the soldiers standing guard told me they were men the general thought were guerrillas. He had them hanged and left them there most of the day for everybody to gawk it. It made me plumb sick to my stomach to see such a spectacle done in the name of the United States of America. Such as that just wasn't called for, not even with the war going on."

Pa sat for a while, gently rocking to and fro. From the look on his face, I could see he was still bothered by what he'd seen and read. He opined that he didn't like the notion that civilians could be arrested on no more basis than suspicion. Folks that General Burbridge suspected of being traitors could have all their property taken over by the government. They could even be executed without a trial.

Deep in thought and running his fingers over his beard, he went on. "This didn't sound much like the country I knew and loved. It just wasn't right. I didn't get to learn more, though. Captain Nash gave orders for us to head out. We mounted up, and Jack and me fell in line as we started our trip down toward Tennessee."

Pa's mood had changed considerably while he was talking about this General Burbridge and what he'd done. He didn't think Burbridge had acted much like a Patriot. I reckoned such an idea as patriotism wasn't as simple a matter as some folks made it out to be. Maybe it wasn't all just a matter of which side you was fighting on. Maybe it was a matter of what you did, of how you did it, and why. Right was right and wrong was wrong, no matter which side of the fence you be on.

"All along the way through Kentucky, we saw forts and military installations being built everywhere. I reckon there were a dozen of them, all strong earth-and-timber structures. One I saw was big enough to hold at least a thousand soldiers. I thought all of this building was right strange. From what I saw in that Union newspaper, General Sherman's march out of Atlanta had distracted everybody away from these parts. I reckon there must have been a good bit of guerrilla activity, but we didn't see any of it. All the way along, we saw no signs of Confederate action anywhere in central Kentucky. Our passage was without incident or threat of any kind.

"All of that changed, though, when we got down near to Tennessee. That's when I found myself in some hot water."

Best Pa could recollect, this was on up into September of 1864. Captain Nash was telling his troops that General Sherman had taken Atlanta. It was burned to the ground, and Sherman was on his way over toward Augusta, headed toward the Carolinas. The captain warned everybody that it looked like Confederate troops under General John Bell Hood was headed right in their direction, and maybe Nathan Bedford Forrest, too. It seemed to the captain like those two was aiming to cut off General Sherman's supply lines that ran through Tennessee, Georgia and Alabama. The 13th Ohio and lots more troops was right in their way.

The look on Pa's face told us he had been sorely distressed at these developments. He was near about to being home, and here it was looking like that wasn't to be, at least not any time soon. That old war was getting in his way once again.

"The captain told us he thought we were about to see some considerable amount of action. When he saw me standing there listening to all this, he came over to talk to me. He said he was right sorry but he didn't see any way for me to get away from there safely. Whichever way I set out to go, I was sure to run into considerable Confederate forces. At the same time, since I was not in the army, he made it clear I was free to do whatever I thought best. I could go or I could stay. His advice, though, was for me to hunker down and stay put until my prospects improved.

"As I found out right quick like, my prospects was not going to improve any time soon. It was clear that Hood had his mind set on taking Tennessee back for the Confederacy. Anybody with half the sense God gave a bill goat could see that to get Tennessee, Hood would have to take Nashville. The Union forces had held the city for a good three years, but there was a whole lot of guerrilla action thereabouts. Such a fight as we knew was coming was going to have to be big, bad and bloody on all sides. And there I was, smack dab in the middle of what was shaping up to be one of the biggest dad burn fights in this whole bloody war. And me with a good horse, a hundred dollars in my pocket and just a week's travel time away from home."

Ma and me didn't have any idea he was that close to being home. We didn't even know if he was dead or alive.

"Our unit was finally joined up with the 13th Ohio Cavalry. There had been some kind of mistake made while we were back up there near Louisville. We were supposed to have linked up with them then. Now we were all coming together down here near Nashville under General George Thomas. The bunch I was with was sent over east of Nashville a ways to a place called La Vergne, Tennessee. Once, I'm sure, it had been a right pretty little town. It wasn't so pretty with all the war had done to it."

I asked Pa to show us where La Vergne was. He sent me to get the geography book, and turned to a map that showed Tennessee and Alabama. The place wasn't named on that map, but he pointed to about where it was located. Then he ran his finger down the map to show us how close it was to where we lived.

"Land sakes, Tom," Ma exclaimed. "You sure 'nough was near about home, wasn't you?"

Pa nodded that this was so, then went on with his story.

"The misfortune of La Vergne is that it was too close to Franklin, Murfreesboro, and Nashville. This was all disputed territory, so both sides had been tearing it apart. There was a small fort on a hill just out of town and a blockhouse closer in for the defense of the town. Both were held by the 13th Ohio. In the climate of this war, even these two small fortifications would be enough to attract attention to the area.

"That was the sad part of it, Mattie. There were lots of little places like that all over the South. There were people who lived there who were on each side of the controversy and lots who held divided loyalties or none at all. Didn't none of that make any matter mind to these two armies. Those good folks were just caught, trapped by circumstances they couldn't do a thing about. I was sitting there in La Vergne watching the good citizens of the place running here and there, wondering what to do, where to go and how to keep their families safe.

I commenced to ponder what they thought it would mean to be a Patriot or to be a Rebel. Could they see any difference? Would any of it matter to them, when what they really wanted was just to keep those they loved safe and sound? I was even starting to doubt what it all meant to me, when I was just focused on getting down here to those I love.

"I'll tell you the truth of it," Pa said as he took out his bandana and wiped away the tears from his face. "There were nights I didn't do anything from dusk to dawn but cry quietly there in my tent. My heart was broke. I couldn't see anything good coming in the future, just more darkness and more killing.

I wasn't sure anymore just what it was all about. Was it worth so much killing and all the dying, all the pain and all the heartbreak? But I knew there was a whole lot more to come before it was over."

Chapter 14

While Pa was camping with those Ohio troops at La Vergne, Tennessee they got the news that Mr. Abraham Lincoln had been re-elected president of the United States of America. Not only that, but Mr. Andrew Johnson of Tennessee was now the vice president. Pa allowed as how that seemed more than passing strange to him. Here American soldiers was in Tennessee fighting against Tennessee's Rebel soldiers, while this fellow from Tennessee was going to Washington to help Mr. Lincoln win the war.

Pa shook his head in wonderment, and he chuckled when he thought about what his friends up North must be thinking about all this. They thought everybody from down South was just Rebels, but now there was a Southerner going to be Mr. Lincoln's vice president. He laughed out loud when he recollected that gang of Copperheads who ran him off because he was a Southern Patriot. He wondered what they was thinking about this development.

The politics of the situation was right interesting, but that wasn't what concerned me the most. I reminded Pa that we was still waiting to hear about what had happened to him over at La Vergne. We knew he was surrounded by Confederates every which way he looked, so he couldn't make his way home right then.

"It was on the fifth day of December 1864 that my luck just plumb ran out. I won't ever forget that day if I live to be a hundred. Battle sounds were coming at us from every which way. It was special bad coming from over in the direction of Murfreesboro. Those two Confederate Generals, John Bell Hood and Nathan Bedford Forrest, were working together. They were dead set on re-taking Nashville. As I said, little La Vergne was right in their way. As it happened, it was Forrest's men who came calling on that little fort and blockhouse.

"When I heard it was General Forrest we were dealing with, I got real worried. I knowed a whole sight more than I wanted to about that Rebel general, so I went to the captain and told him all about what I had seen and heard over there at Fort Pillow. I told him, 'Captain, when the fighting starts, that man goes crazy; he don't show mercy to man or beast.' So, when General Forrest sent in a demand for us to surrender, there just wasn't anything else to do. There wasn't enough of us to stand a chance of resisting, so our choice was a matter of giving up or being massacred. That was how General Nathan Bedford Forrest did business.

"So that's how it happened the first time I became a prisoner of war."

"The first time?" Ma and me both sat up straight in our seats. This was news to us. We didn't know anything about him being a prisoner of war. Now he was saying it happened to him more than once.

"Yes, Mattie. I was taken prisoner two times. This time

I was put in a Confederate prison. A bit later, I found myself in a federal prison."

"A federal prison?" I could hardly believe what I was hearing. Why would my Pa be sent to prison by the country he'd been fighting for?

"Well, you'll have to wait a spell for that part of the story, Fannie. For now, I was taken captive by Nathan Bedford Forrest's men. At first, things weren't too bad. They rounded us all up and used that little fort on the hill for a makeshift stockade. There were only about five hundred of us there to be captured. The other half of our regiment had been split off to go help General Thomas in his fight against John Bell Hood over toward Nashville.

"Now I guess you can understand what happened to that fine horse, Jack. Everything we had was taken away. My gun was the first to go, of course. Jack and all the horses belonging to our regiment were taken to benefit the Rebellion. When they searched me, they found the hundred dollars I was bringing home to you. It, too, was taken into the service of Mr. Jefferson Davis' war. All the benefit I had gained from that trip up North, everything I had worked for all those months, was gone. There wasn't anything to be done for it. That's just the way life happens sometimes; wasn't any need stewing over it."

Pa looked like he aged near about ten years just sitting there. Since he'd had that big breakdown when he first got home, Ma and me always worried about him when he got in this shape. All we could do was just sit with him and hope he'd come around and be all right. After a time, he took in a deep breath and let it out slowly.

"The way things turned out, I was soon going to have bigger problems than that to worry about.

"At first, it didn't go no worse for me than for everybody else who was taken prisoner. The Confederates were short on supplies, so that first day we were just given a bit of stale bread and some weak soup to eat. At least the soup was hot and there were some bits of vegetable in it. There was no meat that I could tell, but the warmth of it felt good on that cold December day.

"We were lined up on the parade grounds and ordered to stand at attention. Next thing was for their first sergeant to make up a roster of who we were. The name of each one of us and what rank they held was taken down for his report. I knew just what he was doing. I had done similar work as first sergeant down in Mississippi.

"That's when things got tough for me. When it came my time to identify myself, I made the mistake of telling him the truth. I identified myself as a civilian, formerly a sergeant with the First Alabama Cavalry, United States Volunteers. I even showed the young officer my discharge papers.

"Well, he came near to exploding right on the spot. His face turned red and his eyes about popped out of his head. He was a redheaded Irishman to begin with, so you can just imagine; the madder he got, the more shades of red he turned. He looked over to where his commanding officer was standing and roared out like a lion. 'Captain, looks like we got us a sorry, no good traitor here.'

"Well, that got everybody's attention. The whole registration process came to a dead stop. Every man in earshot stood looking at me. A murmur of sympathy went through the men of my regiment, but there wasn't anything any of them could do but watch how this was going to play itself out.

"Next thing I knew, three big, burly men had me in hand. They pulled my arms hard behind me and tied them tight with a rough bit of rope. Then they started in cussing at me and beating on me. I was knocked down, with no way to defend myself. One commenced hitting me with a stick, and one was kicking me in the ribs. I don't know how long that went on before the captain finally gave the order for them to stop and had me taken to the stockade."

Pa explained that a stockade was kind of like a jail, except it was just a good size open area in one of the buildings. One of the men threw each prisoner a filthy old blanket, which they had a choice of using for a mattress or a blanket. It was all he had, and all he was going to get.

"All five hundred of us were crowded into one big room. There were several windows but there was no glass in any of them. They were just open holes in the walls, letting the raw winter wind blow through. When I looked out, it was snowing and kept on all that night and all the next day and all the next night.

"They didn't have any isolated cell to put me in for special punishment, so they stuck me as close as could be to one of those open windows. The snow blew right in on me, so my clothes and blanket were always wet and freezing cold. At least they left me with my coat, such as it was. While wasn't anybody being what you could call well fed, I was on half rations. Every time one of the guards or privates came near me, I learned to expect some special attention in the form of a blow or a kick and a cussing out.

"It looked like we might be stuck there for the duration of the war. General Sherman had put a stop to prisoner exchanges with the Rebels more than a year earlier, except for high-ranking officers. That meant we were pretty much on our own. We would just have to make the most of it and hope for the best.

"The floor was hard and cold. We figured out if we slept close together, head to feet, we could share body heat. Our nearly worn out blankets were not much help. They smelled of sour sweat and who knows what all else. In the night, I discovered mine was infested with lice and fleas, and who knows what all else."

It made my skin itch just thinking about Pa having to sleep on that dirty old blanket. The talk about lice and fleas made me scratch my head. I noticed Ma was doing that, too.

"That is how it went for about a month. Off and on we could hear the sounds of battle off in the distance, but that began to change. Increasingly, it sounded like most of it was coming from over Nashville way. We had heard that our General Thomas had taken all of his command there, which meant that was where we would have been if our luck had been different. Instead, we were stuck there in the stockade, wondering what was going on with the war. From the sound of it, we knew whatever was going on was big. It was real big.

"I wouldn't know the truth of it until four or five months later. What we were hearing over at Nashville was one of the biggest battles of this dirty war. What General Thomas brought off in just those few days was the destruction of General John Bell Hood's entire Confederate army. Hood's troops were sent running for cover, with Thomas' troops in hot pursuit. More than six thousand died, counting folks on both sides. John Bell Hood had been beaten earlier at Columbia and at Franklin, so this was his third defeat in Tennessee. Eventually, he retreated over into Mississippi, where he resigned his command in disgrace.

"Fannie, that would have been a sight to see. Of course, I was glad we were kept safe from all the killing and maiming, but wouldn't it have been something to watch John Bell Hood and Nathan Bedford Forrest running for their lives?"

Pa had to take a break from talking, but his face was shining with pride as he thought about such an outcome as that. He'd hated that General Forrest ever since he learned about what he'd done over at Fort Pillow.

"I reckon Christmas must have come and gone during that time, but there wasn't much way for us to know about it. Funny thing was, I had been mustered out of the army a week after Christmas the year before. It made me sad just thinking on it having been a year already. My heart ached at the thought, wishing I could be here with y'all." Pa looked around at each one of us with a smile on his face before going on.

"Those thoughts was the main thing that time of year meant to me. Other than that, the only way we were made conscious of the season was because some of the men had their harmonicas. Every evening they would play some Christmas music. It was the only hint we had of 'Peace on earth, good will to men.'"

Ma and I looked at each other. We was both thinking on our Christmas that year. It wasn't anywhere near as bad as Pa's was in prison, but we sure didn't have any good memories of it. All we'd had to eat was a 'possum Ma was able to shoot, some moldy sweet 'taters and the last handful of unseasoned dried beans Ma boiled in plain water. There wasn't any Santa Claus. Ma said he couldn't get through because of all the shooting going on. She read us the Christmas story from the Bible, and we tried to sing some Christmas songs, but we was crying before we could finish. We had all knelt down and said a special Christmas prayer for Pa, wherever he was and whatever shape he was in. Then we all slept together in her bed. She said at least we could keep each other warm.

Pa managed a little smile through the tears forming in his eyes, then he went on with his story. "It was a whole lot later that I found out that this Christmas season had not been so bleak everywhere. It was on Christmas Day 1864 that General William Tecumseh Sherman presented the defeated city of Savannah, Georgia, as a holiday gift to President Abraham Lincoln. Savannah had been one of the last major seaports remaining open to the Confederate Navy, so that had been a major defeat. But didn't none of us know anything about that until after the war was over. If we had known, it sure would have brought a little bit of cheer in an otherwise dank and dreary winter.

"Yes, it would have helped for us to know things were going good for somebody somewhere, because they sure wasn't going good for us, and we had no prospect for things to change for the better as far as I could see."

The New Year came and went, but Pa said he couldn't tell any difference when 1865 came in. There was some shouting and singing among the Confederates. He could hear them singing "Auld Lang Syne," and some of the Yanks joined in. Pa fell into a thoughtful mood remembering hearing folks singing during those unhappy times.

"Most of us were just too cold, too hungry and too lonely for those familiar words to bring anything but more sorrow, more tears, and a deeper feeling of loneliness and despair.

> 'Should auld acquaintance be forgot, and never brought to mind?'

"Singing those words just didn't make any sense at all because not a single one of those back home were going to be forgot for a minute. They were always on our mind. It hurt too much to sing that silly song."

We could see Pa was having a hard time talking about this. He stopped again, with a distant look of sadness in his eyes. When he got this way, we'd learned it was best to sit quiet and wait. When he was ready, he'd either start talking again or he'd cut it off and say it was time to go to bed.

"Of course, nobody had any fireworks to shoot. The Confederates didn't have any ammunition to waste on such a celebration. When the singing stopped, the night was quiet and cold and dark.

"It was about a week later that something remarkable happened. The officers barked orders for all of us to assemble in the yard. We were given a bit of stale bread and a cup of what was supposed to be soup, I guess, but it wasn't anything but warm water. At least it was warm. I reckon that was something to be glad of.

"After we finished eating, we were ordered to return to quarters and pack up such belongs as we had, and prepare to move out. We were not told where we were going or what was about to happen to us. Given the situation I was in, I was right scared they might be about to line some of us up and shoot us. They considered me a traitor, and that is what they often did to traitors.

"It had turned off real cold. The deep snows of December still covered the ground with more falling as we lined up and started marching out the gate. I looked down and noticed that hardly any of the men around me had shoes to wear. They were walking barefoot through the ice and snow. That made me thankful that my old boots were still holding together, even with soles so thin I could feel every rock and bit of ice I stepped on. We had not gone far at all when our trail was well marked with bloody footprints. Soon after, some of the weakest among us began falling lifeless or nearly so into the snow banks beside the path. Wasn't nobody to help them or even bury them.

"As many of us as survived the ordeal found ourselves at Columbia, Tennessee, or what was left of it anyways. There were signs everywhere that a battle had been fought there fairly recently. Some of the burned out ruins still smoldered, filling the cold air with sharp, acrid smoke. Whenever we could we tried to pause beside these glowing embers to catch such warmth as we could, but the guards soon came along and kept us moving.

"It astonished me to see that the Union had left some rail cars into which we were being herded like so many cattle. The Federals hardly ever left a railroad in shape to be used by anybody. But there it was. Some of the cars were enclosed; most were cattle cars. Our guards stuffed us into them as long as one body could be packed against another. Uncomfortable as we were, it had the advantage of keeping everybody warm and upright. But that was a mixed blessing. The stench was awful, and I could see the lice crawling in the hair of the two men near me."

Hearing about that made my head itch again. And I was reminded of the way Mr. Swindle's pig yards smelled when Penny and me went with Pa to get our new piglets. It made me shiver just thinking about Pa living in such a way.

"When one of the guards came by to close the door on my car I just outright asked him where we were being taken. He snarled and muttered just one word, 'Corinth.' Lardy, mercy, Mattie. They were taking us right back to Mississippi near where I started out in this war. I knew that country and all the territory around it, and knew it right well. I commenced to thinking how I could get home from there, if I could get away.

"It wouldn't take us but two or three days to get there if the tracks held out all the way. As it turned out, they didn't, which meant more walking. We slept anywhere we could find a spot to lay down. We ate whatever berries and nuts we could find that had survived the winter. Mostly it was pine nuts taken from the shriveled pine cones we managed to pick up along the way. Several more men died. They died of hunger or exhaustion or hopelessness or disease; it was hard to tell which, and it didn't really matter much. They just died, and were left where they fell. The dying Confederacy didn't have the resources or the decency to worry about the dead. Not much for the living, either, as it seemed. The whole enterprise looked more and more like a lost cause."

Hearing about all of this tragedy and suffering had plumb wore us out. When Pa fell quiet, Ma quickly got up and hurried off to bed, and the rest of us followed. Didn't seem to be much to say or even much worth dreaming about that night.

Chapter 15

It was a day or two until Pa wanted to get back to telling about that forced march toward Corinth, Mississippi. While it was still real cold, they'd got away from where it had snowed. From time to time they was loaded onto railroad cars and hauled a few miles until the tracks ran out again. The wonder to him was that all the tracks had not been pulled up by one side or the other.

Confinement and lack of nourishment had taken its toll on everybody. To his surprise, despite all he had been through, Pa was in better physical condition than a good many of the others. He still suffered from the beatings he'd got. With all the exertion, his bad lung often left him short of breath. But he found out he had more stamina than most except the youngest of the men.

One of their brief train rides ended with a clashing of cars, the hiss of released steam and the clanging of a bell. The guards half-heartedly shouted orders for everybody to get out of the cars and onto a well-rutted road that ran alongside the track.

"We sure was glad to be free of the crowded quarters we were cramped in. I asked one of the guards where we were, and he said we were near the settlement of Waynesville, Tennessee."

The name of the place sounded familiar to Pa. He thought maybe it was just a few miles north of the boundary between Tennessee and Alabama. A plan begin to take shape in his head. Maybe if he could slip away maybe he'd be able to get down into the Alabama hill country where he could hide out in some of the caves he knowed about, like he did on his trip over to enlist.

If that was the place he thought it was, there was a general store nearby run by a fellow named Amos Hassell. He didn't know for sure, but he had reason to believe Mr. Hassell and his family held to Union sympathies. He thought maybe they'd help him.

"When we got off the train, it was clear there were fewer guards than we had been having. I noticed that the one who had told me where we were headed for Corinth was nowhere to be seen, and several more familiar faces were missing. When we started marching, they made no attempt to line us up like they had been doing. They didn't even bother to take a head count the way regulations required. I took that to mean morale and discipline were breaking down, a sure sign that the army was coming apart.

"I held back so I could fall in near the end of the line. There were just two privates left to guard the rear. They wasn't paying attention to us. They were more interested in talking to each other, complaining about their sorry rations, about not getting paid, and about their families back home, and how homesick they were. One was even talking right plainly about how the South was losing this war and about what their future might be like if the North sure enough won.

"Came a time when one of them ducked off into the bushes

to relieve himself. At the same time, the other one turned away from the wind and paused to light a cigarette. Right then we were passing through a thick stand of pine trees with heavy undergrowth right close to the road. It was the chance I had been waiting for. I dashed into the woods and crouched down behind some bushes. The men right around me saw what I did, but didn't nobody say anything. My Ohio friends just closed rank and kept right on walking. The guards never missed me.

"The weather had moderated a right smart. The ground was frozen but the only snow left was on the north side of the breaks or where it had drifted here and there. Even if somebody came back looking for me, which wasn't very likely, they would have a hard time tracking me without dogs to follow the scent. It looked like I had got away scot-free. Next was to find out just where I was and which way I needed to head.

"Best I could judge it must've been the middle of the afternoon. The sun was no more than a faint disk of light barely visible through the heavy cloud cover, but it was showing me which way was west. I turned south and commenced making my way through the woods. Wasn't long I came upon a little log cabin set out by itself. A wisp of white smoke wafted from the chimney. Cold and hungry as I was, I decided to take a chance and see if there was any comfort to be had from whoever lived there.

"I had no more than got a 'hello' out of my mouth than the door opened and I found myself face-to-face with the barrel of an old muzzle loader. 'What you want? State your business.' The voice was strong and insistent, but I couldn't make out if it belonged to a man or woman. I said I was just a straggler lost in the woods. I was not armed and I needed a little help. I was told to lift my arms up high and come closer. When I did, an elderly lady came into sight.

"She was as tiny a woman as you could imagine and looked to be right smart older than my own grandma, but she had a strong hold on that gun. I could tell she knew how to use it if need be. Her gingham dress was right worn but clean and pressed, covered with a clean white apron. Her silver hair was combed neatly and pulled back into a bun at the back of her head. Wire framed glasses, one lens badly cracked, was perched on her nose.

"'Who be ye and where be ye from?' she asked.

I decided it was best to tell it like it was. I told her my name and I was a soldier just escaped from a prison gang, trying to get to a safe place.

'What kind of soldier be ye?" she wanted to know.

Again, I told it to her plain.

'Ye be one of them Fileses from down south of here in Alabama?'

I thought that sounded hopeful, like maybe she knew some of us. I told her I was. She stood there quiet for a long moment; looked like she was pondering something, trying to make up her mind about me. All the while, that gun didn't move. It was aimed right at me.

"After a minute or two, what seemed like an hour, she lowered the gun but still held onto it as she told me to come up on the porch. She stood there in the doorway, her steel gray eyes staring a hole through me. She wasn't being hostile exactly, but she sure wasn't being friendly either. With a nod of her head she indicated an old rocker and told me to sit. It wasn't an invitation; it was an order.

"That's the way we stayed for five or ten minutes. Now that I was not moving about, I was getting colder and colder and began to shiver so hard my teeth chattered, but she didn't seem to notice. It looked like she wasn't much bothered by the cold.

"At last she drew herself up and stood as straight and tall as a woman her size and age could. She set the gun aside but never took those icy gray eyes off of me.

"'Well, Files,' she said, 'I decided ain't no profit in shooting ye, much as ye deserve it. I got no use for you scalawag traitors. I ought to have shot ye dead right there in the yard. It would've served ye right. It was folks like you done killed off three of my grand boys and left their wives widows with young 'uns to raise. I don't take kindly to men like you. But, here ye be, unarmed and all. What I hear tell is that the South's about done lost this war anyway. Ain't nothin' to be gained by wastin' my powder and shot on ye now. But, mind ye: I ain't as alone out here as it looks like I be. I got a dozen of my men folk scattered out in these woods. One 'whoop' from me and ye'll be deader than a door nail quicker 'n you could lift a finger.'

"She nodded toward the doorway. 'Now as we understand one another, ye can come on in and get warm by the fire. I've got some left over victuals ye can eat. Then I want ye to get on away from here and don't never come back. If I ever see hide nor hair of ye again I'll shoot ye dead on the spot.'

"The cabin was as neat and clean as she was. The stew she gave me was thick and well made with plenty of venison, carrots and potatoes. I was surprised at that. I didn't know there were any deer left in these parts after all the scavengers got finished. She allowed as how not many of them from either side had wandered this far out into these hinterlands. She and hers had been left alone except for the local Confederate conscript agents who came searching for all the able bodied men they could find.

"As quick as I spooned out the last bite of stew she picked up my bowl and took it away.

"'Now, ye get on out of here, ye hear. I meant every word I said to ye.'

"I asked if she could point me the way to get over to Waynesville.

"'Oh, that be where ye goin', is it? Well, ye better not be plannin' on stoppin' there. Ye won't find nary a friendly face thereabouts. Not since some folks took care of that old scalawag Amos Hassell. I shouldn't be tellin' ye this, ye bein' the enemy and all. If ye be headin' down to the Alabama hill country ye best be stayin' in the woods all the way. Stay away from homesteads; ye ain't going to find many folks as tolerant as I been. Now, get.'"

Chapter 16

The next Sunday on the way to church Ma asked me to sit with her instead of singing with the choir. She needed me to help mind Etta, who wasn't feeling very good. She'd kept Ma up a good part of Saturday night, coughing and crying. She wasn't running a fever, though, so Ma decided we could all go on to church.

We'd just gotten settled into our usual pew when Johnny came in complaining about a tickle in his throat, too. He asked Ma if he could please sit with us. She thought it a bit strange that he wasn't going to sit with his own family, who always sat further back and on the other side of the church. Still, she agreed, and we worked it out so Johnny and me could sit together. She didn't know it, but we held hands under the folds of my skirt. It was the longest time we'd ever held hands. Having Johnny hold my hand like that sent a strange kind of feeling up my arm and made my heart beat right fast. I hadn't felt anything quite like it before. When we stood up to sing, it took all either of us could do not to laugh.

As we got into the wagon after church, Johnny stood near the church door with a smile on his face and gave me a shy little wave like he always did when other folks was around. I smiled back and winked at him. I didn't think Ma or Pa saw, but it didn't make no matter mind to me if they did.

Ma fixed a right good Sunday dinner, finished off with a special treat. She had made an apple pie, sweetened with some of the honey Pa stole from the beehive she'd discovered. After dinner we settled in for a little nap, but I didn't sleep any. I kept on remembering what it felt like when Johnny held my hand.

In the middle of the afternoon Pa played his fiddle, like usual of a Sunday, and we sang a song or two. After a time I asked Pa what had happened after he got away from that little old woman up in the Tennessee woods.

"Well," he said, "it took me near onto a week to make my way down into the mountains of Marion County and find the cave I was looking for. Everybody who knew about the place called it the Big Rock House. It was big enough to easy hold a hundred men or more, and had done just that in the early days of the war. My friend Christopher Sheats from 'The Free State of Winston' hid out there before he signed up with Colonel Abel Streight and helped start the First Alabama.

"When I got there, the Big Rock House was almost deserted. There were just four fellows when I got there, all men who had run off from the Confederate army and were waiting for a chance to get back home. When the Rebel conscript officers had discovered it about two years earlier, they rounded everybody up and gave them the choice of enlisting for the Confederacy or being shot on the spot. They signed up, of course, but lots of them got away as quick as they could and went over to the Union side. After that, the Rebels would make a sweep through the area now and again to catch any out-layers who might have wandered in. Now, with the war being in shambles like it was, it seemed nobody was paying any mind to the place anymore.

"Sitting around the fire that first night, I told how I hoped to get on back to home over in Walker County. Two of the fellows were familiar with that territory and said that would not be wise. 'There's been a whole lot of meanness over around Jasper,' one of them said. 'The Conscript Officers and the home guard keep making things real hard for such Union men as have showed back up over there. If they find you, they won't be kind to you, I can tell you that for sure.'

"Both of them got into telling one tale after another about the treatment of returning Union men. Several they knew of had been shot dead. One had been tied to a tree and had his skin peeled off of him. Then parts of his body was cut off and burned in a fire right there in front of him while he bled to death. In another place, a house was set on fire late of a night and anybody who tried to run out was shot. That whole family died together."

Pa stopped and looked at me with a look of surprise. "I'm sorry, Fannie. I wasn't thinking. I didn't mean to tell such a story as that without warning you it was coming."

I reminded him again of the awful things I'd already seen and heard. I didn't like hearing such bad things, but they didn't bother me anymore. They was just part of how it had been.

"The fellows in the cave thought as how things kept getting worse. One was most emphatic. 'It seems like the closer these Rebels gets to losing this blasted war, the meaner they gets.' They convinced me that I couldn't very well keep on this path. Not yet. I needed a new plan.

"I asked where the closest Union post was. Everybody except me seemed to know that Decatur, Alabama, was still in Union hands as it had been for most of the war. That was music to my ears. Decatur was not more than three or four days walk for me, as long as the weather held. So I set my mind to getting over there. If I could see whoever had that command I would seek protection until the war was over.

"One of the fellows was right skeptical. He wanted to know what made me think any Yankee officer would believe a fellow who talked like I did was a Union man. What proof did I have? I told him I had my discharge paper from the First Alabama. That was all the proof I would need.

"I reached into my pocket to show him my paper. It wasn't there. I looked in all the pockets of my pants and my coat, and searched through my haversack. The paper was nowhere to be found. All the fellows helped me search all over the cave. We couldn't find it anywhere. That loss sent me into a great depression. I didn't know what I was going to do.

"I stewed about it all night long. If I went to Decatur, they might suspect me as a Southern spy. Or maybe they would believe me and agree to protect me. Which would it be? About daybreak, I decided I had to take my chances and get myself on over to Decatur. I stood a whole lot better chance with them than I did with them scoundrels back home who had already tried to kill me afore I left.

"I started out walking. The weather had taken a nice turn, the way it can in North Alabama in late February. 'Course, it can also go the other way and put up the hardest snow storm of the winter. Luck was with me and I got to Decatur about noon of the third day. The town was in near total devastation.

"I learned there was a General Steedman overseeing a division of colored troops occupying the place. General Steedman agreed to see me and listened to my story but without comment. I told him all about my service in the First Alabama, and what I had done since. When I told him about how I had lost my discharge papers, he looked skeptical. He put off making any immediate decision, but seemed unmoved by my story. He allowed as how I could have use of a tent for the night but would have a guard assigned to keep watch on me. That was fine with me.

"A tent to myself was the best quarters I had enjoyed since before my capture at La Vergne. I had access to a bath and a latrine. The blanket on my bunk was relatively clean. At mess, I had some real food that had texture and taste and that gave me nourishment for a change. Things had not been this good for me in several months. The familiar sights, the sounds and the smells of a military camp brought a certain kind of comfort. It wasn't like being at home, for sure, but I felt safe and secure.

"I responded to the morning bugle call and promptly found quite a surprise waiting for me. A shock, really. The private who was guarding me said I was to have breakfast with the troops and then General Steedman would see me. He seemed right nervous, and I noticed he never let his hand wander far from his sidearm. At a brisk pace he escorted me to the general's headquarters. As we approached, four heavily armed men surrounded me. The private stepped aside and two of these new men took me by my arms. They tied my wrists behind me just like when I was in the Confederate stockade in La Vergne.

"One of the men, a corporal, informed me they were from the Federal Provost Guard and I should consider myself a prisoner of the United States, on suspicion of being a spy for the Confederate States of America."

My Pa being taken a prisoner of his own country? That just didn't make any sense to me. Couldn't they understand that he was a Patriot? He'd gone through too much in serving his country to be treated in such a way. Pa saw what I was thinking and just nodded.

"I was flummoxed. My stomach turned somersaults. Questions raced through my mind and poured out in rapid order, but the marshals either couldn't or wouldn't provide any further information.

"For the second time in three or four months I found myself a prisoner of war, but unlike in the Confederate stockade, I was the only prisoner. The next day a Federal Provost Marshal and me boarded a train bound for a federal prison in Nashville."

"They took you all the way back up to Nashville, Tom?" Ma was as puzzled as I was. "Ain't that where you had been when the Confederates captured you? Now you was going back there as a federal prisoner?"

"Strange as it sounds, they took me right back to Nashville. The young marshal who went with me was part of what they called the Invalid Corp. He had been wounded right bad at Antietam and couldn't take duty in the field no more. He did light duty with the Federal Marshal Corp for the rest of his time. He seemed friendly enough but was strictly business and well armed.

"We spent the biggest part of a day and a night together on that ride up to Nashville. He brought me up on news of the war. I was especially interested to learn some details about what was being called General Sherman's March to the Sea.

He showed me a newspaper that had some pictures of Atlanta going up in flames. What an astonishing sight that must have been. A whole city on fire was more than I could get my mind around.

"I told him this trip was a whole lot more comfortable that the one I had just had out of Nashville. He got curious when I told him about my escape from Confederate confinement and my walk all the way down to Alabama headed home

"He was from Indiana. I told him about going up to Illinois with Jeremiah and learning about my cousin John Files who had fought with the 27th Indiana. That got his attention. He didn't know John Files, but he had several mates who served in the 27th. I spoke about being with Colonel Abel Streight down in Alabama. When I told the tale about the Mule Brigade he just about busted a gut laughing. I told him Colonel Streight was the first Union officer to give any mind to the fact that there were Southern men strong for the Union. I recounted the story of Christopher Sheats from Winston County, Alabama and how he had put it in the Colonel's mind to organize a regiment of Alabama Union soldiers, by pointing how us Southerners could move about with such confidence and knowledge as Yankees never could. He had never heard that part of the story."

After Pa told him all he knew about Colonel Abel Streight being the one who convinced General Dodge to set up the First Alabama, the marshal fell strangely quiet, turning this over in his mind.

"'Files,' he said, 'if what you been telling me is true, seems to me General Steedman might have made a big mistake about you being a spy. I sure hope things get straightened out for you up here in Nashville.'

"I thanked him for his kindness and assured him again that I wasn't no spy. I told him about all the Patriots in our family, even some I didn't know about until I made that trip to Illinois and Indiana. He just shook his head in disbelief that I should be in such a predicament as I found myself in now.

"When the train pulled into the Nashville depot, he apologized that he had to put handcuffs on me. 'It's regulations, Files. I'm sorry I have to do this to you.'

"As we walked through the depot, everybody was turning to look at me, handcuffed and being led along like a criminal. I found that more humiliating than anything that ever happened to me. My stomach was tied in knots, every muscle was tense and every nerve in my body was at the breaking point. I walked with my head down so couldn't anybody see the tears of hurt and shame in my eyes." The look on his face told how bad that hurt him still, as if he was feeling the shame and insult of it all over again. I went to fetch him a dipper of cool water.

He recalled that the stockade they put him in was right down in the middle of the town. The unfinished building had been a Confederate prison before the Union took it over. It was going to be a hotel called The Maxwell House before the war put a stop to the building of it. Different parts of it served as offices for the Provost Marshal, a hospital, and a prison.

"Even if it was new, it had seen better days. One staircase had collapsed while the Rebels held it. The gossip said that five or six folks died and near a hundred hurt in that fall. That left just one way up and one way down from the upper floors.

"The prison occupied the top floor, five stories up. I hadn't ever been that high up off the ground before. Looking out the window made me dizzy. Wasn't no chance anybody could escape from up there, so some of the windows stayed open for circulation even in the cold winter. The cots proved comfortable enough, and we had plenty of clean blankets to keep us warm.

"The kitchen was downstairs somewhere, maybe in the basement. We had eating tables set up in a big space with a high ceiling. A guard said it would be a ballroom if the hotel ever got finished. They brought the food up to us by a little machine called a dumb waiter. I had never seen anything like it. When we finished eating, it took our dirty utensils back down. After every meal, a door to it was closed and locked. I reckon they thought maybe some of us might try to squeeze in there and escape, but it would have been a mighty tight fit even for a real little fellow.

"The rest of the floor we were on consisted of a guard room and then a bunch of little rooms without any doors, for the prisoners. Four men shared most rooms, with six in some. All told, there must have been at least two hundred prisoners, maybe more. Of course, they were all Confederates but me, some still wearing parts of their gray uniform.

"Being locked up with all them Rebels sure didn't give a body any sense of security. The men were always talking about where they had been and bragging or complaining about what battles they had fought in and what officers they had served under. Everybody had a story to tell about where and how they had been captured. I tried to stay to myself as best I could and avoid any such talk.

"Along about the fourth or fifth afternoon several fellows, including my cell mates, came around laughing and joking and carrying on like men will. They tried to draw me into the conversation. One of them asked what I had done during the war.

"'You been real quiet, Files,' he snarled. 'Don't none of us know anything about you. Nobody has ever run into you anywhere. You don't talk about what fights you been in or who you served under. You've got that limp and you have trouble breathing, so we know you got hurt somewhere along the line. We're right curious about you, Files.'

"I could tell right off they had planned this all out; it didn't just happen. It dawned on me then that I should have anticipated something like this and planned for it. I didn't know what to say or do, and my confusion showed. I just kind of shrugged and looked away. The banter stopped. The roughest looking of them, a big burley man with hands big as hams, sneered at me. 'Well, fellows, I reckon as how we got ourselves a problem on our hands. What is you, Files? You one of them yellow-bellied scalawags? That's it, ain't it?'

"Another one, a tall lanky blond fellow whose nose was all crooked like it had been broke more than once, shook his head. 'If that's true, what would he be doing in here with us? That don't make no sense. These Yankees would be taking better care of their spy.'

"A mousy looking boy, no more than sixteen but with a kind of intelligence to his eyes, chimed it. 'It would make sense if he was a double agent or something. You played both sides and the Yanks caught onto your scheme? That's it, ain't it, Files? They locked you up in here with your fellow Southerners, knowing we would take care of you when we found you out.' He let out a squeaky little sound that was supposed to be a laugh. 'This don't look too good for you, Files. It don't look good at all.'

"With that, they all lit into me. They knocked me down and commenced hitting and beating and kicking me, all of them at once. Wasn't anywhere to go to hide or get away. Soon as I could I turned over on my stomach trying to protect myself, so my back and hips and legs took most of the punishment. I was screaming and crying and calling out for help. Fortunately didn't anybody have a weapon or club of any kind, but their fists and feet were doing a right smart amount of damage. I became aware of the shrill sound of a whistle coming from the guard's station and the pounding of feet running down the hallway. My assailants fell quiet and went slinking off.

"By the time the guards got to me, I reckon I was a right bloody mess. They put me onto a makeshift litter and took me downstairs to the hospital, maybe two or three floors down. With every step, the jostling pained every muscle and joint in my body. I must have passed out on the way."

He stopped and stared down the lane like he did when telling about something that brung him pain. We waited quietly for him to start again. The only sounds was Etta cooing in Ma's arms, and an occasional giggle from Penny and Peggy, who was playing hide 'n' seek out in the yard.

"I came to with a nurse hovering over me, needle in hand about to inject me with something. I asked 'Where am I?" She chuckled and gently reminded me I was in the federal prison and hospital in Nashville. That brought it all back. She said they had been keeping me on morphine for the pain. She told me this was my third day on this floor. I had two cracked ribs but no broken bones. My bum leg hurt something awful and the pain in my back was unbearable. In fact, there wasn't any place on my body that didn't hurt. The nurse said I was fortunate not to have gotten a concussion from the beating I received about the head. If I hadn't turned onto my stomach, my insides would have been busted up beyond repair. So I guess I was lucky in that way. But then, how can not getting beat up beyond repair be luck? Wouldn't luck have been not getting beat up at all?

"Two or three days later I was shaken gently awake by one of the orderlies. 'Sergeant Files, there is someone here to see you.' For a minute I thought it might be you, Mattie. I had been dreaming about you. I dreamed you came to fetch me, and we went walking in the sunshine beside a little stream like we used to do. You remember how we did that every evening when we were first married?"

Ma's face broke into a bright smile in spite of her sadness. She took both of Pa's hands in hers. "Yes, Tom. We had us some real good days before this awful war came along and did such terrible things to us. Why don't we start taking those evening walks again? I would like that."

Pa smiled. "I would, too. Let's take that up again."

They sat looking into each other's face as if they had gone off together to some other time and place. I stayed quiet and still. I had never seen my parents quite like that before. I wondered if there would be times like this for me when I was all grown up and married. Briefly, an image of Johnny flitted in front of me. What a silly thing for me to be thinking on right then! Pa's voice brought me back to the moment.

"I managed to open my eyes and focus on the man standing beside my bed. He was a right big fellow, wearing the dark blue and gold uniform of the Provost Marshals with the rank of colonel. I tried to salute, but I couldn't raise my arm.

"He told me to stay still, and introduced himself as Captain

Carlton Goodwin. I could hardly make out what he was saying. His voice sounded like it was coming from the bottom of a barrel or from far away. I couldn't imagine what he might be doing here by my hospital bed.

"He told me about talking with the young officer who had brought me here on the train. 'He tells me that you are Sergeant Thomas Files of the First Alabama Cavalry, United States Volunteers. Is that correct?' Best as I could, I nodded that this was so. 'He also tells me that you served with Colonel Abel Streight of Indiana. Is that correct?' Again, I confirmed what he said. 'He said you told him a tale about some mules the Colonel got stuck with down in North Alabama. Did you see that for yourself, Sergeant?' I confirmed it with my eyes.

"Turned out my escort was his nephew. They had spent the evening together before the young man went back to Decatur. Over dinner, the entire Goodwin family heard my story. A few days later, Captain Goodwin got my file and read the statement I had given to General Steedman. What I had said about Colonel Streight claimed his attention, and that was when he began to put things together in his head.

"Captain Goodwin asked if I would mind if he had a seat. I didn't know where he was going to sit, or what I could have done about it if that's what he wanted to do. The orderly pulled up a chair and the colonel sat where we could still see each other.

"The captain drew in a deep breath. 'Well, Sergeant, I believe your story. You see, I served in the 11th Indiana Cavalry before I came into the Provost Marshal Service. Abel Streight is a friend of mine; we've known each other a long time. Met when he first moved down to Indiana from New York. That mule business is not a story Abel goes about telling on himself. It is the major embarrassment of his life, one that very nearly cost him his career. If you know that story and all that led up to it, you could only know it because you were there. If you had been on the Confederate side, you would not know those details. So, the long and the short of it, Sergeant Files, is that I believe a serious mistake has been made. The United States Army has done you a terrible injustice.'

"I could hardly believe what I was hearing. Those words sounded like music to my ears. I commenced to bawl like a new-born baby and am not the least bit ashamed of it, either. It near about tore my body apart to do it, but I couldn't put a stop to it.

"When I got control of myself, Captain Goodwin was still sitting there. He said he had given orders for the hospital to give me the very best care they were capable of giving. He assured me that I would have all the time I needed to recover. He had also ordered severe punishment for those ruffians who had treated me so badly. He promised to look further into my situation and what could be done about it. It might take awhile, but he promised to stay on it.

"Just then it dawned on me how everybody was calling me 'Sergeant Files.' They really did believe me, and they recognized my service. That made me feel right good, despite all the pain."

We learned that Captain Goodwin started coming by every two or three days. When Pa was able to talk, he asked Pa to tell him more about himself. That is when he told the colonel about the Patriots in our family. He told him all about Captain John at Cowpens and about his son John, who had joined the Virginia Militia as early as 1776. They talked about this war they was in and how it was going. Both of them was pretty sure it would be coming to a conclusion fairly soon.

"I had been in that hospital about a month, maybe a bit longer. I was able to get around some with help, but not without an awful lot of hurt. The healing was underway, but was taking its own sweet time. But time is what I had the most of.

"I remember it was Palm Sunday, April 9, 1865, about eight o'clock in the evening, when I asked my orderly to help me into a chair so I could sit a spell by the open window. My room overlooked a main intersection of the town, the corner of Fourth Avenue and Church Street.

"My helper stayed with me for a time. When he started to leave, he asked if I would like a drink of water. He hadn't been gone but a minute when I heard him running back. 'Sergeant Files, a messenger just brought this note from Captain Goodwin. He said to see that you got it immediately.'

"Puzzled, I took the note and read the most astonishing news. It was a single sentence: 'I have the pleasure of informing you that at ten o'clock this morning General Robert E. Lee surrendered the Army of Northern Virginia to General Ulysses S. Grant, surely bringing our long national nightmare to an end.'

"Very shortly, church bells began ringing all over the city. The streets filled with people. Musicians came from everywhere and commenced playing patriotic tunes. A band gathered in the street just below me and struck up 'The Battle Hymn of the Republic.' I found myself singing along as best I could:

> 'Mine eyes have seen the glory of the coming of the Lord:
> He is trampling out the vintage where the grapes of wrath
> are stored;

He hath loosed the fateful lightning of His terrible swift sword:
His truth is marching on.'

Pa watched as the festivities went on through the night and into Monday morning. Over the strong objections of his orderly, he sat there and watched the whole spectacle as it developed. It was close to midnight when he finally gave in and went to bed.

"Still, the sound of the festivities blew through my room along with the fresh night air. I never went to sleep. All night long I lay there, vacillating between relishing the cheers of the crowd in the streets, and sobbing uncontrollably at the joyful thought that maybe soon, I could be going home."

Chapter 17

At choir practice on Wednesday, Johnny asked Pa if he could please come out to our place for a visit the next evening. That was puzzling, but Pa allowed as how it would be fine for Johnny to call. He had to work at the general store until closing but would be along just as quick as he could get there. Pa invited him to come have supper if he would like, which pleased him.

The sun was almost down when Johnny's horse turned into our lane. He found us sitting out on the porch. As he dismounted and walked up, I saw Ma and Pa exchange a nervous kind of look. I knew some message had been passed.

We had a good talk around the dinner table, but everybody knew something important had not been brought up yet. Ma cleared away the dinner dishes and served a fresh pecan pie for dessert. Johnny complimented her on her cooking, and then, with some hesitation, cleared his throat and drew in a deep breath.

"I guess y'all are right curious as to why I wanted to come this evening." Ma, Pa and the other girls nodded in unison, but didn't interrupt him.

"Well, I guess there's not but one way to say this, so I'll come right out with it. I would like to come courting Fannie, and I'm here to ask for your blessing. To tell you honest like, I'm hoping we might decide to get married one of these days. If she will have me, that is. I've got me a pretty good job at the store. I want to save up some money. My Pa is going to give me a piece of land where I can start out farming on my own. I want to make something of myself, something she can be proud of. So, anyway, would it be all right if I started courting her?"

He drew in another deep breath and looked first at Pa and then at Ma. Then he sighed and quickly dropped his eyes to the floor. I had never heard Johnny say so much at one time, ever. I went to stand behind him and put my hands on his shoulders. He reached up and took my hands in his.

There was quiet at the table except for Penny's giggles muffled by her hands clasped tightly over her mouth. I'd gladly have spanked her right then and there. I saw Ma scold her with a real stern look and she stopped, but her eyes was still laughing at us.

Ma and Pa looked at each other with a strange expression. I was holding my breath and could see Johnny was, too. At the same time, almost like on cue, Ma and Pa broke out into big smiles. Pa looked at him and nodded.

"Why, yes, Johnny. We would be right pleased to have you come courting."

Ma reached over to take Johnny's hand in hers.

We both burst out into happy laughter. "Do you mean it, Pa? Do you really mean it?" Ma and Pa joined us in laughter.

"Yes, Mary Frances. I really mean it. We both do."

Pa came around the table to shake hands with Johnny. Patting him on the shoulder, he said, "Johnny, God never saw fit to give me a son. Could be, that got left for Mary Frances to do. We'll have to see about that down the road a piece, but we would like to get to know you a bit better and see where things go."

I walked out with Johnny and we stood by his horse and talked for awhile. As he was getting ready to mount up, he leaned over and kissed me right on the mouth. It gave me the most wonderful feeling I had ever felt in all my life.

When Johnny left, Ma and I went off to the kitchen to talk. We spent near about two hours together in girl talk. She took me in her arms, and we cried and laughed. It had never been like this between us before. A body would have thought we was the best of friends, not mother and daughter. I liked it. I liked it a lot. Just before we went to bed, Ma let me know we'd not taken them by surprise tonight. They'd suspected this might be coming since they saw us walking in the cemetery the day of the all-day singing.

With all of that to think on and talk about, it was near a week before we heard any more of Pa's story. He went back and recollected where he had left off.

"Captain Goodwin often brought me *The Harper's Weekly* to read. I learned that General Grant's victory at Appomattox Courthouse was celebrated throughout these United States. Even a whole lot of Southerners were glad it was over, disappointed as they were in defeat. Don't nobody like to be beat. Heaven knows, I been beat a whole lot of times in my life, and I don't remember enjoying a single one of them. Taking a beating does something to the spirit. If a body lets it, it can make you angry and defensive. I couldn't help but wonder what this beating was going to do to the spirit of the South I loved. These rebellious states were being drug kicking and screaming back into the Union, but would they ever feel a part of it again? What lingering spirits of anger, humiliation, and distrust would they be bringing along with them?

"Of course, I was most concerned with what this turn of events meant to me. If the war was over, I guessed I could be on my way home soon. Thoughts like that occupied my mind and filled all my prayers day and night. One big problem remained. I still couldn't walk without help. My bruises were most all gone, but I was still in a right smart amount of pain when I tried to stand and move about. The doctor said it was because of the damage done to my back. Until I could walk, there wasn't any way to get home. I had no chance of getting me another horse. A good horse would cost $2,000 or more. I had no money at all nor any hopes of getting any, certainly not such a sum as that. All that weighted heavy on my mind and spirit.

"It was Saturday, the fifteenth day of April, just under a week after the grand news from Appomattox Court House. The whole city of Nashville was alive with preparations for a grand parade. The place had been in Union hands for several years, and there was going to be a full-scaled celebration of the end of the war. The streets were scrubbed clean. Colorful banners flew from every building. Flags waved up and down every street. Military bands filled the air with grand patriotic tunes. I watched all of this from my room, ready to enjoy the festivities.

"Sitting at my window, I heard somebody coming up behind me. When I turned to look who it was, I knew this orderly was bringing bad news. He could hardly talk through his tears. 'Sergeant Files, I came to tell you as quick as I heard. President

Abraham Lincoln is dead. He was shot last night and died this morning.' He didn't know any more details than that.

"Slowly, the city fell quiet, like a curtain of silence was coming down on it. As the news about the president spread through the streets, the bands stopped playing. People milled around in confusion, not knowing what to do or where to go. Flags came down to half-mast. Joy was turning into sorrow right before my eyes. Troops marched silently back to their quarters. Church bells that last week peeled in joyful celebration now rang out a dirge. Shortly we began to hear the firing of minute guns off in the distance, a military tradition honoring the fallen, which would continue until sundown.

"As darkness took over the city, there came a different sound, muffled at first. From remote, dark side streets came the unmistakable raucous sounds of celebration. A piper and drummer somewhere struck up playing 'Dixie.' Some of the less cautious of the Rebels were celebrating the death of the president. I thought this carried a right ominous prospect.

"Along about midnight I awoke to the familiar sound of troops marching by on the double. Gunshots pierced the night, though muffled by distance. The Rebel celebration stopped. What was going on out there? I was overcome by a spirit of dread. Could the nightmare be starting up again already? It dawned on me that the sunrise, when it came, would announce the arrival of Easter Sunday. Some folks call this day before Easter 'Black Saturday.' That sounded about right to me.

"Next came the news that Vice President Andrew Johnson from right there in that Rebel State of Tennessee had been sworn in as President of the United States. The South saw him as a traitor, and the North didn't trust him. Andrew Johnson was a staunch Unionist, but he also was a slaveholder who had been as strong against abolition as he was against secession.

"With Johnson running with him on the National Union Party ticket, President Lincoln had swept to victory against the Democrat, General George McClellan. I thought that election had been right strange. General McClellan was from Philadelphia, a staunch Unionist, an abolitionist and a military hero. He organized our Army of the Potomac back in the beginning and served as General-in-Chief of the Union army for a time. In that election, the Democrats had split seven ways from Sunday. They never could rally behind McClellan, which was fine with me. I was right glad Mr. Lincoln had won again. But now with his death, our country faced another crisis. What would all of this mean for me and for my burning desire to get home?"

Captain Goodwin and Pa talked about what Pa wanted to do. Both of them contemplated what would happen now with the Confederacy in tatters and the Federal government weakened by the assassination. The captain couldn't see how to avoid a reign of lawlessness in these parts. The remnants of a Rebel state government could provide no security, and the Federals would need some time to take over again. A tug of war was already underway between President Johnson and the Congress. It was over Reconstruction. I had asked Pa about it one evening and he explained it to me. Seemed like the president wanted to go right easy on bringing his native South back into the Union. The Congress wanted to punish the traitorous states for their rebellion. Who won that tussle would make all the difference in the future of the defeated South.

It had got to where Pa could get around some, but he still couldn't stand or walk for more than an hour or two at a time.

After thinking on it, the captain came up with a plan. He offered to let Pa come down to the first floor and help out with the office work. He could pay a modest wage. Pa jumped at that. It would let him be on his feet when he could, sit down when he needed to and earn some money for his trip home. He would be paid the same wage he earned as sergeant in the Army, which came to $17 a month. So that's what he did.

"While doing some filing, I picked up a stack of folders from the captain's desk and started to put them in order. One of them had my name on it. Being curious, I opened it up and began reading. It consisted of the papers General Steedman had sent over from Decatur when he had me arrested, all about how he was charging me on suspicion of being a Rebel spy. Just reading about that made my blood boil. I couldn't understand how a Union general could mistake a Patriot like me for a Rebel. He had not believed a word I had said to him.

"Captain Goodwin came in while I was reading. He saw the anger on my face and asked what was going on. I showed him the file. He motioned for me to take a seat while he sat at his desk. He had the file open in front of him, but didn't seem to be reading it. He just stared blankly at the papers, clearly bothered.

"Finally he said, 'Tom, I've been meaning to talk to you about this, but I just couldn't bring myself to it. You and I both know this charge is nonsense. But the plain fact of the matter is that a general in the United States Army has made a charge against you, and until it is disposed of properly the charge stands.' He reminded me that back in '63, President Lincoln had suspended *habeas corpus*, which meant that General Steedman actually could have had me shot on the spot, with no more evidence against me than just his own suspicion. For some reason he'd chosen not to do that. Maybe he, too, had some doubts. He had sent me to prison instead, which probably meant he intended for some kind of a trial to take place. With all that had happened, this legal stuff had been lost in the shuffle.

"The long and the short of it was that this charge still had to be dealt with and a report sent back to General Steedman. I was stunned. I couldn't believe this could be happening all over again. With all I had been through, here I was facing a possible military tribunal. They could put me to death just on the suspicion of some general who didn't know me at all. The only evidence against me was that I looked and talked like a Southerner, and that I had lost my discharge papers from the First Alabama.

"I could tell that this put Captain Goodwin between a rock and a hard place. He believed me, but he also had a duty to perform, unpleasant as he found it. Finally he said, 'Tom, let me give this some more thought. You try not to worry about it. Let me see what I can work out.' He told me to go on about my duties as usual. As far as he was concerned, nothing had changed.

"As far as I could see, a whole lot had changed. My life and liberty hung in the balance once again. I'd done been through enough already to know that if something could go wrong, it probably would. Worry and dread were eating up my insides and gave me several long and sleepless nights."

About two weeks later Captain Goodwin took Pa aside for another talk. He said he had some good news and some bad news. The bad news was that he had no choice but to convene a military tribunal to hear the charge against Pa. It would be held in about a week. The captain himself would serve on the tribunal along with two other officers. And that brought on the good news.

"He reminded me that he and Colonel Streight knowed each other right well. Except now, Streight was no longer a Colonel. He had been captured by General Nathan Bedford Forrest during that raid on North Alabama with all those mules. He led a bunch of prisoners in an escape from Libby Prison over in Richmond, Virginia. After he returned to duty, he had been down there in the Battles of Nashville and Franklin, fighting against Forrest and Hood. It pleased me no end to realize that Abel Streight had helped make some of that ruckus we heard from our prison in Nashville. Don't you know that seeing those two rascals beat had given him much pleasure? What I didn't know is that after those victories, he had been promoted to Brigadier General. Just before the end of the war, he had left military service and gone home.

"Now here is the best part, Mattie. Captain Goodwin had written to him of my plight and asked if he could shed any light on my circumstances. He told Streight about me being there when them old mules put up such a ruckus, and how I knew details that no Confederate could ever know. The general remembered that there were a bunch of us First Alabama folks there with him. He was proud to say he had been the main one who had set out to organize us Southern Patriots into a volunteer force to begin with. So he took an interest in what the captain was telling him about me. He agreed to look into it and see what more he could learn.

"Well, the long and the short of it is that he would be back in Nashville for a visit. While he was in town, he took over running that military tribunal. Captain Goodwin was part of it and another friend of General Streight's became the third member. The whole event involved just those three, me, and a secretary to take down what happened. The charge against me from General Steedman was read aloud. They asked me if I was guilty of these charges, and I said I was not. Captain Goodwin told what he knew of me and asked me if it was true. I put my hand on a Bible and swore to it.

"Next, General Streight reported that he had corresponded with some folks who had knowed me. One was Major Cramer from Indiana, the same one who had connected me up with Mason, Alexander, and Burdick to travel up north. He had also gotten information from a first sergeant who had been with General Dodge in North Alabama who found a pay record to show that I had served in the First Alabama. That seemed to settle the matter. The third member of the tribunal, whose name I don't remember, made a motion that in light of the evidence, all charges against me be dismissed. Everybody said "Aye," and that ended the matter. They all came over to shake my hand and apologize for the pain and suffering I had been put through.

"The following night, Captain Goodwin invited me to his house to join his family and General Streight for dinner. I told as how I appreciated the kindness, but I didn't have any clothes fittin' to wear to such a fine occasion. He had an orderly take me to a clothes closet maintained by the hospital, where we found a Union uniform just my size. It didn't have any First Alabama identifications on it, but it was a nice enough suit of clothes for me to wear to dinner. That jacket was what I was still wearing when I got home.

"Captain Goodwin did allow as how it would be just as well

if I didn't bring up any talk about those old mules in the dinner conversation."

Chapter 18

The next day, on my way back to the house from the barn, I took a little walk through the remainder of our garden. We still had some collards and a few green beans. The greens could stay until frost, but we'd need to gather the balance of the beans pretty soon. The Goober peas Pa'd planted looked right peaked, all wilted and yellow. I ran in to tell him how they was dying. He slapped his knee and said, "Well, I be swiggered, Fannie! I'd plumb forgot about the Goobers. Let's go take a look at them."

When he saw what shape they was in, he sent me to the barn to bring a spade. Digging into a hill, he turned up some big clusters of nuts attached to the roots. It was kind of like the way 'taters grow, but way lots more of them and way yonder smaller. He broke one open. Inside there was two or three peas. He put one in his mouth, and gave me one to eat. He said he liked the taste of it, but I spit mine out. Pa laughed.

"Let's take a bunch of these up to the house and roast them in the fireplace," he said. "I hear tell that's a good way to fix them. I reckon we ought to try boiling us some in salt water, too, when we can get a supply of salt. That's how most folks talk about fixing them."

After we roasted them, those Goober peas had a whole different taste from what they had raw. I thought they tasted real good. Ma, Penny, and Peg liked them, too. Penny and I went back out to the garden and helped Pa harvest both rows. We had way more Goober peas than the four of us could eat in a month of Sundays. Pa remembered promising to share them with the nice folks who came to help us out after he got beat up. We decided to put a passel of them in the wagon and make those deliveries in a day or two.

We fixed some to have while we sat around talking that evening. Ma came up with the notion of putting them in the oven to roast while she was making our supper, and they came out nice and crisp. That was way yonder easier than minding them in the fireplace and keeping them from burning. Ma said salt cost too much for us to boil any. Maybe we could do that next year if things got better.

While we sat around enjoying our new favorite snack, Pa told us more about what happened to him up in Nashville. It was getting on toward the end of summer and he believed he was about strong enough to start out. The doctor and Captain Goodwin figured if he could hold up to walking eight miles a day, it would take him about twelve days to get on down to Walker County. That is, if the weather held, and if he didn't run into any troublemakers along the way. Maybe it would be best to plan on at least two weeks.

He commenced to gather what he'd need for the trip. He'd earned $51 hard money working for the captain. First off, he needed some new shoes or boots, so he went out looking to buy a pair.

"I'd not been in a store of any kind in more than a year, closer to two most likely. I was plumb shocked to discover how very little there was to be bought at any price. I went into a mercantile establishment and asked if they had any boots to sell. The man looked at me like I was crazy.

"'What you mean, boots to sell? Man, where have you been? We've had no boots for nigh on to two years. The last ones we had was priced at $600 Confederate, and some fool Yankee came along and bought them.'

"I noticed then that all the shelves in the place was near about bare. It was the same everywhere I went. Wasn't hardly anything to be bought. Such as I could find was shoddy. I couldn't believe the prices. Coffee was $70 a pound when it could be had. A sack of salt was $150 and flour was $250 a barrel. I couldn't buy me any pants, shoes, hat or haversack. Nothing. I did find a pair of wool socks that were knitted by a widow woman selling them on the street corner. She was right pleased when I bought them from her. She said it was the first she had sold in several days. Tears came up in her eyes when she saw I was paying with hard money of the United States of America. She said it was the first of that she had seen since right after the war started."

Ma interrupted. "Tom, are those the same socks you was wearing when you got home?"

"Yes. That's the only pair of socks I've had since I left Nashville."

With surprise in her voice, Ma said they sure was well-made socks. "They's showing their use, but they're still good enough to wear."

"I've noticed that, Mattie. I had them on just a day or two ago when the morning air had turned frosty."

She promised she'd set out to knit him some new ones soon as she could get some yarn to make them with.

Pa went on with his story. "When I went back and told folks in the office about my adventure, they all laughed. They said if I'd have just asked, they would've told me what to expect out there. They said most folks all over the South had been living like this for two or three years. The Federal blockades had been right effective in cutting off trade. I made a point of telling everybody about the widow woman selling her socks. Several said they'd go see her. It made me feel right good to think maybe a word from me could help her some.

"That evening when I went up to my room, Captain Goodwin came by to see me. He took me into a part of the building I'd not seen before. It was a room filled with racks of clothes and boots, all well worn. These were things left from people who had died in the hospital or prison. He said the government considered it surplus property. With the war over, he was awaiting orders on what he was to do with it. I could rummage through and see if I could use any of it. I got me a fair pair of boots, two shirts and a change of pants. Figured I didn't need much more than that to tote all the way home. The captain pointed out one lone canvas haversack over in the corner, which I took.

"In the night I dreamed about the men who had wore those things before, thinking on what might have happened to them. I figured every one of them had loved ones somewhere, maybe wives and children, parents and grandparents. The dream wasn't unpleasant exactly, but unsettling. Whose pants were these I was wearing? Whose boots? Did they belong to Patriots who died in the hospital? Or to Rebels who died in prison? And what difference did it make? Wasn't they all just folks like me who wanted nothing more than to get back home to family and friends, and to live in peace?"

Pa was saying just what I was thinking, too. I said "amen," just like I did that day at church. Everybody laughed at that.

"Amen, Fannie," Ma exclaimed, and Pa smiled before going on with what he was telling.

"My dreams turned to what it would be like when I got back here. I dreamed about working in the garden. Soon it'd be time for the sweet 'taters to be dug. I could smell one of Mattie's sweet 'tater pies baking in the oven. I could feel the warmth of the red clay soil of North Alabama under my feet. I could smell the moist leaves decaying in the woods and hear the frogs croaking beside the creek. I saw the smoke curling up out of the chimney and felt the warmth of the hearth. I thought for sure I could hear a baby crying off in the distance, but I couldn't see where it was."

That brought a smile to Ma's face.

"The sun had me up early. I had a really fine breakfast of scrambled eggs with a piece of fried ham, two biscuits with butter and apple jelly, and two cups of hot coffee. I don't know where the kitchen came up with all those goodies for me. While I was eating, several of the hospital staff and folks from downstairs came to say goodbye. I'd been here so long and they'd taken such good care of me, we felt kind of like family. But there weren't any tears, just laughing and telling tales on each other until they had to get back to their work. As we finished our visit, the cook came by and brought me a package with six or eight biscuits, another piece of fried ham and a hunk of cheese for my trip.

"With the haversack over my shoulder, I went down to say

a quick farewell to the captain. We'd already said our goodbyes the night before when he had me for dinner at his home again. He motioned for me to come into his office and close the door. Reaching into his desk drawer, he brought out a revolver.

"'Tom,' he said, 'it's a wild and lawless place out there these days, especially after you get away from the larger settlements. I want you to take this along for you own safety. It's another war surplus item, made for the Confederacy actually. Maybe it can do good duty for a Patriot now.'

"I took the gun and looked it over. It was a right well-made weapon, among the best the Confederacy had. Called a "Griswold," it was about seven inches long, with a six-shot cylinder, and right well balanced. 'Why, captain, this is a fine gun. Are you sure you want to give it to me?' He said he was quite sure, and handed me a small packet of bullets to go with it. Coming around the desk, he put his hand on my shoulder and wished me safe travels as he ushered me toward the door and out into Church Street.

"I was on my way, unsure what further adventures awaited me in this war-torn world. I started out walking toward the south at a right brisk pace, hope and the promise of home becoming real in my mind. But the more I thought on it, the less confident I became. Worrisome thoughts wouldn't go away. A little bit of hope can be a dangerous thing when you don't know what's ahead of you. What if . . . "

I knew Pa had a bad time in prison and a whole bunch of pain in the hospital. The good part was that he got to be friends with that Captain Goodwin. I understood how that helped him get through it all and put him on the path with hope. I knew what hope felt like when it started pushing itself shyly into a place where it had not been in a while.

Chapter 19

Sunday, we got up early to get the chores done so we could get off to church. Hard rain set in just before sun-up, and by the time I headed out to do the milking it had become a sure enough drenching downpour. Nothing to be done for it, so I took the milk pail and made a run for the barn. Time I got there I was soaked as a drowned rat and chilled to the bone. "September rains" is what Ma called it. I sure was thankful we'd gotten most all the garden harvested, except for some greens and things that would stay until frost. By the time I was back with the milk, Ma and Pa had decided we wouldn't try to go to church in such weather.

"Our wet Sunday best wouldn't be looking good at all. After breakfast why don't we build up a good fire to enjoy while I tell about the end of my journey? Maybe Ma will even roast some more Goobers for us."

"I'll fix the Goobers while Ma makes breakfast," I volunteered. Ma and me went to the kitchen while Pa sat with the other girls, with Etta on his lap. I could hear him telling them one of his favorite Grimm tales.

After breakfast, Pa read two of the Psalms from the Bible, ending up with Psalm 150. As he finished, a mischievous smile lit up his face. He remembered how, when he was a boy, he went to a protracted meeting at a friend's church. They had a preacher come from off somewhere to preach it for them. Pa could see right off that this visiting parson wasn't much educated. He started out reading Psalm 150, but when he got to the part about praising God "with psaltery and harp," he stumbled over the word "psaltery" and ended up calling it "peasal-tree." The old fellow admitted he didn't know just what kind of a tree that was, but he knew God was pleased to be praised with it anyhow. When I asked if he made up that funny to get us to laugh, he insisted it'd happened just that way. But he said it with such a twinkle in his eye that I couldn't be sure. Even so, whenever I hear that Psalm read, I'm sure I will get a smile out of remembering Pa and that "peasal-tree."

The smell of Goober peas roasting in the oven let me know they was about ready. I brought a pan of them to the sitting room for us to enjoy while Pa commenced where he left off about his trip down from Nashville.

"I had a great sense of joy as I set out. It was a fine fall morning, with nary a cloud in the bright blue sky. A light breeze kept the heat down. I commenced to whistling a tune as I fell into a comfortable pace, with no pain to speak of. I became aware of all the soldiers on the streets. Union soldiers and freedmen everywhere. Gradually, I began to realize that Nashville was still an occupied city. I noticed that the civilians whose city this once had been didn't tarry long, but darted here and there on whatever errands brought them out. Now and again I noticed an exchange of cautious, unhappy glances as folks passed each other in the street. Hatred and fear glared in the eyes of some as they stared at soldiers standing guard on the street corners.

I began to think on what it would be like to live in such a place. I reckon it had not come to me yet that I would be finding out soon enough."

Etta was ready for her morning nap. Ma went to put her down in their bedroom, because Penny and Peggy was playing in our room. While we waited, Pa and I realized we'd hardly touched the Goobers. I said as how I'd be glad when we could get hold of enough salt to be able to try boiling some. Pa smiled and nodded in agreement just as Ma came to join us again. She'd brought her knitting with her. Sitting down, she signaled for Pa to go on with his story.

"On toward late afternoon, I found myself near the settlement of Oakville. While I'd not been there before, I had heard tell of the place. Many a man from both sides had spilt his blood on this soil during the Battle of Nashville. I recognized the names of places like Peach Orchard Hill and Battery Lane. I decided maybe this would make as good a stopping place as any, if I could find a place to sleep.

"A bit south of the settlement I came upon a comfortable looking homestead set well back from the road. I 'hallooed' to whoever might be on the place. The front door opened a crack and the barrel of a shotgun emerged, followed by the clean-shaven face of a middle aged fellow. He was dressed in overalls, badly worn but clean and pressed, with sharp creases in the legs. 'Yeah?' That was all he said. I told him I was on my way home from the war, looking for shelter for the night. I asked if he could see his way clear to let me sleep in his barn.

"He stood there looking me over. 'That a Yankee coat you're wearing?' he asked. I didn't know just how to answer that. I had never thought of myself as a Yankee. The words that came out of my mouth were something like, 'Well, sir, I don't know just how to answer you with the truth. Yes, this coat is from a Union uniform and that's the side I fought for, but I ain't no Yankee. I was born and raised in Alabama, grandson and great grandson of soldiers of the Revolution. I'm a Patriot, headed back home to Alabama. I sure would appreciate the accommodation of your barn for the night.'

"He was slow responding. A thoughtful kind of look came over his face. 'Patriot, you say? That what you call yourself?' He didn't seem to know what to do with that idea. I could see he was turning it over and over in his mind.

"When he spoke, it was right slow and thoughtful like. 'So, you're a Patriot who fought against your own people. Is that the way of it?'

"There was no hostility in his voice; more like he was puzzled. I decided to push the matter just a little. 'Sir, it ain't quite as simple as all that. If you'd put that gun away, I'd be glad to talk with you about it.'

"He looked at the gun almost like he had forgotten he had it in his hands. The barrel dropped down so it wasn't pointed at me. He stepped out onto the porch and stood there looking me up and down. His gaze pierced me like he was looking into my very soul. Finally, he jerked his head in the direction of the barn. 'Yep. I reckon you can sleep in the barn if you're a-mind to.' He turned and went back in the house without another word.

"I waited for a minute or more, expecting him to come back out. When he didn't, I headed toward to the barn. For the first time I notice how neat and clean his spread was. No clutter in the yard. The buildings hadn't seen fresh paint in a long while

244

but had been kept in good repair otherwise. Fences all in good shape, but no livestock anywhere to be seen. Some chickens and geese scratched for food in a pen off to one side of the barn. A pigsty stood empty. Out beyond the barn, a field looked like it had been plowed up, but nothing planted in it. No corn or anything of the kind was anywhere to be seen.

"The odd welcome I had gotten, if you could call it a welcome, was a puzzle. I didn't even know his name and he didn't know mine. I looked around the barn. It was just like the rest of the place, everything clean and orderly. Tools put neatly in their place, but no sign this was a working farm, not even a horse or mule in the stalls. The only farmyard sound was the clucking of the hens and the honking of the geese, now bothered by my presence."

About then, Penny and Peggy came in from our bedroom where they had been playing. They asked if we could play a game together. Ma and me wanted to hear the rest of Pa's story, but he winked and us and said playing a game sounded like a right good idea.

"I'll beat you all in a game of pick-up-sticks," he said.

We played for near about a hour, but I couldn't keep my mind on the game. I kept thinking about what Pa was telling us. Peggy won.

The rain had let up a fair bit, so Pa went out to be sure everything was all right with the animals. He said he was special worried about the old sow who kept rooting her way out of the sty. He came back with the report that all was as it should be. Just as he walked up on the porch the skies opened up with the heaviest rain we'd seen all day. He slipped his feet out of his muddy boots, leaving them beside the front door. Then he sat in his rocker and wiggled his toes before the warm fire. Ma joined us, and we was ready to hear more about this strange man Pa had met up in Oakville, Tennessee.

"In the loft I found a modest stack of hay, but it wasn't fresh or new. Looked to be at least a year old. I fixed myself a sleeping place with some of it and stretched out to rest for a few minutes. It was still light; wouldn't be dark for another hour, I supposed, so I wouldn't even try to go to sleep just yet. I went back down and stood at the barn door surveying the place. Out behind the house there was a right nice size garden, all neat and well laid out. Sweet 'taters, some greens and tomatoes, played out pea vines and a few stalks of sweet corn. On the far side was what appeared to be a good size grape arbor. Beyond that, an overgrown field was the only unkempt aspect of the place.

"Turning to go back into the barn, I caught sight of another curiosity. On the side over toward the road there was a little burying ground. I could see two weathered headstones, and then beside them three more recent but unmarked graves. One was an adult; the other two child-size. I went to get a closer look. Couldn't quite make out the names incised on the worn limestone markers. The other three graves didn't seem to be real fresh dug. The soil had begun to settle, but there was no grass growing. Fieldstones laid in the form of a simple cross marked each one.

"I stood there for a good while considering what I was seeing, wondering what it might mean. As I turned to leave, I nearly bumped into the strange man standing there directly behind me. I didn't know how long he had been there; I hadn't heard a sound to indicate his arrival. His head was bowed, his eyes closed and his hands folded over his heart. He looked up and our eyes met, but neither of us said anything. Turning abruptly toward the house, he made a silent gesture for me to follow him. He opened the front door and silently invited me in.

"The little sitting room, like everything else, was clean as a pin, no dust or dirt to be seen, and modestly but comfortably furnished. I could see a kitchen through an adjoining door, and what I took to be two bedrooms off to the right. He took a seat by the fire and pointed me toward the other chair. There we sat for a long while, with not a word spoken or glance exchanged. Without looking up or moving a finger, he said, 'Name's Johnston. What's yours?'

"I told him my name, but then went on to tell him some of my experiences that brought me to his door. I figured if we were going to sit here, one of us ought to do some talking. I must have gone on for ten minutes or more. He listened intently with obvious interest, but without interrupting me. Now and again he would nod his head to acknowledge something I had said.

"When I finished, we again sat in silence. Finally, Johnston asked me to explain what I meant when I called myself a Patriot. Again my words to Jeremiah Conway and his friends up in Illinois came to mind. I used them as best I could remember them, recalling all the Patriots who had gone before and my devotion to the nation they had help to create. Without looking up, Johnston now and again nodded to acknowledge what I was saying, but continued just staring into the fire, deep in thought.

"When he looked up he asked, 'Ever hear of Joseph E. Johnston?'

"I was astonished. General Joseph E. Johnston had been commander of the Confederate Army of Tennessee. I'm sure the blood drained from my face.

"'My Uncle Joe. That's his oldest brother buried out there. My daddy.'

"I sat perfectly still, hardly able to breathe, unsure what was likely to happen next.

"Quick as a flash, Johnston sprang to his feet. Startled, I jumped up, prepared to defend myself, quite sure he was coming after me. Instead, he said 'I'm hungry. Let's find some victuals.' He moved into the kitchen and set about preparing a meal. He retrieved the remainder of a baked goose from the warming oven along with two large, baked sweet 'taters. The 'taters he skinned and sliced crossways into a dozen pieces each and put them in a skillet to sear in a bit of goose fat. As they warmed, he scattered what I discovered was crushed dry basil leaves over them. That made a right tasty dish out of ordinary leftover yams.

"In no time, he had two porcelain plates of food on the table for us, along with two mugs filled with a deep red liquid taken from a small barrel in a corner of the room. It was a simple but very fine meal. The goose, I discovered, was well seasoned with rosemary. This Mr. Johnston was a more than passably good cook. The cup contained red wine, sweet but with a pleasant acidic taste. He saw the puzzled look on my face as I tasted it. 'Muscadine wine,' he said. 'Make it myself.'

"We ate in silence. For the first time I realized that Johnston had some kind of disability with his left arm. He could use it some, but with limited movement. He noticed me looking at it. 'Injured in the war,' he said. That left me even more unsure of how to proceed. He looked up, as if he was about to say something more, but then lowered his eyes to his plate and continued to eat in silence."

The talk about eating reminded us that it was getting on toward time for supper. We also needed to do the evening chores. I was right glad that the rain had let up to a light kind of mist. Pa went to feed the pigs and cow, Ma fed the chickens, and I milked the cow. When that was done Ma and me went to the kitchen to see about the cooking. Peggy was looking after Etta. Penny's job was to set the table. We had some of the fried chicken left from noon. Ma mashed up some Irish 'taters, added some butter to them and fried them into patties. While we ate, Pa picked up talking about the supper he had with Mr. Johnston.

"He cleared the table, rinsing the utensils in a bucket of water near the stove, then we moved to sit by the fire again. I decided it was up to me to try to break the ice. 'Where were you in the war?' I asked. He drew in a deep breath and held it for a few seconds before exhaling slowly and deliberately. He planted his elbows on the arms of the rocker and clasped his hands firmly in front of him, still staring into the fire."

I noticed that Pa was sitting in just that same position in his rocker. I wondered if he was doing that on purpose, of if it just happened that way.

'Johnston pursed his lips together and finally blurted out that he was with General Joseph Wheeler up in Tennessee, right on the Kentucky border. There was anger in his voice, and fire flashing in his eyes as the words came tumbling out.

"'Fightin' Joe Wheeler, they called him. Don't know why they called him that. Wasn't much of a commander, if you ask me. Just a scrappy little bantam rooster, too full of himself to give a darn for his troops.'

"He paused and glanced all around the room like he was looking for what to say next. It was the first sign of nervousness or uncertainly I had seen in him. 'I put in for a year. What with General Joseph E. Johnston being my uncle and all, they made me Second Lieutenant right off. We were at Fort Donelson, near a place called Dover, Tennessee, February, 1863.'

"I didn't know the place. He described it as a small Union garrison under a Colonel Harding. Abner Harding. Not a name I knew. 'They were well dug in, with rifle pits and battery emplacements scattered all in and about the town. Fighting went on near all day long. Come dusk, we were almost out of ammunition. Fightin' Joe sent orders for us to go in one more time. The fire was too great. We were turned back, taking heavy losses. Real heavy. That so-called 'Fighin' Joe' finally called a retreat. Yankees chased us a good ways, but we got away. Some of us anyway. The whole thing was a failure. Wasn't the most important battle of the war, but that loss gave your Union folks pretty much unchallenged control of Middle Tennessee. Later I heard that General Forrest swore that he would never again serve under 'Fightin' Joe Wheeler.'"

I wondered if this was the same as General Nathan Bedford Forrest Pa had talked about so much before. That man seemed to have been just about everywhere during that war.

"Johnston's face was a bright red, sweat pouring down his brow, his fists clenched and shaking in front of him. His anger still burned as hot as it had back in February of '63. 'In that last skirmish, shrapnel from a cannon ball caught me on the left side. I thought my shoulder was gone, blown away. They carried me down to Nashville to the hospital where, for a time, the South had its best medical team. Turned out the bones weren't involved, just muscle and tendon damage. They patched me up and saved my arm. By the time I was healed, my year was up and I came home. Wasn't going to sign on for any more of that foolishness. From what I could see, the South's cause was in danger of being wasted away by undisciplined and incompetent fools like that General Joe Wheeler. Troops I served with were underfed, under-equipped, and often just as rowdy as their superiors. I don't care what my Uncle Joe thinks. It was a sad state of affairs and I was glad to be shuck of it.'

"I didn't know just what to say to all this. The best thing, I decided, was to say nothing and see where he would take it. After some considerable time, he looked over toward me and in a quiet calm voice he told me to go out to the barn and get my haversack. 'There's no use for you to sleep on that old haystack when there's an extra bed in here you can use.' He showed me where it was."

When we finished our supper, Penny and me cleared off the table and washed the dishes while Ma put away the food. Pa went out to the woodpile and brought in some wood to build up the fire.

"Could we play another game of pick-up-sticks before bedtime?" Penny liked that game. Pa let us play three games, and he won two of them. Penny won the third one, but the twinkle in Pa's eyes told me he let her win.

Ma got the younger girls in bed. When she came back, she brought one of Penny's dresses that needed to have the hem mended. Seemed like her hands always had to be busy when she was sitting down.

"Now, where was I?" Pa asked. The twinkle in his eyes told me he knew just where he had left off, but I obliged him and told him he had gone out to the barn to move his things into Mr. Johnston's spare room.

"When I came back from the barn he had banked the fire and gone to bed, so I went to the room he had pointed me to. There was an open book on my pillow. The small oil lamp on the table by the bed didn't give off enough light to read it by, but I could see the title: *The Federalist Papers Collected, Volume 1*. It was opened to one of the essays by Thomas Jefferson. Curious as I was, it would have to wait until the morrow. I stretched out on the bed and thought on all that had happened to me that day, and this strange Mr. Johnston who had taken me in. Exhaustion overcame my thinking and I fell off into a deep sleep."

Pa let out a gentle sigh, stroked the neat beard on his chin and smiled a contented smile.

"Well, this long story is coming on down toward its conclusion. Tomorrow you'll be hearing the end of it. Or almost the end. The very end is the part you know already, and that's the happiest part of it all. For now, it's time for us to let sleep overcome our thinking. Off to bed with you."

I went to sleep that night dreaming about that nice Mr. Johnston. I was glad he'd seen his way clear to be kind to my Pa, who was so close to being home with us again.

Chapter 20

The rain that had started up on Sunday showed no signs of letting up. The creek was clear out of its banks in the low lying areas, and Ma was worried that it might get high enough to get into the school house but Pa didn't think so. He allowed as how it would take a right smart of a gully-washer to bring the creek up that far.

Other than the necessary chores like milking the cows and being sure the critters was all fed and safe, there was no work to be done. Us three children was at loose ends, not knowing how to fill the time. Ma and me showed Penny how to churn butter, but she soon got tired of it and went off to play with Etta.

Penny wanted to see if she could win another match of pick-up-sticks, but I was more interested in Pa's story. It was getting on close to the end, and I was anxious to learn the rest of it. Ma told Penny to go and play pick-up-sticks with Peggy. If Penny could win three out of five games, Ma promised, then we would all play. She figured that would give Pa time to finish up.

Ma sat down with her needlework. Pa stirred up the fire and put on another log. Then he took to his rocker and looked off down the lane toward the road. I was watching for him to stroke his beard like he always did, and he didn't disappoint.

"I slept right well in Mr. Johnston's extra bed that night. It wasn't like the one I had at Conway's place, but it sure beat sleeping in the haystack in a cold, drafty barn. My bum leg had not pained me any at all in spite of all the walking I had done, and my breathing was some better, too.

"When I opened my eyes, the smell of fresh coffee and the sizzle of eggs frying welcomed me to the morning. The sun was up, but just barely. I slipped on my boots and went out to the kitchen. Johnston pointed me to a washbasin and a bucket of water he had brought in from the well. The cool water felt right good on my face and arms. The eggs were ready, and we sat down to breakfast. They were goose eggs, a right smart larger than hen's eggs. I don't know what the coffee was made of. I knew it wasn't real coffee, because there had not been any of that to be had for two years or more except at the hospital in Nashville. I never did figure out how they got it. Whatever this was, it was a right good substitute.

"We ate in silence for a time. Without looking up he said, 'Sorry there's no bacon or ham. Had none of that since I got back from the war.' With those two sentences, I thought we had made a hopeful start toward a good talk. I commented that I'd seen no sign of any critters around the place. 'Scavengers. Confederates. My own folks took them, right after I left with General Wheeler. Came home to find my wife and two children nearly starved to death. Don't blame any of the neighbors, though. None of them had anything to spare. It was the Confederate Army came and took everything, Sally begging all the while for them to leave her something to feed the young ones.

self same cause.' They were words of bitterness and anger. 'If it wasn't for some little bit of charity the State of Tennessee sent out for soldiers' families, I don't see how they could have survived as well as they did. Wasn't much of it. Just some corn meal and dried beans and such. Better than nothing, I reckon. Enough to keep body and soul together.'

"I drained the last of the coffee from my cup, but he was right there to refill it for me. 'Back at the beginning of the war, some writer up North put down some words that puzzled me at the time. Lived long enough to know their truth. He wrote something about how the evils of this rebellion would be felt the most by the rebels themselves. Out there in that burial ground, those words stand immortalized.'

"I could see he was struggling with himself, unsure how or whether to go on. Still, he had started on what I could tell was a difficult subject. 'They were shot down by Confederate soldiers. My Sally, my beautiful Polly and my precious little Andrew. Everybody said it was an accident. I reckon it was. But does that really matter? What difference does it make? They are gone, all three of them gone from me. All I have left is those three graves marked with those crosses, right out there for me to look upon every day I live.'

"The tears streamed silently down his cheeks, as I'm sure they must have done through many days and nights since the tragedy. When he was able, he told me the rest of the story. It happened about six months after his return from the army. There was a parade down the main street in Oakville, welcoming some local soldiers home. The little family had gone to watch. At some point, one of the town's people called him aside and he turned to talk with him. As part of the celebration there was gunfire, all of it planned and arranged in advance. Somehow, stray bullets sprayed into the crowd. Three other by-standers were wounded, but Sally, Polly and Andrew were hit directly. As it happened, the town doctor was standing nearby, but there was nothing to be done. They died right before his eyes, with the band playing Dixie and the drums marking dou-ble time."

"'Files,' he said, 'I once thought that people disappeared when they died. Their laughter, their voice, the warmth of their breath, the smell of their skin. Not true. Never a minute passes when I do not hear their voices, feel the softness of their skin. Especially my Sally. In the depths of every dark night, I feel her body close to mine, smell the fragrance of her hair, hear the soft lilt of her voice, the gentle joy of her laughter. And my little Andrew. Oh, my little Andrew.' It was only by force of will that he brought his tears under control.

"After that, there really wasn't anything much a fellow could say. We sat, rocking quietly before the fire for a good part of the afternoon. He spoke the first words. 'You found that book I left for you last night?' I said I did, but had not read any of it yet. He asked if I would go and bring it. He flipped through, looking for some particular passage. He said what he was looking for had come to his mind when I was telling him about being a Patriot and why I had chosen to fight for the Union.

"I can't remember the exact words Thomas Jefferson wrote, but I recall the gist of the matter. Jefferson said there would always be problems when folks started choosing up sides for a fight. He said can't any of us human beings be certain that the side we take is shaped by principles that are any purer than those that shape the opposite side. Ambition, greed, personal prejudices and other such motives are just as apt to operate among those who support what they are sure is a just cause as they are among those who take the other side. And those others are just as sure they are right. Johnston repeated those three words: 'Ambition, greed and prejudice.'

"He turned so as to look me right in the eye. What he said next were words he obviously had memorized from frequent reading. Johnston spoke them with such feeling that they seared right into my mind. He said that in politics, as in religion, *'it is equally absurd to think we can change minds and hearts by fire and sword. Disagreements in either can rarely be cured by force.'*

"Those words from Thomas Jefferson left me stunned. Here we were after all these years of bloody warfare and with God only knows what kind of suffering yet to come. President Johnson had something he called 'Reconstruction,' but there didn't seem to be much of it actually going on. There was more lawlessness than ever afoot, especially in these parts. Had the minds and hearts of any of us been changed, Rebels or Patriots? Where would the future take us, now that our nation was supposed to be united again?

"We sat quietly for a time.

"'So, Patriot Files,' he finally said, not unkindly, 'you are going home to find heaven knows what awaiting you. I am here, surrounded by memories, grief and loss. We have been on different sides, but I am a different man from the one who marched off with General Wheeler. My bet is that you are a different man from the one who went off to join the First Alabama

Cavalry. Both of us have to figure out who we are now, and what we're going to make of it, whatever it is.'

"Johnston and me were both up early next morning. I had told him the night before I was going to start on down toward home. He gave me a chunk of fresh bread and two baked sweet 'taters to take along. As I was picking up my haversack, he asked how I was going. I said I was just going to start walking south and see where it took me. He told as how there had been some pretty bad stories told about bandits and ruffians hiding out in the forests and hills of southern Tennessee and northern Alabama. His advice was that I ought to stay out of the woods and stick to the roadways as best as I could.

"He had heard that the railroad down toward Elkmont had been tore up by General Forrest, so there was no rail traffic down that way. Seemed like that old rascal had been everywhere I turned. The Sulfur Creek trestle between Elkmont and Decatur had been destroyed during a skirmish there, and last Johnston knew, it was not put back up yet. We took our leave, and I thanked him for his hospitality. He wasn't paying me no mind. His eyes and his mind had wandered off down to where those graves lay. Speaking nary a word, he turned and went on into the house.

"I'd been walking an hour or two when a man came along in a wagon pulled by an old gray mare. His strong brogue marked him as distinctly Irish when he asked where I was headed. When he learned I was going down toward Elkmont, Alabama, he allowed as how he sure would welcome the company, if I didn't mind the rough ride of his old wagon. I replied riding sure would beat walking for three days. He introduced himself as Daniel O'Connell, a farmer living north of Oakville.

His daughter and her family lived west of Elkmont, and he was going for a visit. Being a widower and no children at home, he was pretty much free to come and go as he pleased. 'Got no farm animals left to hold me down. Between one of these armies or the other, they were all taken off.' It was the same familiar story. I allowed as how I couldn't help but worry what I what I would find when I got back to my home place.

"I asked if he knowed Johnston. He nodded his head sadly. 'That is a bad state of affairs,' he said. I told him of the hospitality extended to me, and he opined it probably was right good for Johnston to have a friendly body around for awhile. 'I suppose he gets right lonesome out there all by his self.'

"I figured Daniel was well into his sixties, clean-shaven except for a three-day growth of silver stubble on his face. He had a full head of gray hair and his eyes were ice blue. He was sharp as a tack and spry as could be. He seemed relieved, though, to have me riding along.

""Things can get right rough out here in the wilderness these days,' he mused. 'You never know when some of these rogues might come along. We used to call them the Home Guard, but they sure don't guard anything anymore. That is, if they ever did. I was always hearing tales about the way they robbed and mistreated folks. These days that's just their way of life.'

"He asked if I was armed, and I showed him the Griswold that Captain Goodwin had given me. He was glad of it. He had a rifle stowed under the seat of the wagon, but allowed as how he felt safer knowing I had a pistol at hand.

"'And a fine pistol it is, Files. Where did a Union man get a gun like that?' It was clear he knew his firearms.

"Over the next hour, I told him the whole story leading up to how I happened to be in the right place at the right time to acquire it. He was fascinated with the notion that General Steedman had arrested me. I ended up giving him the complete tale of my war experience, pretty much the way I've been telling it to you, but in much shortened form.

"It turned out that Daniel O'Connell had avoided taking up sides in the war. He told me it just weren't any of his affair except as it kept unsettling his life. I remember what he said because I really liked hearing his Irish brogue. He said 'Me boy, that war was none 'o my doing. Wasn't none of my affair."

He commenced talking that way, telling us what O'Connell said. "'Me wife died in childbirth back in the old country. We had only the one child, so I had no kin to send off fighting, and I was too old for either side to want me. I've spent these war years dodging bullets from both sides. Unlike you, I have no ties to the country except as the wonderful place that kindly took us in when we were in distress. Me family and I came here just seventeen years ago, fleeing the great famine that enveloped Ireland. A sad time it was, too. 'The Great Hunger' is what it's called in our own tongue. People dying in their poverty everywhere. Me own branch of the O'Connell clan were a bit more prosperous than most. Not rich, mind you, but not dirt poor neither. That made it possible for us to get away. So, here I be, nearly alone in the world now that me dear parents are gone on to their reward.' He made a brief sign of the cross over his heart.

"I had read some pieces in *The Harper's Weekly* about the great Irish famine, but this was my first meeting with anybody related to it. That evening we camped in a dense copse that gave us some privacy from the road. He unhitched the mare and tethered her to a stob in a good size grassy area near a small spring. Around the fire he continued telling me tales of horror and heroism from his childhood. We slept under the stars in the bed of the wagon with our guns at our sides.

"The sun got us up. 'Top o' the mornin' to ye,' he said with a smile. Each of us had a bit of bread and cheese for our breakfast. Daniel said he didn't drink coffee, but he did have the making of a nice pot of tea. He invited me to join him."

Pa looked over to Ma and smiled. "That made me think of you, Mattie. You and the tea you always liked to have of an evening back before it became impossible to get. I tell you truly, I got terribly homesick when I put it to my lips. It was the only tea I had seen or heard of since those evenings with you."

They reached across and held hands in a brief, silent exchange. I knew some message had passed between them, but no one but them would ever know what it was.

"We arrived in Elkmont in the late afternoon and parted company. As we shook hands we both hoped our paths might cross again someday, but agreed it didn't seem likely. Even so, to this day I consider Daniel O'Connell a friend and wonder how he is getting on.

"I had never been to Elkmont, but still it had a familiar look about it. It was a lot like other little places I had seen during the war. I found a room in a dilapidated rooming house near the closed up railroad station and passed the night alone. Seemed I was the only roomer in the place. The fellow running it confirmed that there hadn't been any rail service down to Decatur Junction since Forrest took out the Sulfur Creek trestle. But he was hopeful that was about to change. Some folks from the

261

Alabama Central Railroad had been in town a few days earlier inspecting the tracks and roadbed, like as if they were going to get it up and running again.

"Being as how there wasn't much to occupy me until dark, I walked the streets looking at how the war had ravaged the town. I began to notice how much idleness there was. Everywhere I looked there were men sitting alone or gathered in clusters on the porches or in the shade of trees. Some were whittling. Now and again one was reading an old, ragged piece of a newspaper, but mostly folks were just sitting. Lots were not even talking to anybody.

"There was plenty of work that needed doing, cleaning up and rebuilding the town. The problem was, didn't anybody have any money to buy needed materials even if they could have been gotten. Something my Grandpa used to say sprung to mind: 'Idle hands are the devil's workshop.' It seemed to me all this idleness didn't bode well for anybody. No wonder there was so much lawlessness about.

"Those thoughts were brought home to me directly later that evening. The sun was just setting. There was a ramshackle little park across from the hotel, and I went there to sit on the grass. I took the last of my bread and cheese and the sweet 'tater that Johnston had given me, intending to have it for my supper.

"I had no more than gotten settled and unwrapped the bread and cheese when I realized I was not alone. There were two men standing in the shadows right behind me. 'Don't you move, mister.' There was a clear threat in the voice. 'Just give us whatever it is you've got there to eat, and you can go on about your business.' I started to protest, but immediately got a hard kick right between the shoulder blades. 'I said, don't you move. Just hold that grub up high in your right hand.' I did as I was told. Somebody snatched the bread and cheese from my hand, and then I heard them running away into the darkness behind me. If 'idle hands are the devil's workshop,' what do you suppose such desperate hunger is?

"I went back to my room, ate the 'tater I had left, and went to bed. I was still hungry but at least I knew more or less where my next meal might come from. How many people were there, even in this little town, who didn't know that? And how many thousands more scattered across the devastated South? I didn't even know how it was for my own family.

"I didn't sleep well with such thoughts invading my dreams. Those thoughts, and the excitement and anxiety of knowing I would be seeing you in a few more days kept sleep at bay for most of the night."

Chapter 21

After three days and four nights of constant rain, we woke up to a sunshiny day. The ground was soaked and lots of the streams was out of their banks. After morning chores was done, Pa walked down to see about the creek behind our house. He came back with the report that it was running higher than he'd ever seen it. We wasn't in any flood danger, but he said he was worried about some of the neighbors who lived on low ground downstream. We hitched Rabbit to the wagon, and he and I went to see about some of them. When we got to the bridge over the creek just past our church, it was under water. He allowed as how it wasn't safe for us to go any further. We knew there was a Secesh family with a passel of young 'uns who lived just past the bridge. Their house went under water right regular, but wasn't any way we could get there to see about them. Pa said we'd just have to hope and pray they was all right.

Near about a week went by before the roads was passable again. Come Saturday, Pa went into town for Trade Day. He didn't have any more stuff to sell or trade. He said he just wanted to talk to folks and see if there was any news of interest. He reckoned as how he'd look in on that Secesh family as he passed, just to see how they'd weathered the flood. Ma fixed up a basket of victuals for him to take for them.

It was late in the afternoon when he got home. We could tell there was something bothering him, but it took a while for it to come out. It was news about a fight going on between President Andrew Johnson and the congress. Best I could tell, it had to do with paying war debts owed to folks like us.

"Now, Tom, that just ain't right," I heard Ma saying. "The government owes us that money. They promised they would pay you for old Rabbit. He was our very best work mule. How come they ain't going to pay you? How we going to pay off what we owe to Mr. John Shaw for them critters we got off of him when you first got home?"

She was near tears. Pa was sure they was still going to pay. It just might take longer than he thought. He told her how he'd read a piece in *The Birmingham Herald* that had to do with paying what he called "Southern claims." He said the Congress had set it up to decide about paying what was owed to folks like us.

"That don't make no sense, Tom. What needs deciding? It's just a matter of them paying what they owe, the same as we have to. That's as plain as the nose on your face."

I could see this had hit my Ma pretty hard. There was deep worry lines around her eyes, and she wasn't herself. Pa sent me to fetch some willow bark like we'd used to make the medicine for him when he was hurt. He said a bit of it might make Ma rest easy. When I had the medicine fixed he helped her drink some and go lay down. Soon, she was sleeping.

Pa, me, Penny, and Peggy went out to take care of the critters. Penny had got right strong and was good help with the chores. She said she wanted to do the milking now, and I was real glad for her take on that job. I commenced helping Pa get the hay out to Rabbit and the cow, and slop the hogs. Peggy fed the chickens.

Time we got back in, it was near dark. Ma'd perked up right smart and had supper ready to go on the table. I saw her and Pa talking in whispers again, but couldn't hear what that was all about. After dinner, Ma and me tucked the other girls in for the night, then we went to sit with Pa while he told us how he got on his way home from up in Elkmont.

"I was awake well before daylight, pacing the floor and thinking on everything that day might hold for me. Decatur wasn't all that far away now. While it would be a significant mile marker, it didn't mark the end of my travels. I still had to make my way to Walker County through the familiar hill country of North Alabama. All the dangers of vagabonds and lawless gangs were still out there, though I'd not run into any myself so far. I knew these parts like the back of my hand, and I knew there would be some sympathetic folks all along the way. I was hopeful I could make swift and steady progress on that last leg of my travels.

"When I set out walking, the sun was hardly showing itself through dark and stormy rain clouds. Before I'd got more than an hour out of town, it commenced to rain right hard, and that's the way it was all the way. It was toward evening when I came to a settlement called Decatur Junction, across the Tennessee River from the town itself. It was where two railroads came together. One was the Tennessee Alabama Central, the one I would have ridden down here it if had been working. When the Union Army departed after holding Decatur for most of the war, they had destroyed the railroad bridge across the river. The other was the Memphis and Charleston Railroad. Seemed like maybe that east-west line was up and running again, though I didn't see or hear any trains."

When Pa got to the river's edge he saw there was an old boat patched-together old boat made up to serve like a ferry, but the ferryman had already closed down for the night. The boat was tied up on the far side of the river.

"I found a spot in a thick copse on a little rise near the river-bank and settled in for the night. It was raining still, so I passed the night wet, hungry and miserable with no sleep to be had.

"The morning saw me up and stirring well before sunrise. I could find no wood dry enough to make a fire, since the rain was now coming down even harder than before. I 'hallo-ed' for the ferryman, and he came over to collect me. When I saw Decatur, I could hardly believe my eyes. Except for extensive fortifications and a vast array of modest structures to house the Federal troops, it seemed there was no town there. Certainly not much of one. There were a few slight evidences of rebuilding here and there, but mostly just the bare foundations of destroyed buildings everywhere. There were not even any churches standing in the place. Walking through the settlement, I counted six intact buildings that had survived the war. There was a place that looked like it might have been a bank building at one time, and the railroad depot. It surprised me to see that the rails were still there but, since there was no access to the town from the north or the south, they were pretty useless. What looked like a bank building turned out to have been used for a hospital. For a time it was used as a headquarters by officers of both sides. There was what appeared to be a hotel but best I could tell, it was nearly unoccupied. I could identify two private residences, relatively magnificent structures that had been spared. I recognized one of them as what had been General Steedman's headquarters, but I tried not to linger on them thoughts. On the riverbank, there was a row of warehouses and military barracks, and something that looked like a guard house near where a bridge had once stood. That was all there was to Decatur except for the fortifications and a few rudely constructed huts here and there.

"I asked the ferry what had happened to the town. He explained that the Union Army had sent all the civilians away and tore down nearly everything to build their fortifications and barracks. Wasn't but just a few like him that had started to come back. The place was still in a right sorry state.

"Being wet, cold, and very hungry, I asked the ferryman if there was any food to be had. He scratched his head and looked puzzled. When I said I was not looking for charity but could pay for my meal, his dark eyes came alive, reflecting the sun rising over the water. He pointed me to a hovel closest to the river bank, a few hundred feet from where we stood. He said there was a widow lady there who might be able to accommodate me.

"He went with me to see about the matter. As it turned out, the widow lady was his own mother. When she heard the part about paying for a meal, she got real interested and invited us into her little hut. The best part of it was that there was a decent fire that kept the little room quite warm. I had not felt warmth for several days. She took my coat and laid it out before the fire to dry.

"She and her son both left right sudden like. I saw her scurrying across to a neighbor's house, but lost sight of him. Soon she was back carrying three eggs. She apologized that this was the best she could do, but she did have half a loaf of bread she had made the day before. In another few minutes, her son was back with a string of fish freshly caught from the river.

"Hungry as I was, eggs, fish and bread for breakfast sounded like a feast. It came to me that this might be the only food either she or her neighbor had. When I asked if they all might join me in the meal, you would have thought I had invited them to a royal banquet. The neighbor woman joined us and brought two more eggs with her. I paid far more than such food would have cost at an inn, and you would have thought the sum I gave them was a king's ransom!"

Ma smiled at that. "Well, I reckon it was to them poor folks, Tom. As much as I wish we had that money to buy things we need, I know it was right Christian of you to give it to them."

The rain hadn't let up next morning when Pa commenced to slog his way into the mountains of North Alabama. Three days of walking and three nights of sleeping on the wet ground in the forest took its toll. He allowed as how the throbbing pain in his bad leg was the worse he could remember since his beating in Nashville. The damaged muscles in his back would knot up, and he had to find a place to lie down 'til he could work it out. With no wood dry enough to burn, he had no heat. Most of all he had no way to cook any food if there was any to be found. He had to make do with such berries and plants as he could find to eat, and I reckon he was glad for them.

"Toward evening I came upon a small cave in the side of a hill. There was the remnant of an old campfire in there with some dry wood collected. Wasn't never any fire felt better to a body since humans first found flame. I shot me one scrawny little rabbit to roast, and that was all there was to eat that night. I continued to be surprised at how little wildlife there was in these woods. The place used to be teeming with deer, rabbit, squirrel, wild turkey and even wild boar. Those two giant armies roaming these parts must have near about hunted these woods out.

"Lying there in that dry cave, I commenced to thinking on how strange it was that I had not run into a living soul since leaving Decatur. When the war was going on these woods was teeming with people laying out and the Home Guard hunting for them. Could it be that most everybody felt safe enough to go home now? That thought warmed me plumb through in places no fire could ever reach.

"It was still raining next morning when I set out. I heard a hoot owl off in the distance somewhere. I reckoned as how he didn't like the rain any more than I did. With raindrops splattering all around, he could hear mice or chipmunks scurrying through the underbrush. I reckoned maybe he was about as hungry as I was, but he couldn't have been near as lonesome.

By mid-day I felt the temperature falling. Being wet clear through, I felt the cold deep down in my bones. I thought I was getting close to the cave known as The Big Rock House where I was staying when I lost my discharge papers and made that disastrous decision to go over to Decatur. If that's where I was, I knew I was getting real close to being home, about a day's walk.

"Sure enough, I found myself on the familiar track that took me straight to The Big Rock House. Cold and wet, I was in a right smart bit of pain. Seemed like it would be a good idea to stop early and get some rest. My leg and back throbbed with every step. I was breathing mighty hard, my body ached all over and a bad headache made it hard for me to think straight. I sure hoped it was just a cold and not something worse. Being sick out there by myself would not be a good thing.

"The cave was deserted. The only sign that anybody had been there recently was the cold remains of a good size fire. Once again, luck was with me. There was some dry wood already gathered in. After getting a fire going, I went to find the spring I knew was back up in the cave, and got me a nice, long drink of cool water. Next up was the worry of finding something to eat. I wasn't feeling real good and couldn't bear the prospect of going back out into the cold rain. I stretched out by the fire to rest a spell and enjoyed drying out and warming up. I drifted off to sleep.

"Some noise jerked me wide awake. There was a sharp trilling sound coming from back up in the cave. When I could focus my mind on it, I recognized the cry of a raccoon complaining about being disturbed in the middle of the afternoon. I reckon the smoke from the fire had roused him. Seemed my supper might be calling me, so I took the pistol from my haversack and went exploring.

"He wasn't hard to find, nesting in the dark among some loose rocks. What if I shot and missed and sent that bullet rebounded off the rock walls and ceiling? I could end up wounding or killing myself, with me so close to home and here alone in this abandoned cave. Luck was with me, though. I got him with one shot. He was a big fellow, probably six or seven years old. He'd be right tough to eat, and it was going to take me into the evening to get him cleaned and cooked. I thought to myself how, if I was at home, I'd soak this old critter in salty water for the most part of a day to get him tender. In a couple of hours I had him roasting over a low fire. I figured I would have a late meal that night, but there didn't seem to be nowhere pressing I had to be for the evening."

There was a twinkle in his eye, and Ma and me laughed. One of the things I liked most about hearing my Pa talk was his quiet kind of humor that just slipped up on a body when you wasn't expecting it.

A frown darkened Ma's face. "Well, we've had to eat 'coon meat a few times when wasn't nothing else to be had, Tom. It sure ain't my favorite, and I know it wasn't yours either, but time comes when a body's got to do what a body's got to do to keep body and soul together."

Pa agreed. "By the time that tough old critter was ready to eat, I was feeling lots worse. I had lost my appetite far before that tasteless meat was done. I was sneezing and coughing, my throat hurt and my nose was all stopped up. By the time I tried to go to sleep, I had a right high fever. I knew I had to bring more wood in to dry. I sure wouldn't do to let the fire go out. I also needed to have some water where I could reach it. It took all I could do to get these chores done. Then I collapsed, plumb tuckered out and burning up with fever.

"All I wanted to do was sleep. I managed to rouse myself just enough to keep the fire going. I had some of that old 'coon meat to eat, tough and tasteless as it was. The water felt right good to my sore throat. I don't know just how long I was in that state. I believe it was three or four days, maybe five.

"In the night my fever broke. Feeling a whole lot better, I went to the spring to wash up and refresh myself. As I was getting up, a flash of something white caught my eye, half buried in sand and pebbles right up against the cave wall. Right off I knew what it was. It was my discharge paper. I sat there holding it, overcome with sadness at what its loss had cost me and with joy at having it back. I knew right then I was going to send it to that ornery General Steadman to show him the wrong he had done me.

"I filled the canteen with water, finished off the 'coon meat and gathered up such belongings as I had. There was nothing but blue sky off to the south. I wasn't going to be moving very fast, but at least I was moving. I shot me an occasional pigeon or dove, but saw no other critters, nor even the sign of any. Lambsquarters growing along the stream banks gave me tender green leaves to eat, and I came upon abundant blackberry brambles now and again. A cluster of pecan trees provided a pocket full of nuts to eat as I walked.

"What should have taken one day took me three. At last I came onto some familiar sights. Passing the homes of old friends and enemies brought both pleasure and fear to my soul. Wasn't anybody out and about, though. I didn't run into a single body until I turned into that little lane right out there."

Pa stopped talking and looked off down our lane toward the road, as he'd done many times in the telling of his adventures. Today it was like he was seeing it the way he did when he arrived back here. It wasn't that far-away kind of look like he had when he was thinking about things. There was a gentle smile on his face and a glisten in his eye.

"When I got to our lane, I stopped down there by the road and took it all in. Didn't none of you look up. You didn't know I was there. What a sight to behold. Right there in front of me, all the people who were most important to me in the whole world. That is when it struck me that in my fear for what might happen to me, I had overlooked something vital. Maybe the most important thing in a person's life. Without family, without those you love, don't any of the rest of it fit together right. Yes, I had kept myself alive, but at what cost? I got back home with a whole lot less than I took away. A whole lot less than I thought I would be bringing. My body was much the worse for wear. I had a bum leg, couldn't breathe very good, looked like an old vagabond, stunk to the high heavens and had barely enough energy to stay upright. But there you stood, the ones who mattered most. The love of my life and two children I couldn't hardly recognize and one I'd never laid eyes on before.

"I wondered if you would welcome me back. Would you hate me for leaving you alone for so long? Had you maybe decided I was dead and found somebody else to care for you? Would my children be too afeared to tolerate me? Would you understand why I had done it all? Could I ever make it up to you? Would you want me to?

"That kind of anxiety near about overwhelmed me as I took them first steps up the lane. My heart was racing like mad and my stomach was tied in knots. Something like dread nearly blinded me. But I started walking. It took all the strength I could muster to put one foot in front of the other."

He reached across and quietly took Ma's hand in his.

"Mattie, you saw me first, and I saw the fear on your face. I heard you call to the children and commence to run away from me. My heart sank down to my feet. It looked like my worst fears were coming to life right there in front of me. Everybody was running away. Everybody but one, that is.

"Fannie, you were the first to know who I was. That surprised me. You had been just a child when I went away. You won't ever know what joy it brought me when I heard you call out to me and tell your Ma it was me coming up the lane. The excitement in your voice was my first clue that everything might be all right after all."

Epilogue

Pa was wrong. Glad as we was to have him back at home, everything didn't turn out to be all right. For a time, we was a whole family again, but that couldn't last. It was true that our country was trying to move away from civil war, but it was a right rough and rocky road.

Not being at war didn't mean we was at peace.

That was why, near about five years ago now, Johnny and I knew we had to move on. Johnny and me got married in our little clapboard church with Rev. McAdoo tying the knot for us. We tried our best to live at peace with everybody, but a body can't live at peace with folks still studying war. We packed up and moved west, the way lots of young folks we knew was doing.

For a long time I cried over leaving home. Still do, truth be told. I get so lonely for Ma and Pa and the girls I just can't hardly stand it. Hard as it was, I know it was for the best. Life back there was filled with just too much meanness, sadness, mischief and grief. And uncertainty. A whole lot of uncertainty. So, once more, that awful war tore our family apart.

The last straw was the evening Pa came back from town with some right unsettling news. Gangs of Confederate veterans was on the roam, doing mischief to the colored and to the Union folks. They'd show up late of a night the way the Home Guard used to do, shooting up folks' houses and threatening to do worse. Nobody knew who they was because they was always disguised. Some wore robes made of white sheets, with pointed hoods. Others of them covered their faces and arms with soot and wore their hats pulled down over their eyes. They traveled in groups of six or eight, and seemed to be covering a right large territory, but nobody could tell how many there was of them. The war was not over. Not even the killing had stopped.

Over time, the terror of war gave way to the terror of Reconstruction and of more bad feelings. It was true that life had gone on and some things had changed, but some hadn't changed and showed no promise that they would anytime soon.

Just because things change, that don't mean they're getting better. Stories came seeping in from all around. Houses being burned, crops destroyed, folks being shot at on the road or in the dead of night. Up north of home there was a Mr. Wilson stripped naked and set on fire because they thought he had money in the house. His grandson was shot in the head and left for dead, and his nephew was killed, when they said they didn't know about any money. Mr. Wilson's sharecropper heard the commotion and came to help, and he was killed while his wife begged for his life.

Nearly everywhere I went in those days I came across somebody flying an old red flag, with a big blue X across it and bearing a star for each of the Confederate states. It was a Confederate battle flag. It was not the national flag of the Confederacy, so flying it wasn't about national pride. It was nothing but a banner of rebellion, strife and confusion. I couldn't help but wonder how come that was anything to be so proud of?

Some nights, from off in the far distance and a time long ago, I can still hear my Ma's strong voice singing a question that most likely will puzzle lots of folks not even born yet.

> *Oh, say does that star-spangled banner yet wave o'er the land of the free and the home of the brave?*

I reckon the fellow who wrote that song must have been wondering some of the same things I was. Is the right flag still flying over our country? And what kind of country is it flying over?

The old questions from my childhood still swirl around in my head, especially as I lie on my bed in the quiet of the night. What is a Patriot? What is a Rebel? Will the time ever come when we can reach out to everybody and anybody and make them all "most kindly welcome?"

I keep remembering an evening long ago when a man came hobbling up our lane, none too steady on his feet and leaning heavy on his staff. All ragged, with shaggy hair and a wild full beard, and so skinny his tattered old jacket hung from his shoulders and flopped in the breeze. It was the fragment of a uniform, one that still showed its Union blue through the dirt and grime.

He was a Patriot.

Author's Notes

"Did that really happen, or are you just telling me this to scare me?" Fannie's question to her Pa is one frequently asked of a writer of historical fiction. As familiar as the question may be, the answer is not always clear cut. While major parts of this story are historical, these parts blend readily with others to heighten interest or dramatic effect. Thus, it is both historical and fictional – a true story imagined.

Tom and Mary Frances Files are real people. In fact, they were my wife's great great grandparents. A Southerner born and bred in the Alabama hill country, he subjected himself and his family to ridicule, rejection and danger in order to defend and serve the Union his ancestors helped to create.

The massacre at Files Creek actually happened. The young John Files survived and escaped with the Tygart family. Whether that John Files was the same person as the Captain John Files of the Battle of Cowpens is a matter of some disagreement. I tend to believe they were the same person, but that is more an assessment of likelihoods than a matter of documentation.

The remainder of the story line follows an actual summary of the experiences of Thomas Benton Files during and for the two years following the Civil War. It is gleaned from several sources, including documents, some written in his own hand, in the National Archives in Washington. His is a tale of patriotism, struggle, suffering and danger, working itself out during the awful final years of America's struggle for survival as one nation.

While his travels are actual events, all of his companions and those he meets along the way are invented. I have made some reasonable assumptions about time frames so as to place him in or near historical events. An example is his nearness to the massacre at Fort Pillow. He could well have been traveling through that area about that time, but I have no evidence that he saw or experienced those events. The three soldiers who escaped from the fort are of my creation, but my description of the massacre itself follows the historical record – though Confederate accounts differ, of course.

The details of his stay in Pulaski, Illinois, including all the people he met there, are entirely fictitious, though the stay itself happened.

I know that from Pulaski, he went down to La Vergne, Tennessee where he was in the company of troops from Ohio. The details of how he got from place to place are of my imagining. The hanging in Louisville and the governance of General Stephen Burbridge are historical, but I do not know that Tom Files was there.

At La Vergne, Tennessee he was captured by the Confederates and imprisoned at Nashville. From there, he was transferred to Corinth, though my description of that journey is fictitious. He escaped, but the details of how he got to Decatur, Alabama are imagined, based on research about the location of safe places. From Decatur, he ended up in a Federal prison in Nashville. While the charges against him are not specified, it was not unusual for Union men from the South to be suspected of being spies for the Confederacy. The partially completed Maxwell House Hotel was used as a prison by both sides during the course of the war and was in Union hands during this time frame. In Nashville, there was a Captain Goodwin whom he credited with helping secure his release. Events and relationships developed there are fictitious, but the external events reflect actual history.

His journey home from Nashville is imagined, though many of the places and events are real. The Mr. Johnston who welcomed him along the way is a figment of my imagination, though General Joseph Johnston himself was a highly distinguished Confederate officer. The account of the battle at Dover, Tennessee under General Joe Wheeler is based on accounts of the event, including Nathan Bedford Forrest's subsequent opinion of "Fightin' Joe" Wheeler.

Fannie and Johnny married and eventually moved westward. Tom, Martha Jane and the family remained in Walker County, Alabama and there were several more children. One, Eva Lucinda, grew up and married the son of another First Alabama veteran, Carroll Cooner and his wife Mahalia, who make cameo appearances in this story. Eva Lucinda, known as "Ma Cooner", was my wife's great grandmother and it was through her telling of it that Tom Files' story survived, though the details of it were not learned until well after Ma Cooner's death at the age of 102.

From Nashville, when the war ended, Tom found his way home. Files family tradition says that his journey ended much as I described it in the opening chapter and concluding paragraph.

Suggestions For Further Reading

Todd, Glenda McWhirter Todd. *First Alabama Cavalry U.S.A.: Homage to Patriotism*. Bowie, MD: Heritage Books, Inc., 1999. [ISBN: 0-7884-1198-5]

Umphrey, Don. *Southerners in Blue: They Defied the Confederacy*. Dallas, TX: Quarry Press, 2002. [ISBN: 0-9714958-1-5]

Current, Richard Nelson. *Lincoln's Loyalists: Union Soldiers from the Confederacy*. Boston: Northeastern University Press, 1992. [ISBN: 1-55553-124-5]

Turtledove, Harry. *Fort Pillow*. New York: St. Martin's Press, 2006. [ISBN: 978-1-4299-0974-1]